D1409780

THE CYTOKINE PLURALITY

THE CYTOKINE PLURALITY

ROBERT JYSTAD

BOOK 1 OF THE NANOBOT TRILOGY

The Cytokine Plurality is a work of fiction. The story line is a product of the author's imagination and any reference to people, events and locations is used fictitiously. Any resemblance to current events or locations or to living persons is entirely coincidental.

A 2021 Bookbaby.com Publication

Copyright © 2020 Robert Jystad.
U.S. Copyright Office Registration Number TXu 2-236-861
Effective Date of Registration: January 30, 2021
All rights reserved.

ISBN: 978-1-09836-672-8
Ebook ISBN: 978-1-09836-673-5

Illustrations by Kim Peasley
Cover design and layout by Bookbaby.com

To my Mom and Dad, rest in peace, I miss you terribly,

and

To my wife Konnie with a 'K'

ACKNOWLEDGEMENTS

If the current COVID-19 pandemic has taught us anything, it is that nothing worth doing is worth doing alone. We are so much better together, and the 'together' of this novel involves several very strong minds upon which I find myself drawing for what are obvious reasons. First, my wife, who has become a blessing to me in ways I did not imagine when I proposed to her on that special Christmas morning, is the inspiration behind Van Eng—whose last name she still doesn't like. Konnie with a 'K' wasn't born deaf but like Van lost her hearing during her childhood and dealt with the humiliation of special ed classes at the hands of teachers not sympathetic to her physical limitations. She is now a top business leader in Upland, California, is well regarded for her philanthropy, and is well known for her women's-only gym and fitness resort called Shirlees. A special thank you to my sister, Sharon Diekman, an avid reader who has lived and worked for many years in the Silicon Valley, and who offered great suggestions and encouragement. I want to thank my illustrator Kim Peasley for her beautiful and artistic maps. Thank you to my aunt, Carolyn Erickson, also an avid reader and history buff, who gave me honest and compelling guidance. Thanks to Barbara Andrews, a good friend and a reader who knows the genre very well and was not afraid to force me to think. Barbara offered several key insights into the story line. My daughter Kaia Jystad graciously took the time to read despite a rigorous and heroic medical residency in the midst of the coronavirus pandemic. COVID-19 was not her first experience with a terrible infectious disease. She also happened to be in Yosemite Valley working as a medical intern when the hantavirus hit, a virus with a mortality rate almost three times that of the coronavirus. This book is a shout out to her courage. Finally, thank you to the Bookbaby.com team whose expertise I trust very much and who has done a great job with my first attempt at publishing a novel.

ABOUT THE AUTHOR

Robert Jystad is an award-winning writer and communications law attorney, living and working in Southern California. He focused his legal career on wireless communications and served as President of the California Wireless Association for three years. Prior to law school, Robert was an editor in New York City, working first as a production editor for Plenum Publishing, and then as a managing editor and administrative director for Professor George Fletcher at Columbia University Law School. He has graduate degrees from Princeton Theological Seminary, Columbia University School of International and Public Affairs, and UCLA School of Law. Robert has had great success with his academic writing, winning top awards at both Princeton and Columbia. He lives with his beautiful wife, Konnie, his two boujee terriers, Fendi and Prada, aptly named by their mom, and finally, his Norwegian Forest Cat, Puff, who is an awnry and really old cat, and who like a good Norwegian complained the whole time Robert was writing. Robert's remarkable chess-mastering daughter Kaia is in medical residency at the Balboa Naval Medical Center in San Diego. She beats her dad now on a regular basis.

CONTENTS

PREFACE

I have had several discussions about the title and considered simpler options, but, in the end, settled on the current title knowing that readers might need a bit of assistance with it. So here it is without giving away the book or the series. The word *cytokine* comes from the two Greek words, *cyto* and *kine,* which when combined mean *cell movement.* A cytokine is not itself a cell, but rather is a very important molecular component of our immune system. It is a special protein that regulates or influences healing cells to move around in the body in response to infection or trauma. Cytokines are like little messengers that instruct white blood cells, for example, to find and attack infections. However, when the immune system overresponds to what it perceives as a foreign element in the body and produces too many cytokines, the effect may be a *cytokine storm.* In a cytokine storm, the immune system's overreaction actually harms the body. For example, a cytokine storm might trigger *anaphylaxis,* which causes the hyper-inflammation of the lungs and other internal organs, and which, if not properly and quickly treated, leads to death.

✳ ✳ ✳ ✳ ✳ ✳

Fred Schmidt knew two things about the petri dish. First, whatever it contained probably had been stolen from another lab, which is why he was not concerned that Ragnor Willowbrook, otherwise known as RW

Labs, would contact the police and accuse Derek Whitestone of the theft. If anything, they would try to steal the dish back and might even come after him, which, to a bored billionaire felt like more of a game than a threat. He also knew that it had to be important. RW Labs, if nothing else, did their research before trying to claim a reengineered invention as their own. The dish bore the label "Risk Group IV," which meant it was not something to be played with. Not only was it dangerous, but it was highly infectious, and the likelihood of an effective treatment or vaccine was so low that if it were released, a widespread pandemic was not out of the question.

But what could it be? He wondered, given Derek Whitestone's report on his visit to RW Labs, if it might be a form of nanotechnology, but he dismissed the thought. Why would it be labeled "Risk Group IV"? Perhaps it was a genetic experiment, and maybe even cancer-treatment related. Maybe it was a weaponized form of a bacterium or virus. RW Labs had made a lot of money finding and reengineering military technology, and not always for the United States.

As he thought about it, he began to get a picture of an opportunity. He needed a high-quality lab that was both capable of handling dangerous substances but also desperate enough to work with him in secret. A Bainbridge Island lab came to mind. The young genius he had heard about there could be tricky to manage if the curiosity of the genius began to give way to moral qualms. But, to Fred, in this case, *tricky* really only meant the experiment might fail and the opportunity might be lost. At the very least, he would learn whether or not the Duc A. Tran Laboratory of Hereditary Biology was capable of working with him.

＊＊＊＊＊＊

She looked at her notes and tried to envision the husband's movements. He falls asleep on the couch watching TV and maybe is a little drunk. His wife wakes him to go change the crying baby while she is cooking. Does he resent her for waking him up? If he came home intending to murder his wife, it is hard to imagine him falling asleep on the couch at all, unless maybe he was so drunk that he simply passed out. Maybe he flew into a murderous rage after she tried to wake him to deal with the baby. If so, rather than carefully attend to the baby, he would have ignored the baby's cries, and would have started pushing her or hitting her until he found a knife to complete the act and satisfy his blood lust.

It was true that he had alcohol in his blood at some point in the evening, as indicated by the breathalyzer test taken by the police at the station, but the blood alcohol content level from that test was too low even to be admissible, and they were still waiting on the blood tests. If the breathalyzer's low reading were accurate, it would be unlikely that he was heavily intoxicated, let alone blackout drunk, just a few hours earlier. Besides if he indicated heavy intoxication at home, why would the police not test him then and take him into custody immediately? They asked him if he had been drinking, and he gave them the timeline mentioned in her notes. Van was beginning to believe that he was distraught, not drunk. In addition, if he had been that drunk, why would a caring mother trust him with her baby? Assuming he is raging mad at being woken up as well as drunk and she just wanted his help. The best he would have done is stumble into the kid's bedroom, rip off the diaper, shield his nose, wipe the baby quickly, and then dump a load of baby powder onto the baby's butt, slap on the new diaper, put the baby in the crib still crying, and leave baby powder trails on the changing table, all over the room, and in the crib. But there were no baby powder trails, and the strongest scent of the baby powder was coming from a small, covered trash bin, in which the last pad from the changing table was neatly folded and placed on top of other dirty changing pads. The room bore the signs of a caring father, not a raging and possibly murderous drunk.

MAPS

Map 1. Bainbridge Island, Puget Sound, Washington

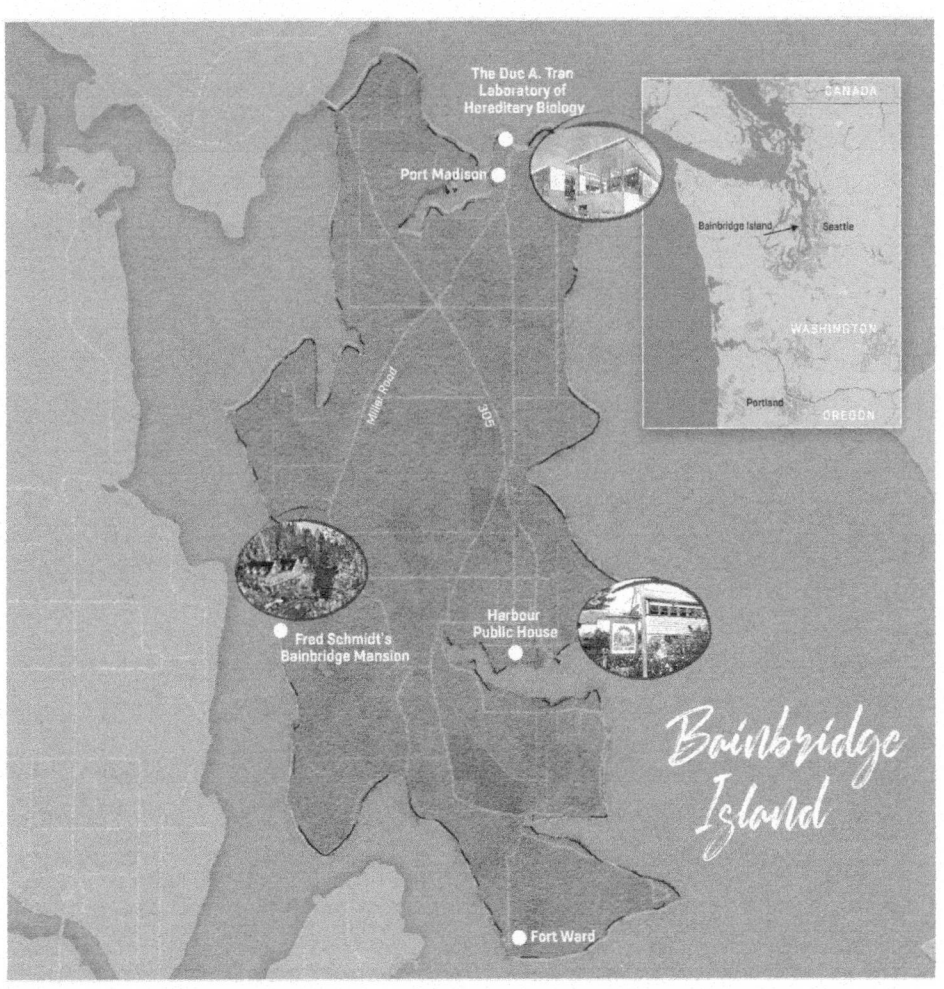

Map 2. Tajikistan, Central Asia

CHAPTER 1.

Butterflies Are Not Always Free

Imagine the world without sound. No sounds of birds chattering in the trees. No hum of summer cicadas as the hot night drops into darkness. Raindrops do not tap the window. Waves do not roar as they pound the sand. The tea kettle blows steam but does not whistle. There is no music.

But imagine if you were able to make a deal with God. He will take your hearing, but in exchange, he will transform your vision so that you capture the brightest reds, yellows and blues in a home garden or in your classroom, and you will learn to distinguish rose, fuchsia, watermelon, salmon, and other varieties of the color pink in the blink of an eye. In addition, you instinctively sort out the scent of wet leather from fresh leather, candle smoke from fireplace smoke, and grass that is wet from rain versus recently watered grass. In short, every other sense that is essential to experiencing the world as a human being will be amplified, and you will experience reality from a fresh and entirely new point of view.

But is it a fair trade? Hearing matters, and as a child, your ability to relate is what is affected and what ultimately matters when your senses are compromised. Van Eng wasn't thinking about any of this as she ran out the front door to greet the summer breeze, the wet grass and the bright dandelions. To a six-year-old, deaf or not, the front yard is its own universe and full of opportunities for delight, surprise and just fun.

She ran and felt her heart beating and lungs pulling for air. She ran until she was exhausted and fell down in the fresh, wet grass that captured her nose and tickled her exposed arms and legs. Mom stood at the door admiring her daughter and stifling the pangs of sadness she felt whenever she thought about what Van was missing by being deaf.

Van was not born deaf. She was a healthy 8 lb. and 4 oz. baby girl reaching out for life with her screams and coos and tears. But when Van was barely a year old, and still not able to walk, the family accepted the generosity of a rich uncle, grabbed only what they could carry, and in the dark of night, ran for the boat that would take them away from a frightening, despotic government. They bounced through overhead waves in a small dinghy and then accepted the help of anonymous hands, who pulled them onto the gangway and shepherded them into the bowels of a large freighter. Wet and tired, they huddled together that night and the many nights to come until Van became sick with fever and dysentery. Fearful for their daughter's life, Mom forced her way to the boat deck to get sun and scraps of food. She found pain medicine and crushed it into powder to add to the little bit of water that now was all that was left in Van's bottle. It calmed the fever and helped Van and her parents sleep just a bit despite their exhaustion.

One morning, after a few weeks of this harrowing existence, men with guns boarded the freighter and found the huddled mass of refugees in the hull. They pushed and kicked them into several small boats, and the refugees who thought they were going to Australia and expected to hear welcoming words in English, found themselves yelled at in Khmer in open pens in Cambodia. Who would have thought that their plans for escape to a better life would go so far astray? But at least the food there was better than on the boat, and there was medical help from a volunteer group called Doctors without Borders, and Van began to recover.

Except that she did not completely recover. Mom noticed that Van seemed to be staring a lot and was not responding to her words. She took the child back to the makeshift clinic and presented her to one of the young doctors. That doctor had a worried looked and took the baby to discuss with her team. When she returned with a steely expression, Mom knew not only that something was wrong but exactly what it was. In addition to having a fever, Van's eardrums became infected and had swollen and burst, coating the inside of her inner ear with scar tissue and Van was no longer able to hear.

Months later, the family found a sponsor and flew to San Francisco, where they settled in a Vietnamese community and began to build a new life. Dad became a chef, Mom found work at a garment factory, and the community supported them and played Mahjong regularly together. Eventually, they found a small house with a nice front yard, where now a spry six-year-old Van rolled in the grass and pulled up dandelion stems to see the milky liquid from the flower's stem flowing into the palm of her hand.

Unlike Mom, as soon as Van ran out the front door, she immediately detected a few minor differences from the day before. The rain from yesterday was gone, and today, the sun baked the grass even though it was still wet from the morning dew. The mailbox had been left open, suggesting that Mommy had run into the rain to retrieve the mail but rushing to get back inside and out of the rain, she had left the box open. Daddy's car was gone, which was odd since Daddy worked very late hours and often slept in until lunch. Maybe they needed him for a special breakfast. Down the road was a single car. It looked old, and the front bumper, instead of bright chrome seemed to be a reddish orange, unlike dirt but not clean and new. The car was running, which Van knew because white steam was coming from the tailpipe.

3

But none of this information meant much to Van. After being locked inside for two days of rain, all she cared about was running and rolling and smelling and looking at the sky. She glanced over at Mommy in the doorway, and felt her love, and watched as Mommy's head spun back towards the house and then, looking quickly back at Van, she held out a flat hand as if to say, "do not move—I will be right back." Van had no intention of moving. The grass was cool, and the sky was full of cottony clouds telling stories of rabbits and elephants.

Which is why what happened next caught no one's attention. Van smelled the smoke of an old cigarette, much like Daddy's brand, only this man was not Daddy. He had mean eyes and dirty khaki pants and one of his new boots was coming untied. But it hurt when he grabbed her arm, and she quickly looked back to the front door—Mommy had not yet returned. She screamed as best as she knew how to, but she was quickly bundled up and pushed into the car's back seat. The cracked leather of the seat scratched her face, and she could smell the old empty cigarette packs that were strewn on the floor. She tried to get up, but another pair of hands pulled her deeper into the back seat and leaned over her to lock the door. She watched as a woman grabbed her hands and pushed them into a hooded sweatshirt that was pulled over her head and her hair tucked into the neck of the sweatshirt. The sweatshirt was soft, like velveteen, and smelled like it was brand new. She felt the car accelerate and a deep uncertain fear made her shake and start to cry as she knew what was now happening was not right. Who were these strange people and why did they take her from Mommy and the beautiful sky?

The car ride seemed go on forever. The smoking man was talking constantly but Van heard nothing. She was learning how to read lips and he seemed to be asking her name, but she was too scared to try to respond. She didn't trust her voice anyway. He quickly gave up, and the woman sitting with her in the back fastened her seatbelt and let her look out the window. The sky had grown dark with the onset of another rainstorm, but this one felt menacing and dangerous. She saw some squirrels scamper off the road and felt the urge to run herself.

The woman sitting next to her was pretty and was trying to be nice. She had lipstick on her teeth and her cheeks were flushed—they resembled the color of Mommy's makeup. Her perfume smelled strong, like rose perfume. But no... it was lighter and sweeter than rose, more like the gardenias in Mommy's garden wet with rain. The woman kept reaching out to Van as if she wanted to hold her, but the effort made Van angry and she pushed her hands away and leaned toward the door. The pretty lady was wearing thick heels that made Van think she was pretending to be grown-up. She seemed very young to Van, much younger than Mommy. On another day, she might have even liked her. But not today. Today was wrong and these people were wrong for taking her with them.

Van saw a flash in the mirror and looked back to see red, white and blue lights approaching very fast.

"Shit," said the smoking man, beginning to accelerate and then realizing that that would be a bad idea.

"Honey!" shouted the pretty lady. "What do we do? Oh no! God, what are you doing? Don't stop!"

"Got to babe. Stay calm. He won't know anything and this one," he said, pointing to Van, "doesn't talk."

"I don't think that's nice" said the pretty lady pouting. "What are we doing?!"

"Look. You have to calm down and you need to do it now!" he glowered, with his voiced rising in a controlled anger.

Smoking man pulled the car over. The patrol car slowed and parked directly behind him and the officer walked up to the driver's window and tapped. "License and registration, please."

"Certainly officer," he said, giving a seasoned smile. "What seems to be the problem?"

"There's been an incident. We just doing a little investigating."

He smiled and looked in the back seat. "Howdy, ma'am," he said to the pretty lady. The lady smiled at the officer, tight-lipped and said nothing. He looked at Van. "Beautiful little girl," he said, and immediately Van felt that he knew she should not be there. "Do you always ride in the back with her?" the officer asked the lady.

Smoking man immediately interceded, "The girl's not feeling well, and it helps her when her mom sits with her." This response caused the lady to try an awkward smile.

"So pretty," the officer said, pointing to Van. "How old is she?"

"She is almost eight years old," said the man, "but she looks younger."

The officer said, "Looks to me like she should be in a car seat, but I guess if she is eight..." he said, with a hint of skepticism.

He looked back at Van and asked slowly and carefully. "How... old... are... you?" Van said nothing and started grabbing her hands as if she wanted to make them work. "What... is... your... name?" This time Van made out the question watching his lips. Smoking man barked a bit too quickly, "Her name is Mary." Van didn't hear smoking man's response but said as loud as she could, "I'm Van," although as it blended with smoking man's answer, it sounded more like "I'm fine."

Van's effort at a response clearly unsettled both smoking man and pretty lady who quickly confirmed, "It's Mary, yes it's Mary, that's right."

The officer furrowed his brow, and said, "Okay. Please sit tight. I need to run these," shaking the documents, adding, "and I'll be back."

The officer walked to the patrol car and got on the radio. Smoking man noticed that he kept his lights flashing and it made him edgy. Luckily, he thought, the officer did not tell him to shut off his engine, so he kept it running. The officer stayed on the radio a long time. Too long. This time, when he got out of the car, his partner got out as well, and rested his hand on his firearm. As they both approached the couple's car from each side, smoking man got spooked, slammed the car into drive and punched the gas. The car took off weaving, showering the officers with rocks from the road. Neither of them fired, and both ran back to the patrol car and took off after the speeding car.

Back in the patrol car, the officer had been able to call in a blockade as a backup. The blockade waited down the road—three patrol cars with armed officers crouched waiting for the couple's car. Its lights appeared at a corner up ahead as the car barely in control sped toward the blockade and then slammed on its brakes just before hitting the lead patrol car sitting in the middle of the road. The first patrol car quickly appeared behind the couple's car and blocked it in from the rear. Officers jumped out and aimed their weapons at the couple's car. "Do not shoot," said the lead officer. "There is a child involved," he added, as if to remind everyone what they already knew. The couple slowly emerged with their hands up. "On the ground! Both of you! Hands above your head!" As they laid down, officers raced forward and restrained the couple. Van was suddenly alone in the car with her seat belt on. She had hit her head on the door when the car first took off, and was thrown forward almost out of the seat belt when the car skidded to a stop. A small cut appeared on her temple. Hands reached into the car and pulled her out. People were talking but she heard nothing. All she saw were people dressed in different colors of blue with badges holding different kinds of pistols and rifles and lights flashing everywhere. Someone wrapped her in a blanket. It was scratchy but made her feel safe and it smelled like a pet dog. She saw lightning flash on the horizon as raindrops began to fall.

Van was returned to her parents, who were weeping and beside themselves with both grief and relief. Mom had stepped inside to take a call, certain she could walk with the handset and cord back to the front door to continue watching Van. Her husband had called to say he was on his way home, and as she walked back to the front door, she saw the vehicle race away and Van was nowhere to be seen. She called the police screaming, and within 15 minutes, a car was there with officers asking questions and getting details about Van's dress and shoes and hair. Mom's English was not very good, but she told them Van was six years old and was deaf and that she was learning to read lips.

CHAPTER 2.

Smart Dust

S tress is as essential to life as oxygen. The Buddha told us the key to happiness is the recognition that "life is *dukkha*," usually translated as 'suffering'. But *dukkha* is more nuanced than simply the idea of pain or emotional suffering. *Dukkha* is about the pain that we feel and experience as we navigate from moment to moment, unable to predict the future but aware of everything in our life experience that is capable of eliminating this moment's experience of pleasure or happiness. As our consciousness shifts toward that unknown future and away from the present moment, it embeds itself in the vast array of terrors that await all of us—such as loss, failure, abandonment, pain, illness, tragedy, or death. It pulls us away from the present and into that next unknowable moment. The pull is unopposable—a basic element of our evolutionary fitness. It is a biological rule of existence, the demand that we survive whatever we might face, never actually knowing what we will face. What and who we are as identities exists only in the space between a present that cannot be grasped and a future that cannot be known. And we know that we cannot change that basic fact of existence—and that knowing is *dukkha*.

It was not, therefore, without irony that the University of Washington's microbiology lab on Bainbridge Island was called the Duc A. Tran Laboratory for Hereditary Biology, after its most famous geneticist.

The luster of his impact had long worn off, and the Lab had had few accomplishments of note since. Lab technicians who worked there now jokingly called it the "Duc and Cover" lab, as senior faculty scratched and clawed for an idea that might be the next big idea and might restore not only the University's fortune but their own as well.

Fred Schmidt, billionaire CEO of the Silicon Valley-based tech giant Grindle, capitalized on desperation. He knew it increased the resolve to succeed and at the same time, weakened the resolve to demand, and for that reason had inherent value. Fred loved inherent value. His latest foray into health care, self-serving though it was, introduced him to the wider world of desperation where a cutthroat competition had developed among university laboratories for the enormous bequests of large pharma and bio-tech companies. He discovered the Tran Lab after reading Dr. Tran's ground-breaking research on biological predisposition. He also knew that since Dr. Tran's unfortunate passing over fifteen years ago, the Lab was struggling. No new ideas were brewing and no new superstars were emerging.

But there was talk about a young assistant professor, who after four short years of post-secondary education had a BA in microbiology and an MA in genetic engineering, and then flew through a doctoral program at the University, completing it in just two more years. Fred knew, of course, that the shelf life of genius was never predictable. The quick burst of scholarly success often ended in depression and self-loathing, if not psychosis. He had seen it too many times to trust it. This kid might show some promise and then—blam!—he goes looney or, even worse, off the grid. Fred hated off the grid. He saw it as the modern version of Luddism. Anti-technology for anti-technology's sake. But if the kid had promise, and he did, at least there would be good reason to test it, conduct a trial, give it a shot and see what developed.

The phone rang. Fred picked up and said nothing. He enjoyed the tension that he created when a caller who reached him for the first time didn't know how to respond to silence. He knew immediately when a caller did not know him, and he could determine quickly whether or not the call was worth his time. Those friends and colleagues who knew him began speaking immediately and the efficiency of that interchange also pleased him.

"Hi Fred, it's Derek. I am heading over to Labs now." Derek Whitestone was Fred's lead investment banker. Fred's account had grown under Derek, and Fred had come to trust him with his money, which was more than he could say about almost anyone else in his life. The business relationship developed into a friendship and their families often dined and traveled together. The tightness of that relationship kept Derek close by and Fred not only could track his investments first-hand, he also often used Derek to explore some of his crazier business ideas, like getting into health care.

The "Labs" to which Derek referred was a local engineering laboratory called RW Laboratories—the RW stood for Ragnar Willowbrook. Also situated in Silicon Valley, Ragnar Willowbrook Laboratories was known for taking certain ethical shortcuts in order to speed up time to market for new products, a characteristic common to most businesses in the Valley, albeit veiled by a leftward-leaning political face. RW Labs did not develop much on its own. It was actually better at reverse engineering new inventions and capturing intellectual property rights faster than most inventors, and it paid a lot of money to the top legal talent from Harvard, Yale and Stanford to harvest those rights. Labs also had a tight relationship with the scientific community in China and exploited that relationship when necessary to bypass outdated regulatory restrictions in the United States.

The latest craze at RW Labs was "smart dust." Based on the principles evolving from the developing field of Micro-Electro-Mechanical systems or MEMS, smart dust in its early development had been viewed as a threshold advance in the fight against cancer. Unfortunately for its proponents, opposition to smart dust developed and slowed the technology on the grounds that it was fundamentally contrary to established norms of privacy, and conspiracy theorists proclaimed it as a new form of mind control. Several top names in technology had come out opposing its use in medicine. Smart dust was perfect for RW Labs, which could not care less about any flimsy political opposition. If the introduction of smart dust into chemotherapy regimens could take a minimally effective and brutal form of fighting cancer and produce spectacular results, it would be worth trillions of dollars worldwide.

Fred had been diagnosed with a form of lung cancer called non-small cell squamous. Doctors had caught it in the occult stage—its earliest stage. His prognosis was positive although not certain, and he had been undergoing treatment for the past six months. But it was this diagnosis that had introduced Fred to the intricacies of the health care system and triggered his investigation into new medical technologies. He was particularly interested in smart dust and its applications in medicine. Derek set up a meeting with RW Labs to look at opportunities for Fred to invest in smart dust.

Cheryl Brown was Derek Whitestone's top assistant. She was intelligent and sexy but mostly street-smart. Her father was an alcoholic and her mother a manic-depressive ex-actress. Growing up, she was left alone for long periods of time. But she did well in school and found respite from an unloving family life in books. She was a history buff and in high school won an award for a paper she had written on the stock market crash of 1929 and how its mismanagement led to the Great Depression. That award and her report card got her into UCLA, and she quickly enrolled in the three-two program under which she would get both a BA in the subject of her choosing—history, as it turned out—and an MBA from the UCLA Anderson School of Business in just five years.

When she was first accepted to UCLA, she was given a scholarship that helped cover her dorm expenses and tuition. The scholarship lasted only a year, after which she was expected to find money to cover her schooling, mostly through loans. She liked to party with her good-looking friends and one of them told her that stripping was an easy way to "make bank." Cheryl was skeptical and was not willing to hook for money, but her friend told her of a particular club near the 405 Freeway that was good at protecting its star performers, many of whom were UCLA undergraduates. She gave it a month, and after pulling in $5,000 in four weeks working just two nights a week, Cheryl knew that she had found her ticket. She gave herself the name "Stormy," even though the other girls thought it was "so negative." But she committed to herself that no matter how much Stormy could make from pole dancing, she would never hook.

"Grab your stuff," Derek commanded, as he rushed past Cheryl's nondescript office cubicle. Cheryl knew that Derek preferred quick reactions and got irritable when an assistant was unable to keep pace. She snapped her laptop closed, grabbed her coat and purse, and popped up behind him at the elevator.

"Do I get to know where we are going?" she asked, batting her eyes and flirtatiously trying to get Derek to laugh and relax. Derek enjoyed having Cheryl with him because she made him look good both by being a looker herself and by softening his intensity. He gave her a Harrison Ford smirk, and said, "Get in the car."

The black Lincoln Navigator Reserve was waiting. Gerard, the company chauffeur, hustled around the back and pulled the back door open. Derek motioned for Cheryl to slide in first and stepped in after her. She knew to slide all the way over. The flirty card only worked before real business would start, and the back seat of this car was considered sacrosanct—a holy space for the most important business discussions, second only to the conference room connected to Derek's office.

"You ever heard of smart dust?"

"I have not."

"It's colloquial for something called MEMS or microelectromechanical systems."

"I have heard of nanobots."

"Exactly. These devices are like molecule-sized sensors and if injected into someone who is sick with cancer, for example, they can be programmed to target and kill cancer cells or paint cancer cells to be killed by other systems that work in conjunction with MEMS."

"Are you sick?"

Derek gave her a "please don't be stupid" look, but then softened. "All you need to know is that this technology is ready to explode and is only waiting for someone to set the trip wire. We are heading to a lab that is working on smart dust and could use Fred's money to help them along. Fred is keen on it."

The SUV jumped onto 85 South and merged onto Highway 17 south, that treacherous windy route over the Santa Cruz Mountains past Scott's Valley to the City of Santa Cruz and the University of California there, which, contrary to its reputation of being a hippy party school, had one of the most advanced biomolecular engineering programs in the country and was one of the key universities around the world working on genetic sequencing for the human genome project. The SUV turned off 17 onto Graham Hill Road, passed Pasatiempo Golf Club, a golf course designed by the famous golf architect Alister MacKenzie, whose other golf course masterpieces included Royal Melbourne in Australia and Augusta National in Georgia, home of the Masters. The car continued on Graham Hill, passing dense groves of redwood trees, and just past Felton, it turned right into a gravel road that looked like the entrance to a Napa winery. After about 20 minutes of windy gravel road, the view cleared to expose the entire Valley dropping away below and a tall glass building popped into view behind a massive steel guarded gate.

The security guard, who bore the air of someone who had served with black ops in the military, approached Gerard. Gerard was no slacker. He rolled down the window and said with grave authority, "I am here with Derek Whitestone." The guard looked in the vehicle and responded, "One minute, please." He checked the register, and, peering out of the doorway of the guardhouse, he waved to Gerard and motioned for him to enter as the gate slid open, revealing tree-lined ponds with fountains and huge metal artwork positioned, it seemed, haphazardly around the open entrance to the glass building.

Derek waited for Gerard to open the door, and he and Cheryl emerged to see a tall, slim woman in glasses, and a doctor wearing a lab coat waiting for them outside the entrance to the Lab. The woman approached first, clearly a senior executive at the Lab. She said with a European accent, "Mr. Whitestone. So good to see you."

"You as well, Belinda. I hear some interesting things are happening here."

"Always. Please come in."

Cheryl and Derek entered the large lobby with marble floor and columns and large paintings, designed to impress and somewhat inconsistent with the idea of the place being a laboratory. It felt to Cheryl more like a mousetrap for the Valley's unsuspecting nouveaux riche than a laboratory. Two 10-foot copper-cast letters *RW* stood behind the security desk, which was framed on both sides by metal detectors. Belinda and the doctor handed Cheryl and Derek badges with their names pre-printed and pulled out their own badges. Cheryl and Derek handed the guard their bags and the guard opened the gates to allow the foursome to pass through the metal detectors.

They were ushered into an ornate conference room with water and diet cokes placed on a credenza. Belinda and the doctor, who seemed ill at ease and was very quiet when they met, now became talkative as the discussion moved onto smart dust. A PowerPoint slide deck popped up with glass screens that appeared through slots in the conference room table and he spoke through the slides in words that meant little to Cheryl, as he grinned and peered lasciviously at her over his glasses. Cheryl knew this look too well, and she knew too well how to play it. She smiled back at the doctor, looking impressed by his words and giving a hint of interest. Derek said nothing and ignored the play as if he was not aware it was happening. What Derek was really interested in was the Lab and the progress the Lab was making toward a marketable product.

"What's the timeframe?"

"You know this product has its detractors," Belinda responded with gravity.

"Let's pretend it doesn't," Derek replied.

"Okay, but we need to take the detractors seriously. Senators Windell and Leumann have mounted an anti-smart dust campaign and the social media misinformation train is in high gear."

"Mobile phones face the same issue with 5G, right? Those companies are smart enough to know anti-technology conspiracy theorists carry no weight with the American majority. The more important question for the people I represent is—is this stuff real, or are we still in the science fiction phase?"

The doctor grew irritated and with an air of authority responded, "It is definitely real."

"So, then, Herr Professor, what is the timeframe?"

"Microbiology is the foundation of all life, and we take it very seriously."

Belinda frowned at the doctor and jumped in, trying to rescue the conversation.

"The fact is, we are making progress, but it is slow. There is AI technology being developed at Providia that could shift us into much higher gear, but they are not releasing prototypes of that technology without co-licensing, and the cost of license is significant."

"What difference can the prototypes make?"

"It will bump us up by 18 months."

"What is the cost of the co-license?"

Derek knew ahead of time this discussion would be about money and it didn't bother him. Belinda began to explain the details to Derek, and the doctor made his way to Cheryl and started talking about his latest skiing trip to the Bugaboos. Shortly afterward, the party of four left the conference room and was ushered into a decontamination zone, where they put on sealed hazmat suits and gloves that were designed to keep the workplace sterile. They entered through an airlock door and walked into a large warehouse-sized room full of white light. Bodies in white suits bobbled around the room.

"There are two different processes for nanomanufacturing," the doctor said through his suit-embedded microphone. "Simply put, we call them top-down and bottom-up." He glanced at Cheryl smiling when he said this. "Top-down fabrication starts with large materials and reduces them to nanoscale. Bottom-up starts at the atomic and molecular level. Bottom-up assembles nanoscale devices by combining molecular material.

The latter process is tedious and more expensive, but the devices are more reliable and seem to operate longer than what are basically shrunken devices. More importantly, we are beginning to detect self-assembling characteristics of molecules. This could take nanomanufacturing into an entirely new realm."

The group wandered around the room and Belinda introduced them to several scientists whose smiles and nodding responses seemed comical or oddly forced. One section was cordoned off, but Cheryl split off from the group and managed to follow a group of scientists into an area marked "Biological." She approached a younger lab technician.

"Hi," said Cheryl. No response.

"Umm, excuse me." She tapped him on the shoulder.

He looked up from his lab desk and it took him a second to realize someone was actually talking to him.

"What are you working on?" Cheryl asked.

"Who are you?"

"I'm with Derek Whitestone. We're investors." She smiled her cutest impishly sexy smile and the scientist almost fell out of his chair.

"Pleased to meet you," he stammered. "Uh, I don't think I am at liberty to discuss…"

Cheryl moved closer and leaned lightly on him as she looked into the plexiglass window that he had been staring at. "Looks fascinating."

With very little additional prodding, he started into a discourse on virology that she didn't follow. But she kept him talking and began to look around the room. Suddenly his phone buzzed and a text message popped up. "I'm sorry. I will be back in just a second." He jumped up and sped off at an awkwardly fast pace.

As he stood up, he inadvertently knocked a tightly sealed petri dish off the desk. Cheryl reached down to pick it up and give it to him thinking it might be important, but he was gone so fast that he didn't see or hear it fall, and she was left standing there holding the dish. It was sealed with red tape and labeled "Risk Group IV," which meant nothing to her. Why she did what she did next even she didn't know, but instead of putting it back on the desk, Cheryl placed the petri dish in a side pocket slit in her hazmat suit.

She left and found the original group moving back to the airlock door. Derek saw her and gave her a stern "why did you leave the group" look. She smiled without any hint of shame and they went back into the decontamination room.

CHAPTER 3.

Sense and Senselessness (Part I)

The history of forensics combines scientific brilliance with the macabre, a deeply disturbing 19th century criminality that is captured compellingly in Caleb Carr's historical fiction, *The Alienist*. The science of fingerprinting, based on the assumption that each individual person has a unique set of prints, was not yet accepted as standard practice. But it caught the public's attention when several brutal New York City murders were solved by a young "alienist," a term in vogue at that time for forensic psychiatry. The alienist who solved the cases did so in part by proving that the fingerprints he identified were reliable markers of a specific individual and were remarkably well-preserved on smooth surfaces like glass and gun metal.

The modern form of fingerprinting, which by no means has replaced its progenitor, is DNA sampling. In cases where the oil of fingerprints is undetectable, the "oil" of DNA can be found at virtually every crime scene through bits of hair, skin, fingernails, blood, or semen. Like fingerprints, DNA sampling is a study in probabilities. But unlike fingerprint readers, which used probability theory to identify a "match," DNA decoders only approximate a match. Still, DNA sampling has been added to the list of evidentiary options selected to prove or to disprove guilt beyond a reasonable doubt. But what DNA sampling does much better than fingerprinting is support doubt about guilt, and by that doubt offer a means of proving innocence long after a judge or jury made the decision that no reasonable doubt existed and convicted some poor innocent to a lengthy prison term or even a death sentence. Accordingly, years and even decades after guilt had been established, it might be shown that the likelihood of a DNA match was so low as to be unsustainable. Even those convicted of the most heinous crimes and buried as it were on death row might find themselves in the now growing class of wrongly accused and returned to freedom.

The trauma of her childhood, and the oft-repeated thought as she grew up that she might have become a victim of an unsolved crime, led Van to develop a deep interest in police work. Even as an adolescent, she watched the news about local crimes with acute interest, and she was a voracious reader of detective novels and true crime stories. When she got to high school, she excelled in science, and in particular chemistry, proving wrong the educators who originally placed her in special education classes as a young child only because of her impaired hearing. In college, she majored in chemistry and completed her education with a dual masters in biochemistry and criminal justice. But when she applied to the San Francisco Police Academy, her deafness interceded again, and she was refused entry not because of some absence of skill or intelligence, but rather because of the risk that her deafness allegedly posed to herself and officers in the field.

Acknowledging her education and skills, members of the police academy selection committee suggested that Van consider forensics and even recommended a couple of forensic labs. She applied to a lab in downtown Los Angeles that had a reputation for excellence forged after the O.J. Simpson trials and the public and highly visible claim made by O.J.'s Johnny Cochrane-led legal team that DNA evidence had been mishandled by the LAPD. Van was pleased to hear that she had been accepted and that it was a well-paying job. Van's parents didn't like the idea of her living so far away, so they sold the small Bay Area house for an obscene amount, and moved with Van to Monterey Park, a largely Asian suburban town near downtown Los Angeles. Monterey Park was a good choice. Several of Van's relatives, who had also escaped from various terrors in Southeast Asia, happened to live in the same area, and they helped Van's parents find a suitable home for a good price.

Dr. Frank Weatherby was the lead forensic medical examiner in Los Angeles and ran the City of Los Angeles Science of Justice Laboratories located in one of several nondescript multi-story buildings clustered around City Hall in downtown Los Angeles and within walking distance of the new police department. Frank had been a young chemist working at the LAPD crime lab during the O.J. trials and watched in horror as several honorable and highly qualified senior chemists had their lives destroyed by the criminal trial. He survived because good people in the lab and in the department protected him and he had helped solve numerous murders and had cemented his reputation as a careful and methodical scientist. Almost 30 years later, Van found herself as one of several assistants who supported Frank in his on-going effort to address crime in the City of Angels.

"What do you think?" Brad Jones leaned over Van's shoulder to see her notes. Brad was cute and gregarious. Everyone liked him, including Van. Brad had completed an internship with the NYPD in New York City and had been accepted along with Van into the current class of Weatherby assistants.

"Ow!" Van winced. Brad heard a small whine as he put his head too close to Van's hearing aid and caused feedback. Brad jumped back and Van turned with a smirk as she put her hand over her notes. "Not yet," she said. "Sorry," said Brad. "I keep forgetting you wear those things."

Van mouthed, "It's ok." She had gotten used to the feedback from her hearing aids and acted like it hurt more to mess with Brad than anything. But it was always irritating—a reminder of an unwanted disability. She turned to focus on the task at hand. Frank wanted a timeline work up on a domestic abuse case that resulted in the death of a young Colombian woman in Baldwin Hills. She was working from emergency dispatch recordings and police notes from interviews and phone recordings made at the crime scene although she had never seen it. So far, the timeline looked as follows:

5:00 pm — husband has verbal fight with boss at work site.

5:15 pm — husband and co-worker meet at bar.

6:00 pm — husband leaves bar after two beers

6:20 pm — husband arrives home.

6:30 pm — husband sits down to watch TV, baby begins to cry, wife asks husband to check on baby

6:40 pm — baby still crying, husband dozes on couch, wife wakes him up and asks him to tend to baby and husband goes to baby's room

[missing data]

7:05 pm — husband hears wife scream and finds her stabbed multiple times and bleeding from stomach

7:08 pm — husband dials 911 tells operator, "My wife has been stabbed and is bleeding."

7:23 pm — police arrive. Husband answers door with shirt indicating blood stains and appears distraught. Wife is lying on living room floor unconscious and bleeding from stomach. Husband claims he was trying to stop bleeding. Baby is lying in crib in her bedroom crying.

7:29 pm — ambulance arrives from County General Hospital. Wife is taken by ambulance to emergency room.

8:36 pm — wife is pronounced dead.

9:15 pm — wife's parents arrive at hospital and take baby. Police handcuff husband at hospital and take him to station for questioning.

11:45 pm — husband is booked on suspicion of murder and remanded to County Jail

Van turned to see Frank approaching quickly. He looked at Brad and motioned for Brad to join him. "Let's hear it," he said. Van grabbed her notes and read through the timeline.

Frank looked at Brad and asked, "So what's missing?"

He answered, "So far, it sounds like the only compelling evidence is the bloody shirt."

Van shook her head. "We have stabs wounds and a dead body, and we have no weapon."

"What else?" Frank asked.

Van responded, "We are missing 25 minutes."

"Ok, you both need to keep thinking about this. Grab your notepads and follow me."

Frank headed toward the door and Van and Brad followed closely behind. They boarded a white Suburban marked 'Forensics Official Use Only' and, within 15 minutes, they pulled up to a small light blue house surrounded by police tape. Frank grabbed the evidence case and all three put on blue gloves and booties. Inside, there were Post-it notes sprinkled around the rooms. The back yard had flags stuck in the ground. Frank and Brad stood over a taped outline of the body. The floor still had blood stains and there were blood stain splashes on the couch and on a counter chair. Unlike Frank and Brad, as they crossed the front yard, Van had taken a mental snapshot and quickly memorized it—something she had done since childhood whenever she encountered a new location. She picked up on a bush on the side yard under an open window that seemed slightly bent. Then, as they entered the house, underneath the overpowering smell of dried blood, she picked up the scent of baby powder. She left Frank and Brad studying the floor around the body tape and walked into the baby's bedroom and looked around. It was neat and organized, almost as if someone had just cleaned it. The changing table was covered with a fresh cloth, and new diapers, wipes, baby powder and a tube of Desinex were neatly arranged in preparation for the next use.

She looked at her notes and tried to envision the husband's movements. He falls asleep on the couch watching TV and maybe is a little drunk. His wife wakes him to go change the crying baby while she is cooking. Does he resent her for waking him up? If he came home intending to murder his wife, it is hard to imagine him falling asleep on the couch at all unless maybe he was so drunk that he simply passed out. Maybe he flew into a murderous rage after she tried to wake him to deal with the baby. If so, rather than carefully attend to the baby, he would have ignored the baby's cries and would have started pushing her or hitting her until he found a knife to complete the act and satisfy his blood lust.

It was true that he had alcohol in his blood at some point in the evening, as indicated by the breathalyzer test given by the police at the station. But the blood alcohol content level from that test was too low even to be admissible, and they were still waiting on the blood test reports. If the breathalyzer's low reading was accurate, it would be unlikely that he was heavily intoxicated, let alone blackout drunk just a few hours earlier. Besides if he indicated heavy intoxication at the home, why would the police not test him then and take him into custody immediately? They asked him if he had been drinking and he gave them the timeline in her notes. Van was beginning to believe that he was distraught not drunk. In addition, if he had been that drunk, why would a caring mother trust him with her baby? Assuming he is raging mad at being woken up as well as drunk and she just wanted his help, the best he would have done is stumble into the kid's bedroom, rip off the diaper, shield his nose, wipe the baby quickly, and then dump a load of baby powder onto the baby's butt, slap on the new diaper and put the baby in the crib still crying and leave baby powder trails on the changing table, all over the room, and in the crib. But there were no baby powder trails, and the strongest scent of the baby powder was coming from a small, covered trash bin in which the last pad from the changing table was neatly folded and placed on top of other dirty changing pads. The room bore the signs of a caring father, not a raging and possibly murderous drunk.

Frank called to Van to come back to the living room. "I need you to work with Joe and capture all footprints in the blood and develop a storyline from the footprints. Brad is working the knife angle."

"Of course."

"Anything from the bedroom?"

"Nothing yet."

Van saw Joe Warren crouching with his digital camera and studying the floor. Joe was the lab photographer and a recognized expert in crime scene investigation.

"What do you see?" she asked respectfully.

"I'll tell you what I see when we are done," he said patiently. "You need to draw your own conclusions first."

Van studied the floor. She noticed immediately that there appeared to be no bloody footprints leading toward the baby's bedroom. They all seemed to be concentrated in the living room and in the kitchen as if whatever happened in the bedroom, if anything, happened before the murder. She asked Joe to take a shot at an angle toward the baby's bedroom. Joe downloaded the photo and together they studied the shot on an iPad Joe had set up on a stand in the center of the living room. Van moved the photo around with her fingers. To the naked eye and to the camera's eye, she was right. No footprints led to the bedroom—all of them were directed to and from the body tape or congregated around in the kitchen and dining room where the phone was located. The floor still needed a chemical wipe, which was technically not a wipe but a spray that turned a light green when it came into contact with blood.

She asked Frank, "Any word from the coroner?"

"I haven't heard back."

Brad was carefully dusting the kitchen for evidence of a struggle or some desperate search for a weapon. The kitchen was clean and the prints he was finding were almost all the wife's prints. There were a few of the husband's prints on utensils and dishes in the dishwasher and a couple on plates in the cupboard where he might have been unloading the dishwasher but otherwise nothing. His prints largely corroborated his story. Brad found them on the TV in the living room, near the phone in the dining room and in the baby's bedroom, the last of which Brad dusted after Van had studied the room.

Van continued her review of footprints. Most of what she was seeing suggested but did not prove that the husband did not commit the murder. Her instinct said they had the wrong guy, but she knew not to lean on her instinct alone. There needed to be something supporting another suspect. She made copies of several of the footprints using contact paper that she sealed in separate plastic baggies, taped them shut, and put a number on each. Her note pad listed the numbers and described the precise locations of the print. Later she would use Joe's photographs to identify further using those evidence tags to show which contact sheets came from which footprints. She took a moment to study the prints and saw no indication that there was a third set. One very troubling thought occurred to her—that it might be possible the wife was suffering from post-traumatic stress and had perhaps stabbed herself. There were several problems with that theory, but the most obvious problem with that was that there was no knife. If the husband found her cut open, he presumably would have no reason to dispose of the knife and would have told the police she killed herself. She made a quick note and set that idea aside for later review. Van studied the footprints and kept looking for a third set of footprints, but nothing suggested a third set. The chemical wipe added nothing new to her findings. She talked to Joe and they agreed on several key points that Van noted:

1. There appeared to be only two sets of footprints in the blood. There was no visual evidence of a third set.

2. One set came from large feet wearing work boots, presumably male and the husband's prints, and the other set came from small flat-soled shoes, presumably female and the wife's prints.

3. No footprints led to the baby's bedroom although a set of male footprints appeared to have come from the bedroom.

4. The majority of footprints, both male and female were in the living room around the body tape, suggesting that whatever struggle occurred, if any, it took place in the living room around the body and nowhere else.

5. There was a line of footprints to the phone and back to the body and then to the front door.

"Anything else?" Van asked Joe.

"Nothing I can see at this point," said Joe. "Good work," he smiled.

"Let's go!" shouted Frank from the front door. Brad and Van gathered their cases and met Frank at the front door. As they walked down the steps, Van remembered the bush. "Give me a second," she told Frank and walked over to the side of the house. The bush, which was under a window next to the dining room, was a hibiscus bush that had started to flower. It was intact except for a section of branches growing toward the rear of the house that looked freshly broken.

"I think you should see this," she shouted to Frank and Brad. Brad was tired and looked irritated. Frank squinted against the setting sun at the back of the house and set down his forensic bag. He grabbed Brad's arm and marched him over to Van. "Be careful," Van said to Brad as he started to walk around the bush to look at the broken branches. At that moment, Van picked a scent. "Stop," she said to Brad. She leaned in and picked up a sweet muskiness that was not from the flowers. It smelled almost like blood, and for a second, Van wondered if the blood smell from inside the house was lingering in her nose. But this was more than blood. It was faintly industrial—like a solvent. Then she saw it, a small rectangular piece of brown fabric was caught in the bush. She put her gloves on and took tweezers out of her case and placed the fabric to her nose and winced.

Frank looked at Brad. "Did you dust this windowsill?"

"No sir."

"Get your gear back on and dust the area around the window from the inside."

Van backed away from the hibiscus bush and placed the fabric in an evidence bag from her case and marked it accordingly. Frank told Van, "Look for prints or impressions in the dirt around the bush and tell me what you see. I am getting Joe."

The sun was setting and the natural light would soon be gone. Van carefully approached the bush on her hands and knees and saw two definite impressions of boots very similar to the boots inside, and then saw a hand imprint in the grassy dirt near the bush that would be roughly where a hand might be if someone had jumped from the window over the bush, landed on both of their feet and then used their hand to keep from falling. The team set up lights, marked the area with crime scene tape and placed flags next to the prints in the ground. They collected samples from the bush and from the grassy ground around the handprint and the footprints. They also took molds of both sets of prints. Joe flashed several shots.

Two hours later, Frank, Van and Brad returned to the lab. "I want you both to know you did great work today. Stow your gear at the lab and get a good night's sleep. We can talk in the morning."

Van was tired but invigorated. The discovery at the side of the house had opened the door to another theory. Brad had been getting sullen, feeling Van stealing the limelight, but he noticeably cheered up at Frank's words.

"Feel like a beer?" he asked Van.

"Not tonight—I have a competition next month and I am laying low."

"Competition?"

Van shrugged. "Fitness—Venice Beach. You should come. It's fun."

"Thank you," Brad flushed. So did Van, and she peered sideways at Brad and smiled.

"See you tomorrow."

* * * * * *

"So, what did we learn?" Van loved these conversations and felt a deep admiration and devotion to Frank.

Brad said, unusually humbly, "Maybe Van should start."

"Ok. Wow. Well, in my mind, as I approached the house, my first thought was about the baby. In the middle of what must have been an extremely violent and chaotic situation, I wanted to know what happened to the baby."

"Interesting," said Frank. "Different angle. It is not uncommon in domestic abuse cases that result in murder for there to be multiple victims, often the children."

"Yes, but my interest was not in what did not happen to the baby but what did happen."

"Explain."

"The baby's diaper was changed—or at least the husband claimed to have changed the diaper and the smell of baby powder was strong enough to match the smell of blood."

Brad said, "Not to diminish your point but houses that have babies usually do smell of baby powder—or you hope they do."

"I don't disagree but there is a difference between baby powder as a residual scent and fresh baby powder. There had been recent activity in the bedroom and the top diaper in the trash bin still smelled fresh."

"Does that lead somewhere?" Frank pressed.

"It does. It suggests—doesn't prove but suggests—that the husband was not contemplating murder when he came home and crashed on the couch. It also suggests that the wife's effort to rouse him to change the baby was not a rage-triggering event and that the husband had a routine with the baby that he followed despite being groggy and possibly a bit inebriated. If all that is true, then two things are possible. One, the husband did not commit the murder and his story checks out. He changed the baby and came out of the bedroom to find his wife already bleeding. Two, he is a cold-blooded killer, who had carefully planned the murder and executed it in a calculated manner that included faking a snooze. But the course of events doesn't really support that."

"Ok. There are a few holes, but I like where you are going. Brad?"

"There was a lot of blood."

"You've hooked me," Frank's sarcasm was not subtle.

"What I mean is there was a lot of blood, but it was not spread all over the house as if the wife was defending herself, fighting back and running for her life from someone she knew could get violent. It was concentrated in one area."

"Okay good—what does that tell us?"

"That she was caught unaware and that her attacker was swift and knew what he was doing. I agree with Van. I don't think this was a rage event. I think it was planned and committed by someone who knew what they were doing."

"Do you make the husband for it?"

"I don't know. The knife is missing. There is no evidence in the kitchen that suggests the knife even came from the kitchen. No fingerprints on other knives or utensil drawers or the dishwasher. The husband could have brought a knife home and then disposed of it but where? The team checked the garbage and the yard and the house and did not find anything related to the murder."

"I don't know," said Van. "This is not a domestic abuse case. Something else happened here and I am willing to bet someone else was involved."

"A love triangle?" asked Brad, trying to get Frank's attention.

"Except that your own theory doesn't support it," Van answered, now feeling competitive.

Frank ignored it. "We don't have much time," he said, bringing the mood back to somber. "They will arraign the husband tomorrow. Homicide wants to know our take. Let's go visit the coroner."

The coroner's office was a tough place to visit, even to the most seasoned detectives. The air was full of formaldehyde and after even a few minutes, which was rarely the case, the formaldehyde stuck in your nose and stayed with you for days, infecting everything you tried to eat. For Van, it was doubly so, and the worst part of her job.

"What's going on, Frank?" Dr. Gilford von de Grassy was a long-time friend of Frank Weatherby and a unique character in his own right. He wore ear spacers in both ears, and as a younger man had been a tattoo model. You could see that both of his arms were covered as well as his neck and jaw, long before boxer Mike Tyson jumped on that crazy train, as everyone thought at the time. You could not see that Gil had 90% of his body covered and had been on the cover of several tattoo magazines along with his wife, also a tattoo model. But Gil was chief coroner of the LAPD for a reason, and he and Frank trusted each other, and had a deep admiration for each other's work.

"Back again, Gil. Seems like no matter what we do, we never seem to work ourselves out of job."

"Ain't it the truth. You are here on Baldwin Hills?"

"Right."

"I got to tell you this one is unique."

"How so?" Gil walked over to the drawer containing the wife's body, opened the drawer and folded the coroner's sheet back to reveal the head of a youngish Latina. Van, Brad and Frank stood respectfully near the body's head. The skin on her face was light brown with the greenish hue of death. It was passive, without emotion. Her lips were blue. As Gil pulled the sheet back further, all three examiners were startled. The stab wounds looked surgical and not what you would expect in a crime of passion. Whoever cut her knew precisely what they were doing and did it with swift precision. The cut pattern resembled a capital H lying on its side with one horizontal cut just below the navel and the second horizontal cut from hip to hip with a single almost perfectly vertical cut midway between the two.

"Cause of death?" Frank asked methodically. Van and Brad glanced at each other.

"Yes," said Gil. "But that's not all." Frank looked up. Gil went over the cuts and with a gloved hand pulled back the cuts on the right side of the body. "She is missing something." All three examiners looked at the body and then each other. "It appears that the murderer took an ovary."

"Damn," mumbled Brad. They stared at Gil as a new realization began to creep in.

Van said it first, "We may have a serial."

"Yah," said Brad. "They got the wrong dude."

Frank looked troubled, "We got a method guy, I agree. Whether or not the husband is the perp, this was not a crime of passion."

Gil closed up the body. "One more thing. We swabbed the nasal passages and found traces of chloroform."

Frank looked at Brad and Van. Van answered his unspoken question. "Nothing was reported, sir, and we found nothing." Brad concurred.

Frank looked back at Gil and repeated, "Cause of death?"

"You're careful, aren't you, Dr. Weatherby?" Gil joked, trying to lighten the mood. "By the time the paramedics got there, she had lost so much blood, she should have been DOA. She wasn't. The paramedics' efforts to stop the bleeding kept her alive a few minutes longer but they didn't see that internal cut. She died from an internal hemorrhage."

The team returned to the SUV. "I am not making the husband," Brad repeated.

"And I'm not ready to release him," Frank responded. "I can't risk releasing a potential serial killer just because his first victim is his wife."

"That's a hard call," said Van, "but I agree for the moment." Her mind was spinning. The footprints on the ground outside the window were an almost perfect match to the footprints inside but if there was a third person in the house, there had to be three sets of footprints. As much as Van's Buddhist culture supported a belief in ghosts, she refused to consider the killer floating out of the house. Besides, something had happened at that window, and her hope was that the small bit of evidence they did find might be a lead.

CHAPTER 4.

Sense and Senselessness (Part II)

The next morning Van woke up early and hit the road for a quick three-miler. When she got home, the sun was still hidden and she ran through a quick routine of band work and floor exercises finishing with a 10-minute plank. Dressed and ready for work, she made herself Vietnamese coffee and scrambled eggs from four egg whites. She loved the hot richness of the expensive Weasel coffee blend that her parents bought for her, especially with a touch of sweetened condensed milk. The condensed milk was a delicacy she allowed herself to enjoy only on rare occasions and never when she was competing. Her strict workout regimen excluded all dairy except eggs, her primary source of non-vegetable protein.

The sun was only beginning to rise as she wished her parents good morning and drove into the LA traffic. The drive from Monterey Park to downtown was only a few miles but it was a slow haul. Van had found a few back streets that at least distracted her if they didn't speed up her commute time. As she drove, she thought about the homicide and found herself agreeing with Brad more than Frank. The husband would have to be both calculating and mentally ill to have planned such a cold-blooded murder. He took time with the baby. He cleaned the baby and set up the room as a courtesy to himself or his wife, whichever would have been called on for the next diaper change. Then he casually walked out to the living room where he clinically dissected a living being who was the mother of his child. It just didn't ring true. And there was no knife and there was no excised body part.

The problem was the complete lack of evidence of a third person in the house. There had to be something. She thought about the bush. It was damaged, and if she remembered correctly, the damage appeared to be fresh. She needed to review Joe's photographs and look for DNA and any other chemical substrate on the torn fabric. She was concerned that the bush evidence was just a distraction and that the husband might have launched himself out of that window and inadvertently damaged the bush for a hundred reasons. She didn't believe that, but the truth might simply be so. After all, the footprints were basically the same.

Frank was impressed with Van's acuity at the crime scene, both her unwavering focus on finding a rational storyline supported by the evidence and her heightened visual and olfactory sensitivities. He had a gift for locating talent and he did not hesitate to encourage it. He saw her enter the lab, remove her coat and replace it with a white lab coat. He could tell she was thinking and probably too hard.

"Good morning, Van."

"Good morning, Dr. Weatherby. Have we submitted the fabric for DNA?"

"Not unless Brad submitted it."

"If not, I would like time with it."

"Let's let Brad get the DNA results first before we handle it anymore. I'm a bit sensitive on that one."

He smiled. "Do you have a minute?"

"Of course," she said quickly, a bit startled by this unusual display of early morning courtesy.

"Follow me," he said.

They left the lab and grabbed an elevator that took them about three stories below ground. The light on the floor was hazy, and Van noticed the air had a scent of mildew from old books and wet paper. The linoleum on the floor was worn and dusty, as if the cleaning crew rarely made their way down here, and the lights would make you go mad if you had to spend much time down there. It occurred to Van for a brief instant that Frank's motives might be suspect. He quelled that thought immediately.

"I am troubled by the body we reviewed yesterday."

Van grimaced. "That's an understatement."

Frank laughed. "Sometimes I find that the best way for me to process something troubling is to get away from it. Not a lot of times, but sometimes, just for a morning."

"I like the idea that your brain works whether or not you are actively thinking about something."

"That's a point. It's a remarkable organ. It works all day and then keeps working while we sleep. It works when we want it to work and then works when we stop. There are some who believe it works actually to fool us into thinking we are making it work. They believe that there is no such thing as pure conscious thought, which they assert is only a neurochemical reaction. Rather, our only true thoughts emerge in the unconscious."

"I don't think I can go there. Sounds as if they think that, without our unconscious mind, we are nothing more than robots. If that's true, then why do we choose when and where to focus our thoughts?"

"Point taken. It's really more about philosophy than neurobiology but no question we are thinking even when we are not thinking." He grabbed keys out of his coat pocket and opened a gray door with mesh covering the window and flicked on the light. Inside were rows of boxes and files.

"Come here often?" Van flirted just a bit. Frank gave her a look that told her that wasn't funny. She flushed.

"These are cold case files. Any effort to solve them was abandoned after no suspect was found or, even if they identified someone, nothing turned up to support an indictment."

Van looked at the size of the room, which was not small and appeared to be packed. "Does this happen often?"

"Our job is to ensure it doesn't, and unfortunately, we are not perfect. But there is a lot to learn here. Very few cases go cold because a criminal is a mastermind. Most criminals become criminals because crime is easy, and they are too dumb to find a legitimate way to live. Some criminals want to be caught. For whatever bizarre turn of events that occurred in their lives, crime and punishment is a comfort zone for them. A small percentage of criminals are just plain evil, but it is remarkable how many of them want to be caught. Bottom line, there are a few masterminds, but it is rare that cases go cold because we are outsmarted. Most cases go cold because mistakes are made by the police, by forensics, by investigators who miss obvious clues. Sadly, some cases should go cold that don't—innocents can become victims of a system looking to lay blame. Study the mistakes of others and maybe you can learn to avoid them."

Van was reflective. "I bet a lot of cases involving prostitutes go cold."

"A fair share I imagine," Frank answered as he pulled the door closed.

"I think about them sometimes."

"You do?"

"Sure. I wonder how they decide that selling their bodies as a way to make a living makes any sense. It's like they tried and failed at a couple of alternatives and then just gave up."

"There are a lot of sad stories to be sure, but they call New Orleans 'the Big Easy' for a reason."

"Yeah. Easy doesn't work very well. I find that living your life trying to avoid the pain of failure becomes the most painful kind of life. You have to find a way to move forward. You can't give up."

Van's spontaneous reflection struck Frank and he reflected on the Simpson trial and how few of his damaged colleagues ever recovered. "This culture is so focused on success that many of us never learn how to manage failure."

"I discovered failure at a very early age. I was six when they put me in special ed. I couldn't hear and the school thought I was slow. When they finally figured it out, they put those giant hearing aids on me and everyone treated me weirdly. I hated them and didn't care if I couldn't hear. I forced myself to learn to read lips."

"You are remarkable, Van. I brought you here because I like the way you think and how you approach your job. Spend some time here. Let me know what you find."

Frank handed Van the keys and left. She walked into the room. It smelled like old, wet cardboard. She wandered around the stacks to see if there was any order or if it was simply old in the back and new in the front. She found the room divided into sections. Each division had a section. Robbery-Homicide, Gang and Narcotics, Vice. The largest section was Commercial Crimes (White Collar). Not a surprise. There was a cage in the back that was labeled Homeland Security. She found the letters *R-H* and pulled down a few boxes, grabbed a chair and started digging. There were a lot of gruesome photos. One picture showed headless bodies. Another showed a woman cut in half. The file said Dalia. Van knew that one and was tripping to be in the basement of an LAPD building reading about it. She looked to see if there were any boxes that linked murders. She didn't see anything immediately. That was not surprising. Serial killers seemed to fall into that category of evil criminals who wanted ultimately to be caught. She found one file about a murder in Hollywood. She read through a couple of files. The coroner's report made reference to semen found on the body of the victim, a young girl. The file contained a sealed bag with pieces of cloth, sheets, underwear. Written on the bag were notes of a lab technician that included the word "contaminated." She thought of the fabric she found on the bush and started to panic. She quickly reassembled the boxes and returned them as she found them, headed out of the room, locked the door, and ran to the elevator.

She found Brad in the lab, intently studying fingerprint scans.

"Where did you send the Baldwin Hills evidence?" she asked.

"I had Karen take it to DNA, Sixth Floor."

"Thanks."

Van found Karen Wasserman in a small cubicle at the back of the lab. Karen was a lab technician who got her forensics science certificate from a local trade college. She was good at her job, recognized by the school with a special award for being the top student in her class. She was also a single mom, trying to work and raise two kids on her own.

"Brad told me he gave you the Baldwin Hills evidence to have analyzed."

"Yes, he did," Karen replied, with a look of concern as if she had done something wrong.

"You followed protocol, correct?"

"I did."

"Good. Who got it?"

"I double bagged it, labeled the outer bag and dropped it with Sam on the sixth."

"Great, Karen. Thank you."

Van rode the elevator to the sixth floor. The floor that handled DNA was reinforced with heavy steel doors and looked more like a mental ward for the criminally insane. Exiting the elevator, she found herself in a small lobby at the end of which was a heavy secured door and a wall with a thick plexiglass window. She peered through the window. The old back room kitchen look of the 1990s had been replaced by stainless steel and hazmat suits. Once evidence entered that room, everything that could be done to prevent contamination had been done; the setting calmed Van's surge of panic. She hit a buzzer and a masked attendant appeared at the window.

"Is Sam here?"

"Just a second."

A tall, lanky African American popped into view. "Van!" She had met Sam a few times. He was a really nice guy and fairly young to be leading a key subdivision of the Forensics Science Division.

"Hi, Sam. I am here to follow up on the Baldwin Hills sample."

"Yes. I have been working with it myself. I'm sorry, Van, but I am not detecting any measurable DNA."

"Are you still working with it?"

"Probably not."

"Can you have it bagged? I'll wait."

"Sure." Sam was gone for about 5 minutes and brought it back. "Always a pleasure to see you, Van."

"You too, Sam."

Van signed out the bag and returned to the lab. She gloved up and opened the bag carefully. With sterile tweezers she lifted it out and dropped it into an open petri dish. It looked to be cotton, which if there had been DNA, would be good and bad. Cotton was a great repository of DNA but also could make DNA very difficult to identify because cotton, relative to polyesters or silks, had a very uneven surface.

But she knew she wanted time with this fabric. She stared at it for a few minutes, looking at the shades of color and tints. Someone without Van's perception might call it light brown but Van could see a variety of tans and even some orange caused, it seemed to her, by a very light stain. She snipped a small piece of the fabric near the stain and placed the snip with tweezers in a separate dish. She placed that dish in a vacuum chamber alongside a small dropper containing disilane. Disilane was extremely unstable and flammable when exposed to air, specifically oxygen. But one if its key properties was that it caused residual chloroform to glow. She turned on the chamber and placed her hands in the rubber gloves that allowed her to work in the chamber. Very slowly she opened the disilane, constantly checking the vacuum gauge. She touched the tip of the thin glass dropper to the fabric and immediately it started to glow. Even though chloroform evaporates almost instantly, there was enough residual to react. Not conclusive, but more evidence supporting the husband's innocence.

She then took the remainder of the fabric and held it closely to her nose. She knew the chloroform was not sufficient to hurt her and unlikely there would be any scent left at all. But she closed her eyes and focused on her nose, taking slow deep draws. At first there was nothing, but soon she began to pick up hints of rubbing alcohol along with diesel, fertilizer, eucalyptus and lavender. It was an odd combination of scents, and she couldn't place it.

She looked up and Brad was standing next to her as he seemed to be doing more regularly lately. It was a little disturbing, but he was trying to be polite and not interrupt her focus.

"Brad?"

"I think I found something," he said.

"Go on."

"There is a third set of fingerprints."

Van's jaw dropped. "You sure?"

"Let me show you."

Van carefully placed the fabric back in the evidence bag and sealed it. As they walked over to Brad's lab, Van asked him, what places would have rubbing alcohol, diesel, fertilizer, eucalyptus and lavender?

"Don't know about the alcohol but sounds like a farm. Maybe a flower farm? Why?"

"Any flower farms you know of?"

"I have seen orchid farms in Oxnard and Mendocino, on the way to Santa Barbara. Could be a nursery."

"Maybe."

Brad brought up the prints on his screen. He explained to Van how his program worked to identify common point on prints to detect positive matches and fails. Van knew a lot about fingerprint software, but she enjoyed listening to Brad. His way of describing things was both simple and smart. He got to the point quickly.

"Most of the prints in the kitchen and dining room area were her prints. I found his prints on the phone and in the living room, consistent with his story. But there was a thumbprint I pulled off the dining room table that does not match either his or her prints."

"Odd that a killer would be so careful and methodical and leave a print."

"It is, but I think he did."

Van got home around 6:15 p.m. Mom was there and preparing dinner. The house smelled fresh, as if there were new flowers. She walked into the kitchen, and said, "Hi Mom, I'm home."

"Hello, Daughter." Her mom rarely called Van by her name when she addressed her directly.

"Smells good, Mom."

"Yes. Nice. Very cheap."

"Did you go to the Dollar Store?" The Dollar Store was her mom's favorite place to shop other than the fashion district in downtown LA.

"No, no. Your father and I drove to Olvera Street. They have a market."

Van looked at the table. Mixed in with the daisies and mums was fresh eucalyptus. "What kind of market?" Van had assumed it was a grocery store.

"Outdoor market. You know it. For farmers."

"A farmers' market?"

"Yes. Farmers' market."

Van saw Brad as she walked into the lab the next morning. "I need to know where there are farmers' markets around Baldwin Hills."

"Farmers' market." Brad picked it up immediately. "Right. I know there is one on Grove Street in La Brea—that is a famous one. There is also one on Olvera Street. Historic."

"My mom went there yesterday. Want to take a ride?"

"I'm in."

Olvera Street had been a Los Angeles icon since the 1930s. The "street" was a brick walkway for pedestrians only and replicated an outdoor Mexican mercado, with small stalls and restaurants. It celebrated Latino heritage and evolved from a small outdoor market into a downtown Los Angeles museum and tourist destination. Some stalls remain owned by the same families that started them nearly a century ago.

But Olvera Street also represented the complicated cultural relationship between Los Angeles Latinos and other LA cultures. Under the veneer of merchandizing and good food was a history of conflict and a battle for recognition and respect that stretched from Mexico down through the Central and South America.

Van and Brad parked at the rear entrance and made their way to the street. Van had never seen Olvera Street even though she worked just a few blocks away. The reds, yellows, pinks and blues of blankets, hats, toys and pottery spilled out of the small stalls, and the smell of *carne asada* and frying breads overwhelmed the market.

Brad entered the street mesmerized by the smell and contentment of Mexican comfort food, but Van's attention was focused elsewhere. She saw the colors and the merchandise and the clerks and managers hustling new business. She saw tourists and the families and older folks out for an enjoyable stroll. She also saw mostly men lurking around shops. Some of the men were probably shop owners overseeing the work, and they seemed to have small entourages. She saw some younger men enjoying the view, potential suitors looking for pretty girls. And she saw others lurking, trying to appear distracted but obviously with more questionable motives.

They walked together casually down the street past stall after stall of the same touristy kitch. "This is not really a farmer's market," Van observed. "More like an open-air pop-up mall."

"Right, except that it's been popped-up for 90 years," Brad noted. Behind the stalls on both sides was a row of mostly two-story buildings. Most of the lower stories were restaurants. Some of the first story rooms were recreations of small 19th century offices, giving Olvera its museum effect. Van studied the buildings, looking for signs of a doctor's office or a medical clinic but the smell of the restaurants was so powerful she thought it unlikely that the fabric evidence spent any time there. She also wondered if her mom really knew where she had been when she bought the eucalyptus.

She walked back to the car with Brad, feeling let down but resolved to go to every farmer's market in LA. Then, as they turned the corner, she noticed a flower shop that was not actually on Olvera Street. It was a good-sized shop with a large selection of mums, daisies and roses set out on the sidewalk. There was a small feminine looking gift shop on one side and a two-story office building on the other side.

Van smiled at Brad. "Check this out," she said, as she grabbed his hand instinctively and started pulling him toward the flower shop. He responded by giving her hand a light squeeze, which startled her and she realized how inappropriate it might have felt to Brad. She dropped his hand and with her hand to her mouth, said, "Oh my god, I am so sorry." He smiled and, in that moment, Van looked at Brad's eyes and felt her stomach drop. "No worries," he said. "I get that all the time." He laughed. She blushed and smiled. "The flower shop," she said determined and turned around this time, letting Brad fend for himself but wishing just a little that she was still holding his hand.

They walked inside and although the roses, gardenias, and jasmine scents seemed everywhere, Van quickly picked up on the strength of the eucalyptus branches that were used to adorn arrangements alone with baby's breath and ferns. She walked to the counter to see an older Latina cutting stems, and from behind a door a small Asian woman appeared. She saw Van and said in slightly forced English, "Hello, may I help you."

"*Ni hao,*" Van responded, hoping to put her at ease. The woman fired back in rapid Mandarin, which, even though Van spoke Cantonese, she understood well.

"I was wondering if you knew of a doctor in this area."

"Doctor? Are you feeling sick?"

"No, I am sorry, but I am from LAPD Forensics, and I am looking for a doctor's office or clinic in this area."

The woman smiled. Her business needed the protection of the police, and she was a frequent caller of 911 when her cameras caught homeless people or other vagrants sniffing around her store. "Very good. I like the police. Very helpful," she said. "Maybe you come back into my office?"

Van turned to Brad, and said, "I'll be back in a minute," and left Brad feeling out of place looking around the flower shop. The older Latina picked up on it and began to engage Brad, asking him if he had a girlfriend. Van followed the shop owner into her office. It was neat and organized but there was nowhere for her to sit.

"May I offer you some tea?" the shop owner asked.

"That would be nice," Van replied, "but my friend is waiting for me."

"I will get him some tea too," she answered and headed to a small kitchen. "Why are you looking for a doctor's office?" she asked from the kitchen.

"We're investigating a homicide."

"Oh. You think a doctor did it?"

"Maybe."

"Why?"

Van wanted to be courteous, but she was wary of the shop owner's curiosity and concerned about interfering in the Department's separate investigations. "I'm sorry but I shouldn't be discussing details."

"Sure. Sure. I'm sorry. I do not know of any doctors here."

"The building next door. Do you know who lives there?"

"Nobody lives there. Been empty for many years."

"Does anybody stay there?"

"No. No. Nobody is there."

"Have you ever thought about buying it?"

At this, the shopkeeper hesitated. "No, I no buy. Very expensive." Van sensed something off about the response. It wouldn't be unusual for a successful business to consider expanding or simply investing in other assets. Downtown Los Angeles was actually growing and multistory condos were springing up all over. Loft style apartments were especially popular and expensive. The land alone under the building would be valuable. But as an empty building, it also might be hard to keep out vagrants who were looking for free shelter.

An Asian man entered through the back door and saw his wife speaking to Van. She saw him, and said, "I must get back to work. Please let me know if I can help."

Van thanked her and walked back out front. Brad was holding a large bundle of flowers. Van thought he might be offering them to her, which would have been very strange, but Brad said, "She told me I need flowers to get the girl. I couldn't say no." They both laughed and walked out the front door. Van wandered over to the front door of the building. She tested it and it was locked. The windows were dusty and had not been washed. She tried to look inside but there was paper covering the windows. She looked up to the second story, and an old shade was pulled down but not all the way. She knocked on the front door but there was no response.

"What did she say?" Brad asked, shifting the flower bundle from one arm to the other.

"Nothing. She did not know of any doctors in the area. But this building is strange, and her reaction when I asked about it was odd."

They returned to the lab. Frank was still there and asked what they had found and why Brad was holding a large bundle of flowers. Van smiled at Brad and said they brought them back to spruce up the office. Brad quickly concurred. Frank furrowed his brow but shifted to the investigation.

"Anything?"

Van described the trip to the market and the flower shop. Frank was encouraging. "Good to follow your hunches. Even if nothing turns up, it expands the window of your investigation. Just be careful of rabbit holes."

"I think it is more than a hunch," Van replied. "I want to test out the florist's claims about that building."

"Fine. If you go back there, take someone from homicide."

✶ ✶ ✶ ✶ ✶ ✶

Charles Darling was a senior detective in the Robbery-Homicide Division of the Detective Bureau. He had been at the Bureau for 25 years and was starting to think about retirement. His approach was old school and he had been fairly successful at solving crimes, successful enough to be kept around. He was never a star in the making and he had seen many stars come and go. He had been passed up several times for chief despite working many more late hours than others and often being the first to arrive. He lived by himself, did not smoke and kept his drinking to special occasions. His one vice was reading, and his small home was lined with full bookshelves. Charlie was getting on, but to say he was losing his touch would be wrong. Charles loved being a detective. But he also liked the company of pretty young women, and when Van reached out and the other detectives on the case declined, he offered to help.

They pulled up to the corner across from Olvera Street, and Van pointed to the flower shop and the office building. Charlie turned at the first corner across from the flower shop, pulled a U-turn in the middle of the road, and parked on the spot closest to the corner. The sun was setting and traffic was beginning to die down. It was the perfect time to start a stakeout. Nothing unusual about a 2010 tan Ford Taurus parked innocently but directly across from your place of business. Van looked at Charlie, as if to say, "Are you serious?" but said nothing. Charlie noticed and smiled at the rookie.

"A bit too obvious?"

"I wouldn't know," Van replied. "I've never been on stakeout."

"Sweetheart," he said, a bit too condescendingly. "I've been on so many of these I can't tell the difference between sitting here and in the office. But one thing I have learned—you don't catch any more criminals hiding two blocks away than you do sitting directly across the street. It is amazing how people fail to see the things directly in front of them."

Charlie didn't know Van was hearing impaired, and therefore that noticing the things in front of her and to the side and sometimes even behind her was how Van lived every moment. Van understood conceptually that people were easily distracted and often missed the details staring at them directly, but that was not her experience and the idea of testing that assumption seemed ludicrous. Still Van was bred to respect others, especially those who were her seniors, and she forced down the complaint just as she slid lower in the front seat.

Charlie pulled out a paperback novel and a pen light and began to read. Van stared at the building. Charlie didn't question Van's intuition about the building. He had learned early on to have an open mind about alternative theories of a crime. It was a key Holmesian principle, as in Sherlock, to allow for alternative theories and not get locked into a specific set of facts. His partners back at the Department were making that mistake now by focusing only on the husband and treating the case as a case of domestic abuse however gruesome. He knew they were making fun of him following the hunch of a first-year forensic assistant, but he also knew they would not mind sitting in his place.

The red-orange hue of a Pacific Ocean sunset slowly faded as the new LED-based streetlamps popped on and began to take over as the primary force pushing back on the darkness. Van noticed that several people walked by the car and were startled to see two people sitting there, but they all gathered themselves quickly and moved on either because it was normal, or if it wasn't, they didn't want to know. Then she saw a man step to the building, stop, look around, unlock the door and walk inside. In the darkening evening, it was becoming hard to see detail, but Van saw enough to know she recognized the man, and it was precisely because Charlie had parked so close. It was the same man she saw enter the back of the florist's shop, who, at the time she had assumed was the florist's husband.

She poked Charlie who clicked off the pen light and looked up. "I know him," she said urgently. "I saw him in the flower shop this afternoon."

"Any reason to suspect him?"

"I don't know. Not yet."

Ten minutes went by. Fifteen. Van thought it odd that even though it was dark and the man entered the building, he didn't turn on any lights, at least nothing she could see. Then another man appeared. He was wearing glasses and a tight jacket and carrying a small case, like an old-style doctor's case. He looked around and then knocked on the door. It seemed like forever to Van but eventually the door opened, and the second man went inside. Van looked again at Charlie.

"Something is up."

"Maybe, maybe not," he answered. "Let's see if we can get a closer look."

Van's heart was pounding as she stepped out of the car. She was both thrilled and scared at the same time. Charlie took the lead and they crossed the street. They were careful to stay away from the front door in case either of the men decided to leave. Van noticed a light coming from a window at ground level. The window was lined by brown paper on the inside, but a small part of the paper had pulled back from the window leaving a slight opening. She walked by the window nonchalantly to see if there was any kind of view and when she looked down through the opening, the light was shining on a white table that appeared to be part of a lab. Charlie had pulled his gun just in case. She motioned to him and pointed to the window at her feet. He stepped to the side and looked down. He saw what looked to him like a sophisticated meth lab. Van leaned forward for a second look and stared directly into the eyes of the florist's husband. She froze. Oddly, the husband returned his focus to the lab without any reaction, as if, as Charlie had described earlier, he just missed what had been staring at him right in the face. Charlie motioned Van to return to the car. He had to think, and he didn't want Van in the middle of something undesirable.

When they got back in the car, Van said to Charlie, "She told me there was no one in the building."

"She the shopkeeper?"

"Yes."

"You think she was lying?"

"I do now."

Charlie made a call back to a friend of his in Narcotics. "Got anything about a meth lab near Olvera Street?" He waited and got a response. He looked at Van impressed. "Well, you might have found something, Van, whether or not it's related to the murder."

"You think it's a drug lab?"

"I don't know but it seems fishy."

"So what's next?"

"Let's talk to Narcotics. They know how to handle this. Let them do their job first and see what happens. They will set up a full surveillance team to check it out. No sense rushing in and ruining an opportunity. They call it a stumble and bumble. Let's not do that."

Van didn't sleep well that night. She was proud that Charlie had complimented her but deeply unsatisfied. What if the second man was the murderer? Had they lost a key moment in the case? What if he disappeared and the case went cold, or worse, the husband was unjustly charged with the murder, or worse still, what if other murders took place that they could have stopped? She knew it was useless to speculate, especially on dire outcomes, but it was hard not to.

The next day, Charlie brought Van to meet the commanding officer of the Detective Bureau's Gang and Narcotics Division, Detective III Elizabeth Sampling. Detective Sampling was not afraid of a fight. She was renowned for her aggressiveness throughout the Bureau and many saw her as a shoe-in for the next chief of the Bureau.

"One of Frank's bright new forensics stars," said Detective Charles Darling, introducing Van to Detective Sampling.

"Okay," said Sampling, looking toward Van. "What do you think you have found?"

"We were on a stakeout for a murder that happened in Baldwin Hills. Detective Darling recognized a lab setup in the building basement near Olvera Street that we were watching and thought it looked like it might be a meth lab. But I was interested in two men we saw entering the office building or lab, whatever it is."

"Do you think they are connected to the Baldwin Hills murder?"

"Hard to say. The facts of the murder are unique. It looks more like surgery than murder, and one of the men was carrying a medical bag," Van explained to Sampling.

"You said she is in Forensics?" Sampling looked at Charlie curiously.

"Right," he responded. "As to the lab, we will follow your lead. But on this murder case, I think we should be listening to her."

"It is possible there is a connection," Sampling offered. "Thank you, Detective, Examiner Eng."

Charlie and Van left Sampling's office.

"What do we do now?" Van asked Charles.

"Wait," he responded. "Detective Sampling will support us, but we need to support her right now."

Sampling called a briefing and invited Van and Charlie. They detailed the events and Van described the forensics team's findings and initial investigations. Narcotics set up a stakeout, only this time the stakeout involved multiple cars and officers located at several angles to the office building. The stakeout team had planted cameras and recording devices around the florist shop and the building. Sampling confirmed that in recent months, the Unit had been picking up noise about high volume meth activity in East Los Angeles but had not yet pinpointed a lab until Charlie had announced Van's Olvera Street discovery. Three days after the stakeout, they noticed a white moving van that arrived at around 4:00 am and circled the building several times before parking at the rear loading dock of the office building. Sampling called Charlie, and Charlie called Van. "It's going down now if you want to get out here," he told Van.

Van was already awake and training. She grabbed her LAPD Forensics Team jacket and left for the Bureau. Forty-five minutes later Charlie and Van arrived at an empty garage set up as a staging area about two blocks from the Olvera Street florist shop and alleged meth lab.

Sampling motioned them over. She noticed Van wearing jogging shoes. "Official Forensics gear?" she queried. Van blushed. "No worries, hun," she said. "Probably appropriate if we get a runner." She looked at Charlie. "Does she know how to handle a weapon?"

He looked at her. Van said, "I have been shooting at the range." They got her a Glock-9. She had fired one before but only a couple times.

Charlie whispered, "Watch out for the slide action. It'll tear your thumb apart if you hold it wrong." He showed her how to keep her thumb low. They headed for the cars. "Stay close to me," Charlie said.

They arrived at the office building and placed two cars at the front door and three cars at the rear, pinning down the moving van. Two officers approached the front door, weapons drawn, and banged on the door. Four officers watched the rear loading area. No one was in the van. Charlie and Van watched the front door, crouched behind the open doors of their car. The front door opened, and the officers began yelling, guns drawn, before they entered the building. Three Asian men wearing lab coats came out with their hands on their heads and one officer behind them. Then a fourth man appeared wearing glasses. "That's him," said Van, recognizing the one they saw with the medical bag. Charlie and Van stood up as the officers cuffed the group, but as the officers started to approach the doctor, he suddenly bolted, directly in Van's direction. Several officers yelled stop and pulled their weapons. Van stepped out from behind the car door directly into the path of the fleeing suspect and pointer her Glock-9. "Stop or I'll shoot!" she yelled. The man froze, just long enough for officers who had started to give chase to catch him and throw him to the ground and cuff him. Sampling came over and stood by Charlie. "Nice work, this one," she said to Charlie. Van found herself shaking a bit but exhilarated. Several officers came over and patted her on her shoulders, and said, "Good job." Charlie smiled. "She never ceases to amaze," he said to Sampling.

About a dozen more people were still at work inside the lab when the police first arrived. As the suspects were rounded up, Van called Frank and, shortly thereafter, Frank and the Forensics team arrived and began setting up for analysis of the crime scene. She heard Frank say, "What do we have here?" and she joined him to watch an officer break open a locked freezer. Inside the freezer were plastic containers heavily taped, but Van and Frank could see that the contents included body parts that looked like human organs. They taped off the freezer and called in a police van to carry the freezer back to the lab.

When they finally were able to explore the freezer's contents, Frank's team found a frozen ovary the blood type of which matched the victim's blood type. In addition, Brad's latest print from the house's dining room matched with the doctor, who eventually confessed to having connections to illicit sex organ sales, although he continued to deny any connection to the murder. He was tried and convicted of the murder, and during his trial, witnesses from the lab testified, giving details about his unrequited fetish for surgery and anger at the institutions that failed to acknowledge his brilliance, which had led to a slew of victims, not all of whom died, but who unwittingly lost testicles and ovaries that ended on the black market. How the doctor snuck in and out of the house without being seen was never revealed, but in this case, he had made two critical mistakes, one discovered by Van and the other by Brad. Van felt great relief that the perpetrator had been caught, but to her, the most important outcome was that the grief-stricken husband and father was allowed to return to the baby he so carefully had taken care of that terrible night.

CHAPTER 5.

The Immoral of the Story

H ans Christian Anderson wrote fantastic children's stories. His first popular work, *Fairy Tales,* which like Dickens he wrote and dramatized episodically, developed enduring characters that resonated beyond the confines of culture and class. A beautiful mermaid willing to sacrifice herself for the ideal of love. A tiny child whose unselfish care for others ended up rescuing her from a terrible fate. A misidentified duckling who endured harsh criticism, only to rise above the gaggle around him. A haughty emperor blinded by the flattery of sycophants into playing the fool. Anderson's art was like much art. It was more than the simple emergence of a natural talent. It was an art born of pain. Like Van Gogh, Anderson peered through a dingy window into a better world, a world where a child of poverty would no longer be discounted among the masses, a world where beauty belonged to and was recognized in everyone, not just a small elite.

Cheryl Brown wanted to be part of that new world. Although already a stunning beauty, Cheryl carried with her the burden of a miserable childhood that she endured first by burying herself in books and then by earning the praise and recognition of academic success. But, like Anderson, it was her books that saved her. That one of those books was *Fairy Tales* didn't matter—any story that drew her in and caused her to forget the yelling and harsh words of her early reality was a lifeboat—a safe and secure vessel to carry her away.

As they emerged from the decontamination room at RW Labs, Cheryl Brown slipped the petri dish into her purse. Derek said good-bye to Belinda and the doctor indicating he would be in touch. Gerard pulled up the SUV and sped them back to Derek's office.

"Any impressions?"

"Yes. Seemed sloppy for a high-end technology lab."

"That's perceptive, Cheryl. They definitely talk a good game, and they have the important contacts that can help them get out quickly, but it is still a question whether or not they can actually produce."

"Do you think the Providia software is as important as they claim?"

"We need to find out. I want you to go there tomorrow and see what you can pick up."

Cheryl blushed. It was a high compliment for Derek to send anyone out on their own, and it meant he was thinking about grooming her for a promotion. She thought about the petri dish. She knew it could go very poorly or very well if she disclosed it to Derek. She resolved to hold onto it for the time being. If he was already happy, no reason to risk it.

Derek called Fred as soon as he was back in the office. "They need money."

"Of course they do. Do I need to be the one to give it to them?"

"I have my doubts, Fred."

"Good enough for me. What do we do?"

"I am sending Cheryl to Providia. Possible building block there if we can find the right lab."

Cheryl asked Gerard to pick her up at her home in Redwood City. Redwood City had always been a bit on the lower end of the economic scale in Silicon Valley, and despite a handful of teardowns, the homes remained mostly World War II prefabricated homes built for military personnel working out of Alameda Bay in the 1940s and 1950s. Even still, the market in the Bay Area turned the smallest Redwood City shacks into million-dollar homes and many of these homes had been renovated using pools of equity, so that, even if they were small, they were now suitable for the rising class of upwardly mobile engineers, salespeople, managers and lawyers of the region. Hardwood flooring, crown molding, elaborate landscapes, and stone chimneys transformed the drywall and pine-framed two- and three-bedroom dwellings into craftsman type homes, almost, but not quite, worthy of the price.

Gerard jumped on the south 101 Freeway that ran through the middle of Redwood City and headed toward San Jose. If Redwood City was on the lower end of the economic scale, San Jose was on the bottom of that scale, at least relative to the cities around it. But even San Jose enjoyed the boom that hi-tech brought to the Valley, and many of the marshes at the foot of the San Francisco Bay between Sunnyvale, Santa Clara and Milpitas, just north of San Jose, had been drained and developed into multi-story glass-covered business complexes, one of which housed Providia within the triangle of freeways formed by the 101, the 880 and the 237.

Cheryl arrived at 8:50 am, in time to freshen up and meet with Providia's leadership team, led by the Chief Financial Officer Christopher Deckwalder. Christopher studied computer science at Stanford, but drawn to the success stories of Steve Jobs at Apple, Larry Page and Sergei Brin at Google, and Fred Schmidt at Grindle, he added an MBA from Stanford Business School where he specialized in technology and finance. He was considered one of the top financial minds of the region, which given the setting, was a remarkable accomplishment.

"Good afternoon, Ms. Brown," Christopher welcomed her into the boardroom. "How can we help you?"

"I will come straight to the point," Cheryl responded. She knew credibility mattered in these high-level discussions, and that fools were not tolerated. It made her proud to know that she learned how to conduct herself in these meetings from one of the best, her boss Derek.

"We are exploring investments in smart dust."

"Interesting. I understand we are still years from a marketable product," Christopher responded. "Why now?"

"Perhaps you can answer that better than I can," Cheryl retorted. "We have been investigating the technology for a client and have been told it is not science fiction and that it is coming and perhaps you have an artificial intelligence product under development that might get us there more quickly. Is that true?"

Christopher looked at his team and smiled. "Maybe," he said. "Let's talk about smart dust."

He turned to his team, who, for the next hour, walked through their view of the challenges and opportunities of MEMS, including the political landscape and growing hostility toward MEMS, which they found to be troubling and problematic.

After that discussion, which Cheryl found to be rambling and highly speculative, she turned to Christopher.

"Do you have it?"

"We do."

"It is ready to implement?"

"As soon as we find the right match."

"What are you looking for?"

"There are production performance indicators that matter to us, but in fact there are two things that matter most: (1) do we believe in your goals, and (2) do we believe in you."

Cheryl smiled. "Seems a bit light for the Valley's most brilliant financial mind."

"They're team goals but I agree with them. I think we are done, Ms. Brown. Thank you for your time."

Cheryl grabbed her coat and bag and was politely ushered out of the boardroom. She was not concerned about how the conversation ended. Providia was not a charity and would be smart about how they packaged and sold an AI product that could revolutionize nanomanufacturing. She jumped in the back seat of the Lincoln, and as Gerard was about to close the door, a young man slid into the back seat.

"Here is my card, Ms. Brown. Don't be disheartened. I am certain we can find a way to do business."

She smiled at the young man, not surprised by the olive branch but that it had been offered so quickly.

"I hope we can," she said, and motioned him to leave and Gerard to close the door.

Back at the office, Cheryl was excited to share the Providia discussion with Derek. She tried to stay cool. He was busy and would ask her for details when he was ready. In the buzz of this excitement, she completely forgot about the petri dish, still lodged in her purse. Derek emerged out of his conference room. He noticed Cheryl was back and moved intentionally toward her cubicle.

"I spoke to Christopher," he said. "You did well—held your ground."

This line of discussion took Cheryl by surprise. She expected to be reporting to Derek, not vice versa.

"Did he tell you what his criteria are for using the software?"

"He didn't need to. I know Christopher. He acts like numbers don't matter, but in the end that is all that matters to him."

Cheryl grabbed her purse. "A member of his entourage reached out to me just before I left." She reached into the purse to get the card left by the young man when the card snagged on the petri dish and pulled it out of her purse, plummeting onto the industrial carpet lining her cubical floor.

Derek initially ignored it, assuming it was a makeup compact, and he graciously leaned down to pick it up for Cheryl, who was impressing him more and more every day. It felt oddly heavy and it was strange to him that a compact case would be made of glass. He turned it upright to hand it back to her and then he saw the label: *Risk Group IV.*

"What is this?" he asked.

Cheryl didn't mince words. This moment, as she knew, was about to go very well or very badly. "It was on the floor at RW Labs. I thought it might be something we should look at."

"Look at? Do you know what Risk Group IV means?"

"I don't."

"Jesus Christ, Cheryl!" Derek put his hand up to his forehead and squinted like he was trying to hold back very bad news. "This dish probably contains a pathogen like ebola or bubonic plague, and if there is any leak...oh my God."

Derek ran back to his office. He shut the door and picked up the phone, but he didn't call the Labs or a hazmat or poison hotline. He called Fred.

"We have a problem."

"Go on."

"I don't know what I am holding, but my assistant took it from the Labs. Risk Group IV."

"Risk Group IV? That is a little risky, don't you think?"

"A little? I sure as hell don't want to get whatever is going on in this petri dish."

"Find a biohazard case asap, seal it and bring it by. I'm not sure what they are doing at the Labs but if they are too stupid to let something like this get away, then they deserve losing it. And fire Cheryl."

"I thought about that. But shit, she was doing so well."

Derek found Cheryl sitting quietly in her cubicle. She was running scenarios though her head.

"This is a problem, Cheryl."

"I appreciate that."

"Grab your stuff and go home. I need to think about it."

Without any reaction, she picked up her coat and bag and left. As she passed the reception desk, she turned back to Derek and mouthed, I'm sorry. He looked back, watching her go. His face steeled and she left assuming she would not be back.

Derek called a good contact at Stanford's principal microbiology lab and asked for an RG IV biohazard transport case. They delivered it immediately. The metal carrying case was lined with rubber and foam and held a dense carbon fiber container that was also lined with rubber and foam. The glass petri dish fit snug in the inner container. Derek programmed a code to lock the case and called Gerard. He thought about Cheryl for a quick second and headed to see Fred.

On his end, Fred knew two things about the petri dish. First, whatever it contained probably had been stolen from another lab, which is why he was not concerned that RW Labs would contact the police and accuse Derek of the theft. If anything, they would try to steal it back and may even come after him, which felt to him like more of a game than a threat. He also knew that it had to be important. RW Labs, if nothing else, did their research before trying to claim a reengineered invention as their own. Risk Group IV was not something to be played with. Not only was it dangerous, but it was highly infectious, and the likelihood of an effective treatment or vaccine was so low that if it were released, a widespread pandemic was not out of the question.

But what could it be? He wondered if it might be a form of nanotechnology but dismissed the thought. Why would it be labeled Risk Group IV? Perhaps it was a genetic experiment and maybe even cancer related. Maybe it was a weaponized form of a bacterium or virus. The RW Labs had made a lot of money finding and reengineering military technology, and not always for the United States.

As he thought about it, he began to get a picture of an opportunity. He needed a high-quality lab that both was capable of handling dangerous substances but also desperate enough to work with him in secret. Bainbridge came to mind, and the young genius he had heard about could be tricky to manage if the curiosity of the genius began to give way to moral qualms. But to Fred, in this case, *tricky* really only meant the experiment would fail and the opportunity might be lost. At least he would learn whether or not the Duc A. Tran Lab was capable of working with him.

He watched Derek arrive through his massive office window. Fred's secretary held the door and showed Derek into Fred's office. Fred stood there waiting for him with a trusted executive assistant. Without saying anything to Derek and before Derek could speak, Fred told the assistant to take the metal case to the hanger at Moffett Airport where he kept his Gulfstream 6 or the 'G-Wagon,' as he liked to call it. It didn't bother Fred at all that he spent as little time as was absolutely needed with the dish. He didn't need to see it himself. He knew enough for now.

"Time for a quick trip?"

"Always," Derek said. He glad to be relieved of the metal case. He knew Fred would find it important, but it scared the hell out of him.

"Send Gerard home. I'll get you back."

"Will do. Thank you."

Fred texted his driver and told him to bring the Bentley and to make sure it was "loaded".

Derek smiled. "Loaded" was a good sign that Fred was excited about a plan. They jumped in the back and Fred poured an old Laphroiag for each of them and began the story of Dr. Duc A. Tran, PhD. His capacity for detail was remarkable and when he started one of these stories, Derek knew he was witnessing Fred's real genius.

"You remember the Vietnamese boat people?"

"Yes."

"Well, several remarkable people made their way out of Vietnam and eventually to the United States. One of them was a young biochemistry student who ended up at the University of Washington in Seattle in the early 1980s. His English was poor, but his handling of complex chemistry was remarkable. He flew through a Ph.D. program and the University hired him immediately as a research professor. Duc Tran had grown up in Vietnam during the war and escaped having to serve in the military only because he was a few years too young. But as he grew older, he watched how the influence of the Chinese cultural revolution under Mao Tse-tung impacted the beliefs in his own country. One of the principal concepts of Mao's revolution was that human nature could be molded, that behavior was not innate and that what they viewed as rigorous education could transform an entire nation into becoming a disciplined and highly productive but absolutely subservient people. Nurture could defeat nature and cultural evolution could be controlled so completely by humans that biology was eliminated as a factor in behavior. Tran questioned that premise and built his entire career around proving it false."

Fred looked out his window and saw the airfield come into view.

"It made him famous. He focused on DNA and called his analysis "biological predisposition." His work laid the groundwork for the Human Genome Project. He won a Nobel Prize in biochemistry and he used the money to set up an independent lab that was eventually acquired by a public university. Then he got sick, but the therapies that emerged out of his research were too far in the future to help him, and he died when he was only 40 years old. They named the lab after him, but nothing significant has come out of it since."

Fred went on to talk about the Tran Lab and his confidence that they could handle an RG IV dish but, moreover, the possibility that they may have a unique angle on the contents of the dish. He also wanted a test for the new young genius. Derek was concerned that Fred might be more interested in testing out this remote lab for purposes other than actually exploring the contents of the dish and its opportunities, but he trusted Fred, and more importantly, he served Fred and Fred's money. They boarded the plane, with Fred still holding his glass, and headed to Seattle. He buckled himself into a plush captain's chair and turned toward Derek.

"By the way, Mao proved he was right at least to some degree. He was able to eliminate gender distinctions in the low ranks of the military, and his female foot soldiers became every bit as technically proficient and savage as his male foot soldiers."

"So is it nature or nurture?" Derek asked.

"Exactly," Fred smiled and poured another glass.

The jet landed at SEA-TAC 90 minutes later. A car pulled up to the plane, picked up Fred and Derek, and sped north to a ferry that shuttled them over to Bainbridge Island. The Puget Sound ferry boat system was unique. It originated as an uncoordinated fleet of privately owned boats that served the inhabitants of the islands and connected them to Seattle and the mainland. Starting with a sternwheeler from London and then an American manufactured steamer called the *Fairy*, the fleet grew into a mass of boats that was nicknamed the "mosquito fleet." Ferry traffic today is managed by the Washington Department of Transportation (WDOT) and, more specifically, the Washington State Ferries System. The hop from Seattle to Bainbridge Island is a mere 35 minutes. Fred and Derek relaxed in the back of stretch limousine as they crossed Elliott Bay to the landing dock where the ferry let them off to continue on Highway 305 north through the heart of Bainbridge Island to the Tran Labs.

Derek had never been to the Island but what he saw looked like a wealthy bedroom community combined with a nature lover's travel destination. He watched as they flew past walking and biking trails and chain bridges in multiple nature preserves containing cedar, pine, Japanese maple and birch trees. Fred told him of a small mock Norwegian village called Poulsbo holds a Viking Fest every year in July. On the north end of the Island, just off Highway 305, they reached a large irregular bay called Hidden Cove and glided along the Cove up to where Dr. Tran built his lab looking north out onto Port Madison Bay and the Sound.

A team of scientists was waiting outside the Tran Labs for Fred and Derek. Derek was holding the metal biohazard case, which he quickly handed to one of the scientists. It was breezy and cold, and the group hustled inside to a modest lobby and elevator bay. It took two elevators to carry the group up to the third floor, where the main offices and conference room had large windows looking directly out onto the Sound.

Dr. Stanley Meisner welcomed the two men to the Tran Lab. He gave a brief history of the lab and a summary of their current projects, which

Fred and Derek patiently endured. He looked at the metal biohazard case and concluded with a question. "So, what do we have here?"

As Derek opened the case and carefully placed the petri dish on the table in front of Dr. Meisner, Fred responded, "Our hope is that you can tell us. All we know, as you can see, is that it is labeled Risk Group IV."

Dr. Meisner studied the two men and then looked at his colleagues, who had been quiet but now focused intently on the dish. "It's likely to take some time, Mr. Schmidt."

"Not a problem. I am certain you can handle it." Fred studied the group. The young genius was not present. "By the way, how is Dr. Johannsen doing?" The group looked at Dr. Meisner, who smiled. "He is coming along quite well. We are very proud of him, thank you for asking."

"Very good." Fred smiled graciously. "We'll wait for your results."

Fred liked Bainbridge Island and its nature preserves, and had envisioned spending several weeks and possibly months at the Tran Labs. In advance, he purchased a large estate on a remote portion of the island in a community called Westwood, just off Crystal Springs Drive. No one at the Lab knew that he would be staying around. He invited Derek to stay as long as he liked or to take the jet and return home. Derek had much to do and he felt the need to address the Cheryl Brown issue as quickly as possible. Fred would respect his decision on Cheryl one way or the other, but Derek knew that he could not make the decision from Seattle. "Thank you but I must return," he told Fred, and Fred immediately called the jet hanger and instructed them to fuel up for a return trip.

The Tran scientists returned to the boardroom.

"What do you make of it, Stan?" asked Dr. Leonard Whisk, head of the lab's biochemistry unit and Brian Johannsen's immediate senior.

"He wants something else here," he responded. "I don't think it is about the box."

"I feel the same. I'll leave it with Brian. Let's see what he comes up with."

Dr. Whisk had very little time for curmudgeon billionaires. He was chasing his own vision and had been for many years. No one was going to distract him, not even the CEO of Grindle. He took the petri dish over to Brian's lab and set in on the floor next to his desk and walked away.

Derek landed back at Moffett and Gerard was there to pick him up. They drove directly to Derek's business park and Derek raced in through the front door and up to his office. It was 10:00 pm and no one was around. He called his Stanford connection.

"Do you have it?"

"Yes."

"And it is secure?"

"Yes. We placed it in the same type of metal casing that we gave you. It is in the safe."

"Very good." He disconnected and set his phone down. Derek had spent a lot of years in Silicon Valley and he saw the many ways in which the game was played. Before taking the dish to Fred, Derek had had the foresight to have the microbiology lab at Stanford split the contents of the dish and hand just a portion to Fred. He now had a lot of options. If RW threatened him, he could return it. Like Fred, he too knew, if they did anything, it would be covert and designed to avoid public display. But it could be nasty and that was not a preferred outcome. He also could take it back, plead innocence, throw Cheryl under the bus and possibly use it as leverage to gain a better foothold in a partnership with Belinda. Derek not only had money, but he had connections in the Valley beyond Fred Schmidt. It wasn't out of the question that he might facilitate a deal between RW and Providia that didn't involve Fred's money.

He called Cheryl. She was at a club, drowning her sorrows and trying to find a way to get a cute boy to take her home.

"You realize how stupid that was?"

"I'm listening," she said, trying to maintain her composure.

"The people at RW are snakes. You saw the security there? There is a reason they prefer black ops to off duty cops or ex con security detail. They would not hesitate to kill you Cheryl. Or me."

"If you are trying to scare me, you're doing a good job."

"Yeah. Okay. Meet me in the morning. There is work to do and I don't want to talk about this anymore."

That went well, he thought. She will be a star if she finds a way to stay alive. He needed to find a way to stay alive, and it was quite possible Cheryl Brown would be the key.

CHAPTER 6.

The Theranos Syndrome

Washington D.C. was in chaos. A ragtag New York billionaire playboy with an ego the size of Manhattan had won the presidential election and had become the forty-fifth President of the United States. The liberal media was in utter shock at his victory, having battled claims of fake news for the past two years of his campaign, and their heroine, wife of a former President and the brains behind that effort, had just been swept away by the playboy. The conservative media was overjoyed and stunned themselves. The shock jocks who had been riding on an anti-establishment and pro-capitalist wave, suddenly found themselves a legit and a startlingly credible voice for the new establishment.

The new President started right out of the gate. "We are going to change America and restore its pride. We are going to stop being fodder for the world's anti-American rhetoric and we are going to stand up for ourselves and the capitalist power that we have become. No more apologizing for the wrongs of history. And we are going to clean up Washington, dredge the swamp. Eliminate the stupid laws that keep our companies' brightest minds from shining and taking America way over the top. That is exactly where we are going. Way over the top!"

The world didn't know how to take this new leader. A leader of a global power who had no fear. A leader who would look them directly in the eyes and actually say, "You don't think I have the balls, do you? Try me."

Washington didn't know how to take this new leader. Regulatory department heads and their reports all gathered up their belongings, called their private sector counterparts and fled the Beltway like rats off a sinking ship.

Wall Street did know how to take this new leader. They knew this guy personally. He lived Wall Street and had played Wall Street many times, and they knew that he was someone to be taken seriously. Crazy? He was a little. Just crazy enough to keep everyone around him off balance, and to keep himself in control. They knew that if he set his mind to something, nobody could stop him—nobody but himself. The word went out. Buy! Buy tech! Buy health care! Buy natural resources! Buy media! Buy telecom! Buy commodities! Buy! Buy! The stock market exploded and climbed close to 50% in a few short weeks. And then, despite a massively powerful liberal media and long entrenched liberal left out for revenge and fearful of losing its own credibility, the stock market held its gains and the playboy president had just what he needed to do exactly what he wanted.

What he didn't want was, in his estimate, to subject the American economy to the restraints of the Paris Accords and the pressure of an unrealistic reduction in the country's carbon footprint while other superpowers paid lip service to the effort in order to make rapid gains in the global economy. Environmentalists under former administrations had won the regulatory battles only to risk losing the war. He believed the Paris Accords were a fraud on American labor and American-based business, and his proof was that the largest of American companies had not only gone multinational, they were staffing down their American presence and setting up shop in countries where light regulation and a cheap labor force allowed their returns to pop. He believed he could convince these companies to return to American soil, but he could only do so if he eliminated the harsh regulatory climate of the country, chief of which was environmental regulation.

In order to succeed, his first step was to debunk the belief that the climate was out of control, and that the rise in the earth's surface temperature was a danger caused by human activity. He went on the attack, calling climate change junk science and defunding and even dismantling the departments like the EPA, which under federal law had become the single most challenging impediment to economic growth. Moreover, it was not lost on him that environmental controls had also boosted the authority of local government, which used the power to withhold or delay environmental permits as a corrupt means of securing political influence over and benefits from business, most of which were small local businesses. The president knew this impact only too well, having battled local government on his own hotel and casino projects all across the country. Environmental protection was, in his mind, the giant curtain behind which not only the Washington regulatory complex, but also all state and local regulatory authority in the country hid and pretended to be the Grand Protector of the American Preserve. If he could tear that curtain down, expose the regulatory complex for the hoax that it was, he would end the giant sucking sound and American labor would love him, American business would love him and the American public would fawn at his feet as the Great Savior of the Dream. In short, he would become the greatest president that ever lived.

He was remarkably close to succeeding. But a series of his own ego-driven missteps looked to be his undoing. He refused to cater to the liberal left and called out American media at every opportunity whether or not his ideas were being opposed. He was comfortable only when he was at war, and he delighted in not only making enemies but in baiting his enemies to confront him or risk looking weak. Some might say he was caught up in the very same game that he rose to power opposing. But whether or not he made enemies intentionally or as a byproduct of his own radical pro-American ideals, they came at him and they were relentless. He spent all of his time swatting at his opponents like mosquitoes, rather than creating an effective shield by enhancing the credibility of his original position. He was having some success, and to a degree, Washington politics was shifting, and the regulatory complex actually did fall to one knee, but it was not going down and only history would tell whether what he was doing would hurt or help the country. For the moment, the jury was still out, way out.

Marshall Turner loved Washington, and he knew how to work Washington regardless of who was in office. He was enjoying the chaos and hysteria caused by this new president, and his firm, Blue Ridge Consultants, was doing better than it had been doing in many years. Companies saw the new president as an opportunity to reduce and possibly eliminate the high costs of regulatory compliance, and Marshall had deep connections not only to office holders but also to almost every agency in the city. His firm doubled in size in the first six months of this president's first, and as it would turn out, his only term. Many of his new employees were former regulators and although they disagreed with the new president's view on climate change, they enjoyed the money. They knew the Washington regulatory maze well, or what was left of it, and how best to navigate it.

The key to standing in line with the new president was, as some thought with no small irony, a belief in science. But he refused to believe in just any science, his knowledge cult was new science. "Set the inventors free" was one of his favorite new mottos, and anyone with a direct line to the

Environmental Protection Agency, the Food and Drug Administration, or the US Patent and Trademark Office found themselves in huge demand.

Marshall's phone played a short Aerosmith sample and he clicked on it to answer. Sandra Wellington, an older EPA recruit whose not so hidden agenda was still to fight climate change, said, "Good morning, sir."

"Hi, Sandra!" Marshall answered brightly. He was always positive with his employees. There was no reason to be otherwise. If they screwed up, they were fired and replaced—simple as that. Sandra was anything but a screwup. She was a scarred warrior, and unlike many of her former colleagues who became disgruntled and had abandoned Washington, she chose to stay and keep fighting. Sandra was not a believer in regulating as an end in itself, and if regulations needed to be sacrificed to make way for advances in technology that might become potential solutions to the challenges of the age, then so be it.

"Providia is talking about MEMS again."

"Really? Not a surprise I suppose but I thought the last administration pretty much killed it. What do they want?"

"They want a lock on all artificial intelligence rights related to MEMS."

"Good God. Not asking for much."

"A lock on all AI related to MEMS won't work. But it might be possible to secure special rights to most aspects of AI supporting nanomanufacturing."

"Smart, Sandra. Call Senator Quibley. He is one of the few who never gave up on MEMS. We might be able to build a wall around nanomanufacturing that gives Providia what they want. But it'll be a tough battle and it is going to cost them."

"They'll pay."

"Of course, they will." Marshall smiled. He had endured some tough losses and difficult times, but this was not one of them. He loved it when money came easy. In this case, very few in the old or new Washington establishment would have any idea what Providia was even asking for. The naysayers could be bottled up and discarded as conspiracy theorists. This was exactly the kind of new science this president would support, and the only ones that mattered in the final decision tree would fall in line. So would it actually be a tough battle? Possibly. There were always surprises, but he doubted it.

Aerosmith played again and he answered. There was a pause, but it was not the pause of a robocall. He heard the sigh of exasperation and recognized it immediately. "Hello, Fred. How is my second favorite billionaire?"

Fred Schmidt burst out laughing. "Not as good as my second favorite lobbyist!"

"What can I do for you? Legalize meth?"

"Definitely not that! You'd break up my monopoly!"

"Can't have that." Marshall chuckled. He enjoyed messing with Fred and pretty much anyone he knew to be powerful. It was part of his charm and a key to his success. "What's up?"

"What are you hearing about bio-terrorism these days?"

"It's a dark path, Fred. I wouldn't go down there."

"Actually, I am quite serious. Are you aware of anything the Pentagon is working on?"

"Nothing out of the ordinary. They'd be violating dozens of international treaties."

"Any we care about?"

"Let me put this way. There are a couple of companies allegedly working on antidotes but it's no secret that you can't develop a cure without a disease."

"Risk Group IV?"

"Well, that would be very dark because, as you know, by definition there are no cures, only quarantines."

"So unlikely."

"Yes. Very unlikely."

"That's what I thought. Thank you."

"Fly low my brother." Fred hung up. Marshall blinked back any ideas that Fred was walking down a dangerous path. Fred was too smart for that. At least Marshall hoped he was. He turned back to Providia. He could not help them without getting greater clarity on what they were doing. He called Sandra. "Been to San Francisco lately?"

＊＊＊＊＊＊

RW Labs' Chief Scientist and CEO Belinda Maria Armendáriz gazed through the rain at the massive grounds at the entrance to RW Labs. She smiled at the hidden design created by the iron sculptures and gardens that from her angle resolved itself into the heart-shaped image of her Basque Country. Joan Miró, her favorite Spanish artist, would have been proud. She turned to face the large gathering in her boardroom.

"You think Schmidt is really interested in MEMS?" asked the doctor, who had made the presentation to Derek and Cheryl.

"The better question is whether or not you are really interested in MEMS," she replied. "You need to be more subtle, Leonard."

Dr. Leonard Freund huffed and shrugged his shoulders. He couldn't care less about what Dr. Belinda Maria Armendáriz thought about his dalliances with young female interns. He styled himself as a ladies' man, albeit a late bloomer, and truth be told, he was far more interested in his sexual escapades than MEMS, which wasn't going anywhere anyway. If Belinda could get money out of Fred Schmidt to support MEMS—and she seemed to be able to get money out of a dry turnip—then good for her. Leonard already had more money than he could spend in a lifetime, and pretty much everything other than sex bored him.

At that moment, one of the pretty young interns pressed herself into the room and motioned to Belinda. Belinda walked over to the door, and the intern whispered in her ear. Belinda's eyes narrowed and she nodded to the intern who left.

"We may have a problem. Biological is missing a dish."

The group acted shocked and angry. Surely their protocols were so advanced that stupid accidents could not occur.

"Have they been looking for it? Are they certain it is missing?"

"I need the details," Belinda retorted. "Sam Waterford had it last. Find a secluded office and let's have a little discussion. Leonard, I want you in on this."

They pulled Sam out of the lab and into a small empty intern office. Sam knew it was over for him. He would cooperate with Belinda and Leonard, only because he knew they could kill his career, but he was so depressed it almost didn't matter. He had been waiting about 20 minutes when Belinda and Leonard walked into the office with Belinda's assistant who was holding a note pad. Belinda started off as gently as she was capable of.

"I take it we have a problem, Sam."

"Yes, I think we do," he answered dispassionately, his eyes gazing at the table.

"What can you tell us?"

"I've explained it already several times but here it is again. I came back to my desk and found a petri dish labeled Risk Group IV. It was sealed tightly, and I was preparing set up. I assumed Dr. Stein had placed it there, and I didn't know what it was. I got an urgent text to go to the vacuum lab. They needed my help immediately. I dropped everything and ran to the vacuum lab. When I returned, the dish was gone. My first thought was that it had been placed there inadvertently and that whoever set it down had come back to retrieve it. I went over to Dr. Stein's office and asked him if he had removed it, and he told me he did not know what I was talking about.

"Did you find out how it got there?"

"I did." He looked up at Leonard. "I believe it was one of Dr. Freund's technicians."

Belinda looked at Leonard. "Do you know anything about this?"

"Nope. But I will find out."

She looked back at Sam. "So you asked around and nobody knows what happened to the dish."

"Yes. If it is still here, we can't find it. That is what I reported to Dr. Stein."

"Ok. Anything else?"

"Well..." He paused. "I had a strange interaction before I ran to the vacuum lab."

"How so?"

"A young woman came up to me in the lab and asked me what I was doing."

Up to this point, a missing Risk Group IV was a serious matter, but it was more likely a failure of protocol and a stupid mistake than corporate espionage. Belinda knew corporate espionage well and her skin started to prickle.

"Did she tell you her name?"

"No. She said something about investors."

Belinda felt herself go hot. She thought about her interactions with Derek and didn't think it was his style. But she didn't know Cheryl Brown.

"Did you tell her anything, Sam?"

"Absolutely not." He looked directly into Belinda's eyes, as if to say you can't doubt me on this.

"Okay, Sam. You can go."

Sam walked out of the room quickly. Leonard looked at Belinda, and said, "He'll be terminated in the morning."

"Not yet," Belinda replied. "We might be able to use him."

Belinda and Leonard returned to their offices. Leonard shut the door and walked over to his window. He knew that his office was probably bugged so he didn't take out his phone, but he thought about calling General Warner at the Pentagon. The dish that was left with Sam had been created in Tajikistan. Its contents were still unknown but had something to do with a mechanical virus directly in line with Leonard's work on MEMS. He had it placed in Biological as a screen, and wanted to see if the lab could identify it as a virus or as smart dust. His hatred of Belinda and the control she exercised over the lab justified his keeping it a secret from her, at least for now. But he was upset that it was missing, and like Belinda, Leonard was willing to do anything to find it. He thought about making a visit to Derek Whitestone's office, but he was concerned that word of the missing dish would leak. Belinda was smart to keep Sam around if for nothing else. Even if Sam had not explored the contents, he was more likely to stay silent while he was still here at the labs. He thought about Cindy, the cute intern that had come into the boardroom to report the dish. He sighed. He needed a good distraction right now.

He called her, and said, "I could use some good coffee."

She perked up and whispered, "You mean the rich and creamy type?"

"You got it, fair lady."

They met at the entrance and jumped into Leonard's Porsche Cayman GT4. Belinda watched from her office as they drove away. She turned back to the large screen monitor in her room. A new story was breaking about a Silicon Valley company in biotech that had allegedly defrauded investors out of $11 billion dollars by claiming they had developed a new machine capable of diagnosing blood disorders. Belinda knew about Theranos. They had approached the RW Labs for assistance and for a short time, the Lab had investigated the technology choosing, in the end, to let this one go. It had been Dr. Stein's group who helped make the decision, and Sam Waterford had been part of the team. She remembered with some disgust the pathetic look on the two Theranos representatives' faces when she announced her decision. She had thought to herself, "Do something else. Your leaders are smart. Some ideas are just not worth it." Of course, they refused to abandon their dream. But they chose the wrong path—in the battle for Silicon Valley supremacy everyone steals good ideas but even if outside investors can be dumb, the Valley is way too smart to accept falsified results. Fake it until you make it works in Hollywood. But the wolves of the Valley will tear you to pieces, and that is exactly what happened to Theranos, and it was not unexpected and not pretty. Belinda mused on her own good fortune: lying about results in the Silicon Valley kills the golden goose every time.

CHAPTER 7.

A Cold Start

The road to success is rarely a straight shot, and when success comes, it often comes in unexpected ways. The story of Lebron James is instructive. Everyone knows that no team in the NBA can win a championship without a superstar but having a superstar does not guarantee a championship. The New York Knicks have not won an NBA championship since 1973, almost a half century ago, despite attracting multiple superstars for, in part, being in the same sports market as the New York Yankees. They made it to the finals twice with Patrick Ewing in the 1990s but ran into the buzzsaw of the Chicago Bulls under Michael Jordan and missed out on NBA glory. Since then, the tale has been mostly sad and disappointing.

Owning a superstar and trying to win is one thing. Being a superstar and expecting to win is something completely different. Many acclaimed high school and college superstars have gone down in flames in professional sports. The world, as commentator Jim Nantz likes to say, is littered with wasted talent. Lebron James burst into the League in 2003 and was so confident in his abilities that he made a big show of signing with the downtrodden Cleveland Cavaliers and promised to bring a championship to his hometown team. For eight years, he battled management and the press but was unable to get the job done. In 2010, without a championship and fearful that he would have no enduring legacy, he made one of the most controversial free agent decisions in sports history and signed with the Miami Heat. The move worked out and in joining Miami, Lebron helped form the dominant 'Big Three' in combination with Dwayne Wade and Chris Bosh. By 2013, the Big Three already had won two rings. But despite the wins, Lebron was jeered in his hometown as a sellout and the drama prompted ESPN to produce a special about the move called *The Decision*. The challenges and painful years that Lebron faced in the glare of the public eye in Cleveland honed Lebron and, in another remarkable move, he returned to Cleveland in 2014 to bring them their first championship in 2016, and then earn another with the Lakers in 2020. He is widely recognized in the NBA as a championship machine but the road he took to get there was extremely rough and anything but predictable.

Frank Weatherby called Van into his office.

"Detective Darling was very keen on your work in the Baldwin Hills case."

"I've been hearing a bit. Thank you."

"Well, you not only uncovered a massive drug operation, albeit inadvertently, you saved an innocent man and kept a case from going cold."

"Thank you, sir. Would not have happened without you and Brad."

"Well, I have some good news for you, assuming you think it is good news." Van leaned forward. "Does the Detective Bureau interest you?"

Van felt her stomach leap. Becoming a detective had been a dream of hers since she was a little girl.

"But I didn't even qualify for the police academy? They thought my deafness would be a risk in the field."

"Apparently they are admitting that they made a mistake. But they don't want to send you to the Academy. They want to bring you in immediately as a Detective 1."

"What about the detective tests and the interviews?"

"Bypass. They will put you in special weapons training. They also have advanced courses in investigative analysis and scientific investigation, but my guess is that you would be able to teach those courses."

Van winced at the compliment. Suddenly, she felt like she would be getting in over her head, that she knew nothing at all about being a detective and would look foolish. Frank could tell she was getting scared.

"Van," he spoke encouragingly. "Your insights in Baldwin Hills far exceeded the insights of the detectives we have on the beat now, even some senior detectives. You will be a great detective. If you have any concerns, I am here. Come by any time. Do not pass this up. You were meant for it."

"Thank you, Frank. I am a little overwhelmed. Are you sure?"

He smiled. "Collect your things. You'll be meeting with Detective Darling tomorrow morning and he will introduce you around. Congratulations."

As he watched her leave his office, Frank had his own mixed emotions. He loved watching his young stars grow and develop, but it was hard to let quality go, and he could see in Van great promise and a great loss for the Lab. He walked to his door and leaned out. "Brad!" He shouted. Brad came running over. "I have something I need you to look at."

✻ ✻ ✻ ✻ ✻ ✻

"Good morning, Van!" Detective III Charles Darling welcomed his new protégé.

"Good morning, sir," replied Van not certain what to call him. She wasn't even certain what to wear when she woke up that morning, if that is what you call not sleeping all night and then getting out of bed in the morning.

"Charlie, please. You know me, Van."

"Good morning, Charlie."

"Better. Welcome to the Bureau. I have something for you." He reached into his pocket and pulled out an LAPD Detective badge and handed it to Van. "Congratulations, Detective. Now, follow me."

Van stepped in line behind Charlie, as he made his way across a sea of desks. Van noticed detectives gathered around in clusters drinking coffee and staring at her. A few seemed friendly but most just stared. He stopped at an empty desk surrounded by other desks. "Here is your new home."

Van looked at the desk, then looked back at Charlie and forced a smile. She immediately felt homesick for her desk at the Lab and the freedom and respect she felt under Frank. She started to panic and think again this was a huge mistake, but she remembered Frank's words to her and forced herself to calm down.

"You'll be fine," Charlie whispered. "If you need anything at all, my office is right there." He pointed to the door at the end of a long row.

Van's first day flew by. The Chief held a daily briefing and introduced her and then added ominously, "No shenanigans." Van had no idea what shenanigans he was talking about, but chose to ignore the comment, smiled and nodded. She went to HR and completed a ton of paperwork. They gave her a fob and a parking space. They said she was eligible for a handgun but not until she completed special weapons training, which would start the next day. "They don't fool around here," she thought to herself. Charlie took her out to lunch and invited a few of her new colleagues.

They found an Italian restaurant near the Bureau. It was dark with red carpet and dark brown leather booths and framed photos of downtown Los Angeles in the 1930s. As they slipped into one of the booths, Van leaned over to Charlie, and asked, "A bit stereotypical, isn't it?"

"What do you mean?" He looked at her and smiled.

She bit her tongue and replied, "Come here often?"

Charlie laughed. "Actually no. This place is expensive. This is a treat in your honor." Van blushed. "And if you don't like it, I promise we will never come here again."

They ordered drinks, no alcohol, and Charlie began, "Boys. I want to introduce you to Detective Van Eng."

"Welcome to the Bureau," they said in near unison. They lifted their glasses in her honor.

"Thank you," replied Van cautiously.

"You are going to learn some things about Van that will amaze you, just as they amazed me," he said. "I want her taken care of, if you get my drift."

"Absolutely, Charlie," the team responded. "Anything you want."

"So," Van leaned in. "Thank you all but I am starting to get the impression that I need to be taken care of. What am I missing?"

Charlie looked at her very seriously. "This is a great opportunity for you. But do not be fooled. Every single detective in this Bureau fought for recognition, and each of them guards it very jealously. Many of them do not understand how you got here through back channels. They will not be so supportive. I am confident that you will do very well here, but it is not an easy job, and it is not an easy atmosphere. So when we offer to watch out for you, it means we have your back. Whatever you need, you can come to us." Everyone at the table looked equally serious and nodded their heads.

"Okay, I will. I am grateful."

"Now, I usually order the eggplant parmesan. It's to die for." He looked at her and winked.

"Charlie," she said. "You're killing me."

The next morning Van drove out to the LAPD weapons training facility in Granada Hills. The training lasted three days. She spent the first day in classes and on the range, trying out various pistol styles. She didn't like the Beretta or the Glock. They both felt too heavy and were harder to aim than the lighter Smith & Wessons. But she fell in love with the Kimber Classic bone handle .45 caliber. It was relatively light and she could control the kick. She learned how to load, how to shoot and how to carry, and most importantly, how to avoid having to use it. Charlie called her and complimented her on her choice. He also told her that given her background in Forensics, she would start her training in the Cold Case Homicide Special Section.

"You know a lot about DNA, right?"

"So I have been told, Charlie," she responded, barely holding back a smirk.

"Good. Have great weekend and report to Chess on Monday."

"Chess?"

"That is what they call it. C.C.H.S.S. right? It's where all the smart people start. Anyway, great place for learning about detective work." His comments reminded her of Frank and her experience in the cold case files over at the Lab.

On Monday she showed up bright and early and brought coffee with her as much to blend in as to enjoy it for breakfast. When she arrived, there was a large stack of files on her desk with a Post-it note that said, "Take copies to Detective Young." She set her coffee down and asked about the copy machine and proceeded to copy the files and create duplicate folders. She carried the originals and copies over to Detective Young's office. He was a Detective II in Robbery-Homicide. He barely looked at her and told her where to set them down. When she got back to her desk there was another stack of files with a note, "Please copy and return to Detective Black." She suspected something was up but took the files, made copies and carried them to Detective Black's office. She returned to her desk and this time it was empty and she grabbed her notebook and went up to the sixth floor where Chess was located. As she walked out of the elevator, Charlie was standing there and he looked at her a bit cross, and said, "It's 11:30. Where have you been?"

Van was confused by the question but before she could respond, he said "At least you are here now. Follow me." She walked with him down the hall and into an over-stacked and disorganized file room. There were multiple carts overloaded with file folders. They pushed past the folders and found an office at the back. Inside the office sat a bored-looking detective staring at his smart phone.

"Detective Broad, let me introduce you to one of our newest in the Bureau." He motioned to Van and she reached out her hand. He looked up without reaching back, and said, "I've heard of you. Thanks, Charlie." Charlie left Van in the office with Detective Alvin Broad. Alvin Broad had been at the Bureau as long as Charles Darling—same class even. Like Charlie, Broad was nearing retirement but, unlike Charlie, Broad was never even considered a candidate for chief. He was a good detective, quiet, reserved and unambitious. He became a detective not to be a hero but to solve puzzles. Tough puzzles. He had a reputation for cracking more cold cases than any other detective, and when Broad decided that he had seen enough of the street, he requested Chess, and as a courtesy and out of respect, the Bureau put him in charge. Broad was also a teacher, at least philosophically. He enjoyed working with new recruits, and Charlie had placed Van with him partly because he knew she would learn from him but also to protect her. Broad would not be threatened by Van like the other detectives.

"Charlie tells me you have a hearing issue," he said to Van, when they were alone.

"I hear fine with my hearing aids," she said. "But I lost my hearing due to illness when I was an infant."

"Can you read lips?" he asked.

"I can," she replied.

"How many languages?"

"My parents speak Cantonese, and I was exposed to a lot of Vietnamese, so my lip reading is limited to Vietnamese, Cantonese and English. But I speak Spanish fluently and I am fairly fluent in Mandarin."

"Incredible," he said. "What do you know about cold cases?"

"Forensics has a cold case filing section and Dr. Weatherby introduced me and required me to spend a lot of hours reviewing files. He told me that a lot of cases that go unsolved are not complicated cases. Rather, a detective or cop or lab technician made a mistake and overlooked something obvious."

"Very good," Broad answered impressed. "Sounds like you are ahead of the game."

"What would you like me to do?"

"Well, for now, just acquaint yourself with what you see around you."

The first thing Van noticed about the room was that, unlike the Lab where everything was labeled and the files were organized by Division, there was no order other than a loose association with dates. The oldest files were on one side of the room and the dates progressed as you made your way to the opposite side. The newest files were lying on carts and it seemed that when detectives downstairs found their file cabinets over-loaded, they would simply identify a younger detective to pull all their older files and leave them in Chess, which really meant dump them in a cart in the Chess file room. She asked Detective Broad if she could organize the room and if he had any objection to a more systematic arrangement. Broad didn't care. His activities in Chess were not guided by the files, but by detectives who might stumble across a new fact in an old case and would call him to check in and see if the information rose to the level of pulling the case out of Chess for further review. It wasn't always easy to locate the original files and what Van was proposing might make that easier.

Van got to work organizing the room. She spent several weeks on the project. Occasionally Charlie would stop by and ask Van to accompany him to a crime scene and Detective Broad never objected. Charlie was often impressed with Van's insights at a crime scene, but he was careful not to compliment her in front of other detectives and soft-pedaled her ideas when sharing them with others. Hiring Van had been a bit of an experiment and Charlie was smart enough to keep Van out of the lime-light, and quite literally, given her placement in Chess, in the dark. But Van didn't mind. Detective Broad was very friendly and helpful, and she was not in any rush to show off her skills or to show anybody else up. Besides, the cases she was coming across were fascinating. She decided to organize the files by type of crime—similar to the Lab but not, like the Lab, strictly by Division. It wasn't easy because some cases involved multiple crimes and, in those cases, she selected the most serious crime as the principal category and developed a color-coded Post-it system to show multiple crimes in a single file. She started with all the homicide files and divided them up between gang-related, drug/alcohol-related, sex trafficking, robbery, prison, domestic and other interpersonal, juvenile, domestic and international terrorism and espionage, and then subdivided them into first degree, second degree, manslaughter, negligent homicide, suicide, and finally, cases that were simply accidental deaths. She developed similar systems for robberies, mayhem, assault and battery, white collar and financial crimes, computer crimes like hacking and piracy, etc.

Detective Broad enjoyed watching her develop her system. Sometimes she would ask him where he thought a case belonged, and he began to own the new system as his own. But Van had another idea that was bigger than simply organizing the file room. As she was doing that, she was also building a database that not only would help her locate specific files, it also was grouping the files and connecting them by type of crime, type and name of victim, location, property, details about suspects, evidence, and anything that drew her attention. She had IT help her assemble the database and she started running cold case reports identifying number and type and frequency. Her capacity for remembering detail stunned Broad and they spent long hours sitting and discussing cases from the 1930s and 1940s. She also was able to sort cases by types of forensic or investigative errors that allowed cases to remain unsolved. After several months of work, Detective Broad began to share some of the reports Van was generating with the Bureau Chief, who shared it with the Chief of Police. Van was invited to top-level meetings to share the data, and she noticed, with some concern, that internal affairs started to attend some of those meetings.

She never took seriously the taunts she got from other detectives and the games they played trying to get her to do grunt work. Most of the time, she took the steam out of the joke by simply taking care of what was asked of her. She got coffee, ran errands, made copies, wrote up reports, and did so without complaining, and after a while, most of the detectives began to give her some respect. Then one morning, she came in and someone had placed a single bullet on her desk. She took it to Charlie, who got very serious and said he would find out what was going on. She told Detective Broad, and he suggested she start carrying her Kimber with her all the time. It was unnerving to her. She had noticed that fewer and fewer files were being left at Chess.

Van started spending less time with Detective Broad in Chess and more time at her desk, almost as if she were taunting the person who threatened her. She went over to Detectives Young and Black, and asked if they needed any assistance with anything. They both shrugged, looked disinterested, and said not now. She wandered into the kitchen and made coffee that she pretended to drink, starting up conversations with other detectives lounging there and chatting. She went outside and relaxed at the rear door near the parking lot where the smokers liked to hang out. No one she talked to gave off any strange vibes, and she began to learn more about the variety of cases that were being investigated but picked up nothing that would expose the person who had threatened her. She asked Charlie if he had uncovered anything, and Charlie had nothing to report.

One day, one of the young detectives who joined the Bureau around the same time that Van joined, invited her to ride along on a stakeout. The detectives were investigating a new Vietnamese/Latino gang called "The Rush" thatwas making a play for the Macarthur Park side of Koreatown. They had made a lot of money in human trafficking all around Los Angeles and were headquartered in a couple of karaoke bars off Wilshire Boulevard around Sixth Street. They drove hopped up Camrys and WRXs with green neon lighting on the undercarriage and used Hummer limos to shepherd gaggles of young Vietnamese girls to parties in Hollywood, Malibu, and Marina Del Rey. They had been linked to a couple of brutal murders of other gang members and had developed a reputation for being ruthless.

The Gang and Narcotics Division tagged a 25-year-old Vietnamese immigrant, Danny Kang, as the self-appointed leader of the gang.

The detective's name was Robert Johnson. Robert made detective as a police officer in Rampart Division and had been reassigned to Downtown. He knew Koreatown and spent his first three years as a police officer patrolling MacArthur, Rampart and Koreatown. Many of the local business owners knew Robert well, and his ability to get information impressed his commanding officer enough to suggest Robert apply for detective. He did and passed the test with flying colors. They pulled him in under Detective Young in the Downtown Gang Unit. Young had taken to calling Robert "BJ." Now he was back in his old hood chasing a new gang that was making a lot of noise. He had heard Van spoke Vietnamese, and asked Detective Young if he could bring her along. Young didn't hesitate. "Pull her in, BJ," he told Robert.

Wilshire Boulevard was not an easy place for a stakeout, and the karaoke bar where Danny Kang ran his operations was actually a multistory mall with an underground garage, so sitting out on the street was not very effective. Still Robert pulled into a space across from the garage entrance and down the street about a block where they could see fast cars and limos entering the garage. They sat there for an hour.

"Does this feel like a good location to you?" Van asked Robert.

"You can call me BJ, everyone else does," Robert answered.

"Ok, BJ, does this feel like a good location to you?"

"As good as any."

"What are we looking for?"

"Waiting to see if we see Danny Kang or his chief lieutenants leave the garage. Then we will follow them."

"Ok, but maybe we should get a bit closer."

"We can't be obvious, Van."

"We won't be," she said. "Do you mind pulling into the garage?"

"Are you out of your mind?"

Robert, or BJ, had not had the benefit of working with Detective Charlie Darling and learning the "they don't look at you anyway" approach to stakeouts. Van had been on several stakeouts with Charlie and every time they went out, Charlie had successfully unnerved Van by where he positioned the car. Van wanted to be respectful of Robert and his knowledge of the area, but she now knew this was a rookie mistake. Besides, she didn't want to waste time waiting for an imaginary car to pull out of the garage.

"Just drive in and around the garage. If it feels uncomfortable, we can drive out. I want to take a look."

Robert looked at Van at first irritated but then he smiled. If she wanted to know his moxie, he would show her his moxie. "You got it," he said. He pulled the car out, narrowly missing a gold WRX that was speeding up the street. He followed the WRX into the garage and, as they pulled in, they saw the WRX stop at a valet station next to a bank of elevators, and Danny Kang and an unusually tall and beautiful Vietnamese woman stepped out of the car, flipped the keys to the valet along with a large bill, and headed to the elevator bank. The valet played cool and crawled into the WRX. Robert and Van passed the valet and drove around the garage acting as if they were looking for a parking space.

"That was Danny Kang," Robert whispered.

"I wondered," Van replied. They turned down another lane, and Van said, "Pull in right here." He slowed the car. "You want to stay here?" he asked incredulously.

"Yes, we can see the elevator bank and the valet." Robert looked a little scared but backed into the space. "It's ok," Van replied. "If anyone gets suspicious, we can act like we are making out." Robert looked at Van wide-eyed. "I am not saying we will make out, Robert," she chuckled.

"Of course not," he said. "I knew that."

They sat in the space for two hours undetected. A couple of people walked by the car and didn't even notice they were sitting there. Robert secretly hoped something would force them to play act a little, but at the same time he didn't. Van pretended to be playing with her phone and took several photos of the incoming cars and drivers. Robert started doing the same. She also made notes as she watched the cars pull in. She saw five lime green WRXs, an orange Mustang GT, two cherry red Nissan GTs, an old, refurbished Porsche 911, a black Acura TLX and six BMWs, one M4, four 3 series, and a 750i. Most of the drivers were young men in their 20s and 30s. The orange Mustang was being driven by a young woman. She saw an older gentleman get out of the 750i. Many of the drivers were high fashion. A few were dressed in all black. All of them went to the elevator. She looked up karaoke bars and discovered that there was a bar located on the third floor of this mall. "I'll be back in a few minutes," she said.

"You sure?" Robert looked at her and then scanned the garage. He wasn't completely certain they were not being watched. She removed her blazer and unholstered her Kimber. She unbuttoned a couple of buttons on her blouse and got out of the car. She walked toward the valet nonchalantly. The two young guys at the desk gave her a quick look but were distracted by a black Hummer limousine that pulled into the garage right after she passed them. The Hummer and two young men jumped out of the driver's seats to open the side doors. Fifteen girls who looked to be in their late teens piled out of the car. There were all wearing K-Pop gear and were wearing too much makeup. Van picked up various perfume scents: Marc Jacobs, Cloe, Dolce & Gabbana, and Chanel. They laughed as they crammed themselves together into the elevator. The men watched them ·

emotionless, and Van strolled forward as if she was simply going to the mall. Inside the mall were several Asian shops, similar to the shops that her parents liked. There were two escalators that carried her to the second floor, where it was mostly clothing stores. Back in the corner, she saw a neon sign and a single slightly heavy-set young man standing next to a gold stanchion with a red velvet rope and an elevator door. There was a colorful poster set up next to the elevator showing someone singing. She went up to the young man who smiled at her. She asked in Vietnamese how to get to the karaoke bar, and he pointed to the elevator. He pressed the button and when the door opened, the elevator was empty, and he directed her to enter. She smiled and nodded at him, which drew a quick smile and nod in return, and walked into the elevator.

The elevator opened into a dark but colorful lobby. There were two velvet couches, and a Chinese coffee table to Van's right. On the left was a cashier behind a chrome counter. Disco lights were running, and a heavy door stood at the back of the lobby.

She walked up to the cashier and said in English, "Hi. I have never been to a karaoke bar like this before. I would like to bring my friends. What is the arrangement?"

He looked at her as if to size her up, and responded, "This is a good karaoke bar, one of the best in LA. We have rooms here that you rent for an hour or more, and each of the rooms has its own hi-def sound system with a monitor that has many catalogues of music." He pointed to a bank of black microphones. "We will give you microphones and take you to the rooms. We have a great menu of foods, and if you like alcohol, we have a nice collection of vodkas, gins and whiskeys as well as beer and wine."

"Would you mind showing me?" she flirted with the young man. He looked up at a camera and a green light flashed on the desk behind the counter.

"Sure," he said. "Just a minute."

He disappeared through a door, and when he returned, he brought a young woman who was wearing the same uniform as him—black jeans and a black button-up Oxford shirt. Van noticed that it was the same woman who had been driving the orange Mustang.

"Follow me," he said.

She walked through the door into a hallway lined with black glass and metal doors with small windows. She could hear various songs being played at the same time and different voices screaming out old rock songs or Chinese melodies. A couple of the rooms had small parties going on and food spread out on the tables in the middle of the rooms. She caught a glimpse of a few rooms in which there were older men sitting and drinking but not singing. As they turned the corner, two young men passed her, and behind them was a line of girls from the Hummer. They stopped at a door with one of the older men, knocked, opened the door and brought in the girls who stood in front of the men.

The host was quick to explain, "The girls serve the men and help them with the sound system. It can be difficult to operate."

Van leaned forward to the host who was taking her around, and said, "This looks like a fun place."

He turned and smiled, "Just one big party!"

Van thanked the host and returned down to Robert, who was not too happy.

"They know me here. This was part of my beat."

"Do you think anyone recognized you?"

"I don't know but we are done here," he said, almost pleading.

Back at the Bureau, Robert and Van stood in Detective Young's office. "Did you follow Kang?" Robert answered, "No sir, but we scoped the garage and took an inventory of cars and drivers." "Good," Young replied. "Put a report together. She can draft it." He looked at Van and said, "She is good at reports." The comment was directed at her, and to Van, it seemed loaded. She noticed that he did not say "reporting," and she thought to herself, if he is involved in the bullet threat, he is not being very careful.

Robert left the office, and Van turned back to Detective Young. "I think I should go back," she said.

"Back where?" he asked.

"To the stakeout site. I think I can get more."

Young looked at her, slightly impressed. "What is your plan?"

Van closed the door. Robert could see that they were talking and was worried that Van might be throwing him under the bus or, alternatively, encroaching on his turf. As she opened the door, Robert could hear Young say, "Be careful, Detective."

Van waited a couple of weeks before returning to the Koreatown mall. In the meantime, she and Robert collected their photographs and descriptions into a report and hijacked a conference room to serve as a war room. They tacked photographs to the wall and created a test hierarchy. BJ and Detective Young downloaded all the intel they had gathered on The Rush mostly through stakeouts. In recent months, Rampart Division had apprehended a couple of gang members for petty theft, and obtained warrants to search their homes, where they found guns and narcotics. The possession charges added leverage, and through those interrogations, they learned about Danny Kang and a couple of his top lieutenants. In exchange for the information, the members served a few months' jail time and were released. The murders that had been attributed to the gang were not simple drive-by executions. The gang kidnapped leaders of a rival Latino gang called *El Muerte*, tortured them before they executed them, and left the bodies in public view. The Gang Unit had interviewed El Muerte, and they pointed the finger at The Rush.

Van needed support, and Robert was too well known in the area to go undercover. She enlisted three officers from the Asian Crimes Unit in the Narcotics Division, two women and one guy. They agreed to play it as Friday night clubbing and dress the part. Van had explained that the look of the bar was high end, and she convinced the Bureau to pay for wardrobe, hire a limo and give them cash for the night. She called the karaoke bar and reserved a room and ordered food.

The limo she hired was a black executive sedan, but it served the part. Van knew she did not want to overdo the look. If it were too rich, she might artificially distance herself from the bar's operations. They pulled up to the valet, who opened the door and saw four Asians laughing and ready to party. They stumbled out of the car and were shown to the elevator. The men at the elevator door told them to raise their arms and did a quick pat down. When they emerged from the elevator, Van went to the counter, and saw the young man who had hosted her when she toured the bar. She smiled and waved at him. He recognized her and stepped to the counter, motioning the others to let him check her in. She was giddy and couldn't wait to start singing and flirted mercilessly to send the message that she was single and not involved with the guy in the group.

He led the group to the heavy door and as they walked to the room, he looked at Van and said, "My name is Jack. Anything you want, please ask for me. I can get you anything."

She giggled and thanked him. He led them into the room, where there was food already set up. He gave Van one of the microphones and turned on the monitor. He asked if they wanted English or one of a handful of Asian languages and they agreed on English. He showed them how to use the catalogue to pick songs, and as he left, Van tried to hand him a $20 bill. He looked at her for a second to see if she wanted something, then when it was clear she didn't, he shook his head "no," smiled, bowed, and left them in the room.

They played around in the room for the next couple of hours. Jack came by after about 20 minutes to check on them, and they said it was fun singing rock classics from Abba and Journey and the Stones. They ordered beer and vodka but drank very little. After about 45 minutes, Van walked out of the room and looked around. She saw the young men leading the girls around to different rooms. Typically, one or two would stay in the room. She walked back out to the front lobby and flirted with Jack barely nursing a vodka tonic. She saw the green light flash several times, and when it did, one of the staff would run into the back room. She was able to see a half dozen staff dressed in black working back there. She noticed the woman who drove the orange Mustang acting as if she were a manager. She returned to the room. The group had agreed to play their roles the entire time they were there, cognizant that they might be being watched through hidden cameras. So they said nothing about what they were seeing and acted as if they were simply partying the night away.

After about 90 minutes, Jack returned to the room. He motioned to Van. "Come with me," he said. He took her arm gently and led her to another elevator door at the rear of the bar. She was concerned that he might be making a move on her and strategized how to play it lightly and discourage him, but he made no moves. They emerged from the elevator into a lavish almost overdone loft studio with sateen couches and chairs, and a plush white carpet. There were green neon lights in the corners, and a fully loaded kitchen at the back right corner. In the back left corner, where the dining room might have been, was a large mahogany desk with two black leather chairs. The tall Vietnamese woman whom Van had seen in the garage, was sitting on the corner of the desk, and Danny Kang sat in a large leather chair behind the desk. A half dozen men and women lounged in the room.

Jack brought Van to the center of the room directly in front of Danny Kang.

Danny gave her a stare, and then smiled, and said, "Welcome to Oasis."

Van looked back at him and stood her ground. "Thank you. My friends and I are having fun. Did we do anything wrong?"

"No. No. Not at all. Jack here was telling me you are an interesting person."

"I suppose that is a compliment," she replied. She smiled at Jack. "I think he is interesting as well."

"Yes. I would agree that Jack is very interesting." As he said this, he stood up and came around to the front of the desk. He sat on the edge of the desk next to his Vietnamese companion and studied Van.

"Are you a cop?" The room became very quiet.

"Excuse me?" she said. "Why would you think…"

Danny stood up slowly and leaned forward. "If not, then, my darling," he said very quietly, as he grabbed her ear, "what are these?"

It hurt her and a small whine pierced the air. She jerked her head away from him and stepped back. "I am deaf," she responded angrily. "You never met a deaf person before?" She pulled them out of her ears and held them out in her hand. "These are my hearing aids," she said, disgusted. "Here. Check them!"

He glanced down and then back at her face, assessing her reaction. Then he backed away and held up his hands in mock surrender. "My apologies. You can never be too careful."

Van was shaken up but gathered herself, only not too quickly. Anybody would have been upset by the aggression. She took a deep breath. "Yah, I understand," she said, as if she was biting her tongue.

"Well then. Please, accept my apologies. Jack," he added, "what is our lovely friend's name?"

"My name is Van," she said, not letting Jack answer for her.

"Well, Van, pleased to meet you. Please join me and my friends for a drink."

"I think you need to work on your charm," she answered, and he laughed out loud. The room relaxed. She took her time, considering the offer. "Thank you," she finally said. "But my friends are waiting, and I don't want them to worry." It was the same line she planned on using with Jack if he got frisky. "Maybe another time?" He smiled and handed her a card.

"Call me," he said. The card had one word on one side and a number on the back. The word was "Oasis."

She took the card. "Have a nice evening," she offered to the room and then to Danny she said, "It's been interesting." She motioned to Jack, who looked at Danny. Danny nodded and Jack escorted her back to the elevator door and down to the bar.

"I'm sorry," he said as opened the door to the room. "It's okay," she responded. "You have interesting friends."

Van and the team gathered their things. The two female cops made a show of being concerned, and Van pretended to waive them off. By the time they got downstairs, the limo was waiting for them. They jumped in acting boozy and were dropped off in Downtown next to a converted loft apartment building where one of the team lived. As the car drove away, Van said to the others, "Let's discuss Monday." "In the meantime," she added and patted her purse. "I'll submit the card for prints."

Van called Charlie on Saturday morning and walked through the events of the evening. Charlie was scared for Van but knew she would do what she felt was necessary. She also told him about her interactions with Detective Young, and he told her that if she sensed anything was wrong to contact him immediately. She called Broad and told him about the night as well. She opened the cold case database and searched for Kang and Vietnamese and Koreatown, and a few cases popped up. One case caught her eye that involved the execution-style shooting of a young Vietnamese couple that was survived by two children—a boy and a girl. The family had not been cooperative, and the police were unable to identify suspects, so it was determined to be a family dispute and not pursued. The city placed the children in Child Support Services and there were no additional notes.

On Monday, Van reported to Detective Young. She had already sent the card to Forensics for prints. Young continued to be impressed by this rookie detective. They agreed that her hearing aids were an unfortunate and probably dangerous mistake, but now that Kang had seen them, that she should continue to wear them. Van asked if any hearing aids had ever been developed that functioned also as two-way radios but Young had never heard of anything like that. "The Detective Bureau doesn't hire many deaf detectives," he acknowledged. He suggested that she talk to the Department's Technology Division and see what they had. "Have you been to FBI and met anybody there?" "Never." "Check with Technology first."

Forensics recorded the clean prints on the card and confirmed they belonged to Danny Kang. They returned the card to Van and Young handed her a new phone. "Use this." Van called Danny. The Division recorded the call.

"Hi."

"Yeah? Who is this?"

"It's Van."

"Van? Oh, yeah. You're the chick from Oasis."

"You gave me the number. Did you not want me to call?"

"Maybe. What's going on?"

"I'm in the mood for singing again."

"I see. You need someone to hold the microphone?"

"Or maybe just sing with me."

He paused. "All right. I'm busy until about six. Can you get here?"

"Of course."

"Okay, Van. See you then."

She hung up and looked at Young, who was nodding. "I am putting a couple of cars nearby. Anything gets uncomfortable and you call. Got it?" They set up '9' as a speed dial or as the code to text to Robert, who would be in one of the stakeout cars. Van took an Uber to the garage. She dolled herself up enough to look interested but wore jeans and a loose sweater. When she arrived, one of the valets walked her to the elevators but rode with her to the penthouse where Danny was waiting. The same supporting characters were there including the tall Vietnamese woman.

Danny smiled when he saw her. "Welcome back to the scene of the crime," he said extending his hand to take hers and gallantly bowing and kissing her hand.

"Well, I would say this is much better than last time," she smiled.

He looked pleased. "What are you in the mood for?" he asked, motioning toward the alcohol at the bar.

"Diet coke is fine. Are we going to sing?"

Danny furrowed his brow, "You were serious?"

"Well, it is a karaoke bar."

"So it is." He motioned to one of his lieutenants, who opened a cabinet to reveal a PA system and a monitor. They turned on the system and Danny handed Van a microphone. Van loved music and had spent long hours listening to all types of music, sometimes with her hearing aids and sometimes without just to feel the music. She knew her voice was a bit off pitch but she didn't care. Danny was amazed by her total fearlessness as she belted out *Dancing Queen* by Abba and a sultry rendition of *Toxic* by Britney Spears. She gave Danny the microphone and he sang a favorite Vietnamese song, the only song he ever performed at karaoke, just to show that he could. Van smiled and laughed. "You aren't half bad."

"Yes, I am," he confessed. "You want to take a ride?"

"Sure, but please introduce me to your friends."

"You are right," he responded. He went around the room naming everyone there, and they were gracious to Van as Danny would have demanded. "And last but never least," he said, leading her to the tall women posing at the desk, "this is my sister, Min." Van studied her and could make out that Min had reservations about her.

"Your sister?"

"Yes."

"It's an honor." Van dipped lightly. Danny seemed pleased but Min rolled her eyes. "Come on." Van grabbed her handbag and followed Danny to the elevator. Downstairs the gold WRX was waiting. The valet held the door and Van got in. It smelled like smoke and new car scent combined. "Are you a smoker?" she asked.

"Nah, that's Min." He pulled out onto Wilshire and gunned it. The car took off and sucked Van back into her seat. He turned up Vermont and headed up through Rampart to the 101. He got off at Mulholland and whipped around the corners until he reached the top of Runyon Canyon. He pulled onto the dirt on the side of the road.

"Are we hiking?" she asked.

"Follow me." he said.

The trail was crowded with a mix of locals and young starlets walking their little dogs and aspiring actors showing off their bodies and hoping to meet someone famous. They started down the main trail and then Danny took Van's hand and climbed a small hill where he found a knoll next to an abandoned home and sat down. The view looked right down on Hollywood Boulevard and a building the entire side of which was covered by a six-story rendition of Lindsay Lohan. Beyond Hollywood Boulevard in the distance was downtown Los Angeles, beginning to glow golden in the sunset. Van had to remind herself what she was doing. It felt incredibly romantic and Danny was being surprisingly gentle and not aggressive.

"My favorite spot in LA," he said.

"Why is that?" She pushed back at this point knowing that he liked that in her.

"I've always been in love with that picture of Lindsay Lohan," He looked at her and grinned.

"Right."

"Not really," he said, almost sheepishly. "That's not it. I just find it comforting to get above the fray. I imagine its mine and I rule it and I am king."

"You realize you are sitting on a throne of dirt, Mr. King?" she poked him. He laughed and took her hand.

"You want to be my queen?"

Van blushed. "You need to do a lot more to win this queen," she said.

"How about ice cream?"

"Yes, that might be enough."

He jumped up and they went back to the car. As he was getting in, he got a call. He took the call outside the car and Van could hear him shouting as another side of Danny began to emerge. "Fuck 'em," he said. "Fuck 'em good." When he got in to drive, Van looked at him a little scared. "What was that?"

"Just business."

"Some serious karaoke business?" She tried to calm him down, but he wouldn't look at her.

"We have to go back." He punched the gas and after weaving through traffic, they got back to the mall.

"I'm sorry," he said as they pulled up to the valet.

"Get her a car," he told the valet and then looked back as he headed to the elevator. She could sense he was torn. "I'll be in touch," he said and disappeared.

The next morning at the Bureau, Van, Robert and Detective Young all stood in the war room that Van and Robert had assembled. Van pinned the picture of Danny at the top and a picture of his sister Min next to him and slightly below. She began to sort the remaining photos of Danny's team according to an order that in her mind reflected the hierarchy she saw in the loft office of the Oasis.

"We didn't know you were in Kang's car, but one of us followed anyway," Robert said. "We followed the car up Mulholland to Runyon and thought he might dump your body in the canyon."

"Right," she said. "Right in front of all those hikers." But she wasn't irritated and appreciated that she had back-up so close. "Did anyone follow him after he took me back?"

"We tried. But we lost him in Silverlake."

"Any gang news?" she asked.

"Nothing concrete. A neighbor reported shots fired but could not identify where and no one reported any crimes."

"I think I need to show you guys something," she said. She went to her desk and pulled out the cold case folder of the Vietnamese couple and brought it to the war room. I don't know if this is related," she started, "but this murder left two orphaned Vietnamese kids, a brother and a sister." Detective Young looked at the file and said, "Seems like a stretch but I'll go with it. What do you think it might mean?"

"At this point, I don't know. I just thought you should see it," Van replied.

"Okay," he said disinterested and laid the file on the conference table. "But remember we are chasing a gang that is known to have tortured and murdered their victims. Whatever you do, Detective, do not take Danny Kang lightly. We don't need to lose a valued member of the Bureau."

She thought his tone was off a little, like he meant it, but didn't really mean it. "Thank you, sir. I'll be careful."

Danny called Van a couple days later. They met at a coffee shop downtown and he took her to Bar Marmont, a high-end restaurant connected to Chateau Marmont, a famous boutique hotel frequented by Hollywood A-listers. He asked about her life and background, and she explained that she was a biochemist who worked at a lab. She talked about her family and the journey from Vietnam when she was young and how she had lost her hearing. They ordered diver scallops and halibut and a Stag's Leap chardonnay. She asked about his family and he told her it wasn't very interesting and didn't seem to want to discuss it. They walked on Sunset and held hands. He talked about his dreams of running an empire, how he wanted to buy a mansion and have his own helicopter and pad. She asked how he would make his money, and he told her it was easy to get people to pay for stupid things. For example, he said, his team liked to recruit pretty Asian women and take them to fancy parties in Hollywood. He said it was amazing how rich Hollywood elites, young and old, would pay thousands of dollars just to have beautiful women attend their parties. "I'm not a pimp," he said. "I don't care what they do on their time and we don't control what they do. We just round them up and bring them to the parties and get paid." He laughed. "It's ridiculous but it taught me a lesson. People will pay for stupid things."

"Do you want me to go to parties?" Van said with a bit of an edge.

"Oh my God, no," he responded. "I want you to be my queen." He leaned down and kissed her and Van's first thought was that she had made a terrible mistake and was getting in over her head.

As they headed back to the car, Danny got a call and as he listened to the voice on the phone, Van could see a dark cloud start to come over him. He got cold and angry and again said they needed to get back to Oasis. But this time when they returned, he took her with him up to the loft. Danny's sister Min was talking to two of Danny's chief lieutenants. They turned when he entered and were surprised to see Van with him. "Help yourself to a diet coke or whatever," he told her. He approached Min and they started talking rapidly in Vietnamese. Van could pick up something about a fight and heard one of the lieutenants mention El Muerte. She watched Min whisper in his ear and could pick out her lips saying, "You want her here?"

Danny turned and looked at Van, and said, "I am going to be busy for a while. You probably should go home."

"Whatever you need me to do Danny," she said.

He paused, wanting her to stay with him, but he knew he didn't want her where he was going. "Go home," he said gently, and walked her to the elevator. He called the valet and told one of them to take her home. Van gave him a hug and left.

She reported to Detective Young her impressions of the night. When she revealed that Danny said he wasn't a pimp, Young laughed. "Right.

And BJ here is the president. Christ. Are you the president, BJ?" Young was a hard guy. Van had seen it often and wondered where that came from.

Van continued and described the conversation back at the loft. "They talked about El Muerte." "They did?"

"Yes. I am certain the problem Danny was dealing with had something to do with them."

He looked at BJ, who had been keeping the stakeout going. "Did they go out after Van left?" "Yes. We followed them through MacArthur Park and Filipino town and then up to Mulholland but all they did was drive."

"Something is about to happen," Young said. "We need to pull you out Van."

"No, don't do that. I am close."

Young paused. "Ok, let's give it time. But don't take any unnecessary risk. I have a feeling I am going to regret this."

Danny pulled up on Flower, and Van jumped in. "I've got some business and then we can head out."

"That's fine, whatever you need to do," she said.

They sped down Olympic and turned left on Normandie. As soon as they passed Venice, Van saw several Rush cars pull in behind the gold WRX. Danny slowed and turned into a cemetery called Angelus Rosedale Cemetery. It was an old school cemetery with headstones so close they seemed to be stacked on top of each other. They drove near a large cannon and pulled over and stopped. The cannon was set up on a large, white, carriage-shaped pedestal, and on its base inscribed were the words, "With Malice Toward None." It seemed eerily out of place.

"Wait here," Danny commanded and he and about six of his lieutenants all got out and gathered next to the cannon. Van looked in the side mirror and saw Min pull up behind the row of cars and jump out. Two of the lieutenants, whom Van knew as Tak and Toshi, started smoking. A line of smartly outfitted 1950 Chevy pickups pulled up on the cemetery road opposite the cannon. A group of Latino guys all wearing black jeans and multicolored bandanas got out. Danny stepped away from his group and the leader, an older male in his forties, approached Danny. He smiled and said, "*Oi Vato*, my Asian brother, whazzup?"

Danny looked back without reacting, and said, "We gonna fix this or do we gotta fix this?"

"Fix what, my friend? There ain't no problems. *Todo está bien!*" As he said it, his members gathered closer around him.

"Yes, there are problems," Danny said, and stepped closer to the leader. "*Todo no está bien.*"

At that point, the guns and knives came out on both sides. Danny looked at the leader and said, "You got two options" and added "*vato*" sarcastically. "We kill each other," he said. "Or we become one."

The leader laughed. "Kill each other? You mean you die."

"You think so?" Danny responded. He motioned to Tak, who pulled two bandanas out of his pocket and handed them to Danny. Danny held out the two bandanas. The leader raised his gun and turned it sideways, execution style.

"You motherfucker," the leader said, and spit on the ground. "Now you die." He looked back for support and he noticed that his members had all lowered their guns. "Shoot these *putos!*" he shouted, but before he could fire his gun, one of his own gang members pulled out a burlap bag and pulled it over the leader's head and shoulders. Two others quickly wrapped him in duct tape and as he was screaming, they took him behind a large gray headstone and shot him. They carried his wrapped-up body to one of the pickups and threw it in the back. Another member walked forward to Danny and reached out with a closed fist. Danny bumped the fist, and when he gave a signal, around the corner came a new lime green fully loaded WRX. It stopped, and Danny pulled a set of keys out of his pocket and motioned for the member to accept the car as a gift. The other members came back from the pickup. They smiled and patted the guy on his shoulder as he took the keys and strolled over to the car. Danny turned and headed back to Van.

Van in the meantime watched the entire scene in horror. She knew something like this was coming, but to be there felt entirely different than what she imagined. Danny was unmoved and emotionless the entire time. The execution was quick and vicious. She had started punching the number '9' into her phone to get Robert's attention but he had not yet responded. As Danny returned to the car, she turned off her phone, fearful that Robert might call her or text her, and Danny might detect that something was up. As Danny came toward the car, one of the other El Muertes caught up with him and said, "See you soon, brother."

Danny nodded, and the guy looked over at Van and his eyes grew wide. "Who is she?"

Danny looked at him like it was none of his business, and the man said, "She's a cop, bro! I seen her at the station!"

Danny turned and grabbed him by the throat. The man held his hands up and shook his head furiously, and gasped, "I'm serious, man. I'm sorry."

Danny dropped his hold and looked back at Van. The cloud came back over his eyes. He jumped into the driver's seat.

"What did he say Danny?" she asked quickly, panic rising.

"He said you're a cop," Danny replied. Then grabbing her purse, he opened it, rifling through it for a gun or a badge. Van knew not to bring them, and they weren't there.

"Danny. He doesn't know what he is talking about. Maybe I look like somebody," she said, starting to shake.

"Well, babe," he said, coldly, "we'll see." He reached back in her purse and pulled out the phone and held it up. "Yeah. We'll see."

She could tell as they drove back that he was betraying that same conflicted sense she had felt before, and that helped her to relax and act like she had no idea what he was talking about. They got back to Oasis and instead of taking her to the loft, Danny took her to one of the karaoke rooms and locked her inside.

"What are you doing?" she asked.

Danny said nothing and disappeared. She waited, wondering if she had made a fatal mistake. She heard a tap on the door. She walked over and looked out of the small window. The door unlocked and standing there was the woman who drove the orange Mustang.

"You gotta get out of here," she said, almost mechanically. "You must leave. Now."

Van didn't hesitate. She grabbed her purse and followed the woman to a stairwell. She turned, said thanks, and then ran down the stairwell, which opened onto an alley adjacent to the building. She looked around and ran to the backside of the mall and then turned down the street and walked quickly away from the mall, trying not to be conspicuous. She was about a block away when Robert pulled up beside her and urged her to jump in, which she did.

As he drove, she asked, "Are you being followed?"

He kept driving and looked back. "I don't see anything and nothing like a Rush car."

Van looked down. The trauma of the moment overwhelmed her. "Don't take me to the Bureau," she said. "Can I borrow your phone?" She called Charlie and explained what had happened. They agreed to meet and Van asked Robert to take her there.

"Who is she?" Van asked Robert as they drove on.

"She is a plant. FBI. It's a joint operation."

"You didn't tell me?"

"You didn't need to know. You were too close to Danny Kang."

Van was unhappy but what Robert said made some sense. "Is she going to be okay?"

"We don't know that yet. We are watching."

In fact, the joint operation had been in place for over a year. The woman in the orange Mustang's name was Mindy Wong. She worked for the FBI as an undercover agent, and had been planted in the Oasis, and through that, the Rush for the entire time. But she was not getting close to Danny Kang, although she had gotten close to Min and through her adopted as a part of the gang. Min bought her the orange Mustang.

Shortly after Van witnessed the execution, and Mindy rescued Van, the FBI raided Oasis and what remained of El Muerte. They found what they considered to be evidence of human and drug trafficking, and arrested Danny Kang and his lieutenants including his sister and several members of El Muerte. Van filled out an affidavit describing the scene at the cemetery. She added to the affidavit the possibility of a connection to the cold case file of the murdered couple.

Danny was convicted on several counts including conspiracy to murder and sex trafficking. His crimes were considered aggravated because of his affiliation with a gang, but his sentence was reduced after it was learned that the couple in the cold case actually were his and Min's parents. Van went to visit him in prison.

"You got a lot of nerve," he said, through the bulletproof glass that separated them.

"Something about you, Danny," she said.

"Yah? Like what?"

"Don't give up on your life."

"I am a fucking felon, and anyway who are you to tell me…?"

"I am serious. You are an empire builder. Get through this quickly and do it right next time. You can still be the King of LA."

He laughed. "Still wanna be my queen?"

"Get out of here quickly and look me up," she said. "You never know."

Six months later, Danny Kang was murdered in jail. Old school El Muertes found him and hung him in his cell with a twisted sheet. Min Kang was released after two years in the Century Regional Detention Center for Women in Lynwood, California, just southeast of downtown Los Angeles.

CHAPTER 8.

The Cytokine Singularity

Between 1990 and 2010, the computational speed of computers doubled every 14 months. Computer memory capacity doubled every 18 months. Computer storage capacity doubled every three years. These hyper-rapid advances in computer technology were the result of human intelligence. Computers did not make themselves smarter. Humans made computers smarter. But as computers continued to become smarter, the distance between human intelligence and machine intelligence narrowed. Enter artificial intelligence or AI. AI is a quantum leap advance in machine intelligence. The difference between pre-AI software and post-AI software is the ability of AI-driven software to adapt and recode itself in response to new stimuli, a change in circumstances, or a logic problem not previously encountered. In short, unlike operating systems before AI, post-AI operating systems have the capacity to learn. This capacity accelerates the advance of machine intelligence toward human intelligence, and when the distinction between the two evaporates—when that line is crossed—that is the moment of singularity, the moment when human intelligence loses control over machine intelligence.

Fred Schmidt looked out over the bay. The sky was gray, as it usually is in this part of the country. But it was a quiet morning. The water was still, and dark green islands dotted the horizon. He stared at his multiple monitors for just a few seconds, enough time to get a snapshot of the markets. The country was in an upswing, buoyed by the new president's anti-regulatory posture. Fred's personal fortune increased $20 million in the first three minutes of open. If it were that easy, he thought to himself, then why waste time and energy on yet another new venture? He knew the answer before he asked the question—because otherwise he would be bored, and he hated the feeling of being bored almost more than anything. Of course, his personal health crisis had ratcheted things up a notch. Finding some way to stay alive captured his interest, and combining a new scientific discovery with solving his own personal cancer riddle was, in a kind of perverse sense, the best of all possible worlds.

He called Derek. "Good morning, Fred. How's the weather?" Fred knew he wasn't asking him about the actual weather. He liked that about Derek—very few people really knew how to communicate with him. "Calm," he said, "but I could use a good storm."

* * * * * *

Dr. Brian Johannsen loved Bainbridge Island. He often thought of it as its own petri dish. Unique flora and fauna dotted the island, battling invasive species brought by birds and bicyclists and hikers, who thought they were simply enjoying the views. He found a small apartment in Fort Ward, as far away from the Duc A. Tran Laboratory for Hereditary Biology as possible, and he rode his Honda Gold Wing through the back roads to work every day. The traffic on 305 had gotten oppressive, even for a small island, and he could relax and think as he rode on Fletcher Bay Road past Port Orchard and then through Grand Forest West on Miller Road up to Hidden Cove. He parked his bike and pulled off his helmet. As the sun was creeping up and through the thin line between the horizon and the gray sky, an orange light lit up Tran Labs and the pines and lush vegetation that surrounded it. He took a deep breath and walked to the back entrance that he preferred to use. By the time he got there, the sun had disappeared, and the morning returned to its standard gray. He climbed the stairs to the third-floor laboratory and found his office, where he set down his helmet, removed his riding gear and pulled on his lab coat. He loved this office. He was glassed in from the busy-ness of the Lab and he had a floor-to-ceiling window that looked directly out onto Hidden Cove and Port Madison Bay.

Brian pulled his chair back, and as he was about to sit down, he noticed a biohazard transport case on the floor next to his desk. A note from Dr. Meisner was taped to the handle. It read: "Highly Infectious. Follow BSL IV Protocol." He jumped up, opened his Hazmat case and pulled out a jump suit, booties, sleeve covers, two pairs of surgical gloves, and a Halyard N95 Fluid shield respirator and surgical mask. He put everything on and grabbed the case, walked it to a secure lab that the team used for highly infectious substances, and locked the door. Inside, he placed the case on chrome table and carefully opened it. He noticed that an enclosed petri dish was properly stored inside two watertight containers packaged in black sponge. He reached inside to pullout the petri dish and read the label: Risk Group IV. He gently carried over to a gas tight Class III glove box, one of two at Tran Labs. The glove box had been constructed inside a small, sealed room. He entered the room, placed the dish inside the box, gathered his working materials and set them next to the dish. He snapped down the lid to ensure a tight seal and then sealed the door and went over to the intercom and buzzed Dr. Meisner.

"Good morning, Brian."

"Hi Stan. Saw your message. Nice way to wake up."

"You're talking about the bio case?"

"None other."

"Sorry about that. Couple of Silicon guys dropped it off yesterday. One of them asked about you. You know Fred Schmidt?"

"Fred Schmidt, CEO of Grindle?"

"The very same."

"Never met him. How does he know me?"

"Word's out I guess."

"Word's out?" he chuckled. "Right. So what do you need me to do?"

"Take a look. Let's figure it out."

"Thanks, Stan. I'll try not to spread it around."

Brian could sense that Dr. Meisner had very little interest in the case. The fact that he had left it on the floor was a pretty clear signal that Meisner had other concerns. Silicon Valley CEOs were a dime a dozen these days, even Fred Schmidt. Bill Gates wasn't a regular with Meisner, but he had stopped by a few times, and they both were members of the same country club. No reason to get worked up.

He sat down at the glass in front of the glove box, place his hands inside the rubber arms that allowed him to work on the dish. He carefully opened it and began to separate the contents into five other dishes. He tested the contents for RG IV's "big three": Ebola, Marburg and Lassa, and the results were negative. He tested for HIV and SARs, just to be sure, and the results likewise were negative. He ran backup tests on all known RG III and IV microbes and could not get a positive result. He isolated a small specimen on a slide, placed the slide in a glass containment capsule and closed up all the remaining samples for storage. He pulled his arms out of the gloves, entered the room and grabbed the containment capsule. The particular lab he occupied had its own Scanning Electron Microscope or SEM, with which Brian used to view microscopic organisms. The SEM was fitted with a special slot for the containment capsule to handle potentially infectious microbes. He slid the containment capsule into the slot and turned on the SEM.

At first, the images were blurred. He tried several different resolutions before an image began to appear. At its core was a small globe about 0.3 microns in diameter. The globe appeared to be spinning around an axis of two spikes that were north and south respectively, the north spike was the same size as the globe, and the south spike about double the size, more than 0.5 microns. Around the equator of the globe were four additional spikes also measuring 0.3 microns, each at 90°, 180°, 270°, and 360°. The spiked globes seemed to cluster in groups of six. Brian noted the perfect symmetry of the globes. He ran a spectrometer to determine composition and the globe came back as a mesh composed of carbon fullerenes, and magnesium diboride, which is a key element in ceramics. The spikes appeared to be a titanium alloy. The spectrometer confirmed what he had already begun to surmise—these microbes were not organic. He suspected, though, that that didn't mean they were safe, and whoever packaged them as an RG IV organism was sending the message to be extremely careful. He pulled the containment capsule out of the SEM and stored it with the other samples. He returned to his desk, removed the hazmat gear and put his lab coat back on. Then he went to see Dr. Meisner.

He walked quickly downstairs to Meisner's office. He wasn't there. Brian wandered around the floor looking in the conference rooms without success. He asked Meisner's assistant if she knew where he was working, and she thought he might be in the main lab on the first floor. Brian bound down another flight of stairs and into the Lab. He found Dr. Meisner standing with a group of faculty members from University of Washington Microbiology Department or what he now called U-Dub. They saw him approach, and everyone smiled. "Dr. Johannsen! So good to see you! How have you been! Cooking up anything new?"

Brian smiled back and was cordial. As he approached, the group returned to discussing a proposal put forth by Bill Gates to prepare for a global pandemic. The question was whether or not they might get a jump on any research by anticipating what the source of the pandemic might be. One of the faculty members mentioned Wuhan and the virology work that was being done there. Another faculty member responded that possibly, but more advanced work was being conducted in Zimbabwe in response to the recent Ebola outbreaks. Brian waited for what he felt was an appropriate amount of time and tapped Dr. Meisner on the shoulder. He whispered that he had information on the package. Meisner looked at him a little irritated, and said, "Thank you, Dr. Johannsen. Feel free to put it in a report and send it to me. I will take a look when I finish here." Brian looked at Meisner as if to say, if you are not interested, why did you ask me to look at it, then shrugged it off, and said "Certainly. Nice to see you gentlemen." He added "…and gentlewoman," to the one female faculty member who was present.

Brian returned to his office and shot Meisner a quick email. "Check again with Schmidt. The microbe is not a biologic." He put his lab coat back on the hook, tossed his leather riding jacket over his shoulder, grabbed his helmet and left for the evening.

✳ ✳ ✳ ✳ ✳ ✳

Derek Whitestone mused for a quick minute on the storm that Fred Schmidt either was waiting for or possibly even contriving. He knew the health care industry was in a protracted state of chaos. The last administration, after two decades of political stalemate, had passed a health care bill designed to meet the needs of the 20 million souls that high-cost managed care allegedly had abandoned. In so doing, that administration recast a mostly privatized system as a quasi-governmental program that measured success more by the pool of covered entities than by profit. The new administration now seemed hell-bent on dismantling that system and returning health care to a pre-managed care proto-capitalist state driven by profit. But the administration never actually explained how the existing state would end and how that new state might be resurrected. Tidbits here and there made it look like something real, but the health care battles actually had morphed into a purely political battle—nothing more than a proxy for one administration's opposition to a prior administration. The back-and-forth whipsaw effect of the political wrangling left the health care industry without clear direction and the scientific community that fed the industry its high-cost cures and treatments and devices found itself floundering. The pressure to survive by being the first to succeed had grown so great that the same community that once prided itself on its independent objectivity now found itself under the allure of bad science, announcing accomplishments and publishing results prematurely and without adequate verification. Fred Schmidt already had his storm. All he needed was the killer app that would bring him his next billions, and Derek knew he was banking on Bainbridge.

The problem with that strategy was the petri dish. Its actual origins were still unknown, and the question of its ownership was complicated enough to qualify as a law school fact pattern. Derek needed an alternative. RW Labs had the infrastructure. Derek could go hat in hand, as he had already considered. He would have to throw Cheryl Brown under the bus for taking the dish, which didn't really bother him. But if he went that route, he wouldn't be able to predict the outcome—a skill he based his entire career around. Belinda could be vengeful. She would want his money for the Providia AI engineering product, but as soon as she had her results, she could try and cut him out. He knew her legal team to be vicious, but Derek had been down that road, and he knew his way around it. Unfortunately, there was a bigger problem. Derek had already split the contents of the dish, and Belinda's team would figure that out. He needed to look elsewhere and he had an idea.

The Lyndon A. Rutter Center for Cellular Engineering at the University of California in Los Angeles had recently announced a breakthrough in cancer treatments. Using self-renewing pluripotent stem cells, researchers at UCLA successfully manufactured T cells capable of enhancing immunity and fighting cancer cells. T cell therapies had been around for years, but in patients with low T-cell counts, they didn't always work. This new breakthrough allowed for the production of T cells without having to harvest them from patients. Derek had met Lyndon Rutter but didn't know him well. Rutter made his money in the lucrative LA real estate market. Lately his focus had shifted to philanthropy, and he had donated large sums to UCLA for the fight against cancer. Rutter's position reminded Derek of his own client, the one who now lived on Bainbridge Island.

Cheryl Brown sat in her cubicle. She didn't feel particularly well and had not taken her coat off. Derek called her into his conference room.

"I need to know what you were thinking."

"I think it is obvious I wasn't thinking."

"I disagree, Cheryl. You have your weaknesses but being thoughtless is not one of them."

Cheryl looked down and then up again to meet Derek's stare. "If the RW Labs was that careless, then there were two possibilities. One was that the contents of that dish were not really that dangerous, and two, that we didn't want to be working with them. I thought that if the dish had anything to do with MEMS, it might give us a leg up, and I figured you would understand that."

Derek smiled. He knew he would not trust Cheryl with the full story, but he could enlist her as part of his Plan B.

"How would you feel about returning to Los Angeles?"

"I'm not sure I understand. Are you firing me?"

"I'm not, but I gave it pretty serious thought. You took a great risk and have potentially implicated me and this company in a crime that could ruin us. You have also risked the wrath of RW Labs, and that part of the story is not over yet."

"I'm sorry, Derek."

"Well, I'm not. I want to know more about this dish. I want you to take it to UCLA Medical School, and shepherd its review. You might need to stay down there a while. I will arrange for an apartment. You need to address your lease here. Work out an arrangement with your landlord. You have two days to get your affairs in order. Meet me back here on Thursday morning."

Cheryl left, and Derek looked out his window. He told himself, "This is a good idea." He called Stanford, and arranged for the delivery of the petri dish first thing Thursday morning.

The UCLA Labs had benefitted greatly under the Rutters' generosity, but in fact, it had struggled over the years since another T-cell-related controversy had smeared its reputation. Decades prior, the UCLA Labs was accused of harvesting T cells from patients who were being treated at the University's medical center and storing them for its own research. When the news broke, utter chaos broke out, senior faculty members were fired, multiple lawsuits were filed, and the University was forced to settle claims to the tune of hundreds of millions of dollars. The only thing that kept the lab in operation was its affiliation with UCLA Medical School, which found itself forced to keep the lab open simply for teaching purposes. It took the school more than 20 years to recover from the debacle.

Cheryl was happy to be back in LA. She still had friends there, and the intensity of Silicon Valley had been wearing on her. It felt as much like a break as it did like another job, and Derek had found her an amazing apartment near the Grove, an outdoor high-end mall in Park La Brea built around LA's historic Original Farmer's Market. She spent the weekend partying with old friends, and the transport case rested under the floor in one of her many empty closets.

Cheryl was not alone with her friends. A nondescript black Ford Explorer had picked up her trail on the way down Interstate 5 as she sped past the fields of grain, hay, cotton, grapes and citrus trees grown in the California's central valley along the California aqueduct. It followed her as she made her way over the Grapevine and through the Tejon Pass. It followed her that weekend as she bounced from La Brea to Santa Monica to Malibu to the Hollywood Hills and back to La Brea. On Monday, the Explorer reported that she had gone to UCLA, parked in Structure No. 2 and carried a backpack into the Biomedical Sciences Research Building just off Charles Young Drive.

Cheryl Brown had seen the black Explorer and reported it to Derek. He pressed her to be certain she wasn't being paranoid, and she confirmed that she had seen the same Explorer in her rearview mirror several times since the Grapevine. She was pretty sure the Explorer had followed her all the way down the 5 Freeway. He wasn't certain but he suspected Belinda, and if so, he would not be surprised if Belinda was having them followed. He urged Cheryl to be cautious but to go about her business in the normal course and not act as if she were hiding something. There was nothing unusual about Derek sending Cheryl to UCLA. He might be exploring the same opportunities for investing Fred's money that took him to the Labs in the first place. UCLA's medical complex housed one of the top microbiology labs in the country and the scientists who worked there had been researching MEMS for years. The California NanoSystems Institute sat directly across the medical plaza from the Rutter Center of Cellular Engineering and Medicine. Derek told Cheryl to use her UCLA backpack, which she still had, to carry the transport case. He called Rutter in advance to let them know she was coming. When she arrived, two students met her at the main entrance and escorted her into a small room off the main lobby, where a team was waiting for her.

"Good morning, Ms. Brown," said Dr. March Fielding, who led the virology team at Rutter. "Derek Whitestone told us to expect you."

"Good morning."

"Mr. Whitestone told us you were carrying a substrate of some kind. He could not tell us what it was, but that it might be highly infectious. Is that your understanding as well?"

"It is."

"Can you tell us a little more about what you are bringing us today?"

"Not much more than what Mr. Whitestone has already told you."

"Do you know what it is?"

"It is a petri dish labeled Risk Group IV."

"Nothing more?"

"No."

"Do you know where it came from?"

"I do not."

"Do you know who might have worked with it?"

"I don't."

"Do you understand what Risk Group IV means?"

"Not entirely but I believe it might contain a virus or something like that that is very dangerous."

The team looked at each other. Either she was not telling the truth, which seemed likely to them, or Derek had entrusted one of the world's most potent and untreatable diseases to someone who had no idea what she was carrying. If so, the possibilities were frightening, and Derek Whitestone was committing gross negligence by placing this microbe in incompetent hands. They smiled at Cheryl condescendingly, and took the transport case out of the backpack and took her back to the lobby. She went into the women's bathroom and pulled a folded cardboard box out of the backpack. The dimensions of the box were roughly the same as the transport case. She unfolded it and placed it in the backpack and exited the building. She decided to take a different route to her car. She had lunch at the cafeteria adjacent to the student center. It reminded her of being a student there and how nice it was to be worried about nothing more than finishing a paper or getting ready for an exam. She could almost feel the same comfort just by sitting there and watching the other students. She waited an hour before heading back to Parking Structure 2.

When she got to the parking structure, she climbed the concrete stairs and crossed the lot back to her car. That's when the Explorer rushed up on her and two men jumped out and grabbed her. Almost instantly, she heard a whistle, and a UCLA Security Guard was running toward her. The men ripped the backpack off Cheryl's shoulder and jumped back in the Explorer and took off. The security guard caught up with Cheryl and asked if she was okay and if she knew those men. She started crying and told him they had stolen her books. He took some information from her and said he would report on what happened and would tell the security administration to look out for a black Explorer. She wiped her eyes and told him how brave he had been. She wondered if he had any idea how close he had come to being shot and possibly killed.

She sat in her car for another hour. She was afraid to leave the structure, as if it were watching out for her and keeping her safe. Eventually she pulled out, called her friends in North Hollywood and drove out there to stay with them. They had a joint ready when she pulled up and her hands shook as she lit it and took a draw. Exactly what I need, she thought to herself. Her immediate second thought was—what the fuck did I get myself into?

Derek waited for a call. He expected her to follow up as soon as she left Rutter. When she didn't call, he got concerned but another matter captured his attention and he let it go. Several hours later, his phone rang. It was Cheryl.

"What the hell, Cheryl? Did they get it?"

Cheryl was high. "Man, I got jumped."

"What happened?"

"They stole the empty box, those idiots."

"So you delivered it?"

"I did and they jumped me in the parking lot after I had dropped it off. You were right about the box. They grabbed me and a student security guard saved me. They took the backpack."

"You certain it was a security guard?"

Cheryl paused. "Well, he had a yellow jacket on." She started giggling and found it difficult to stop.

✱ ✱ ✱ ✱ ✱ ✱

When Brian got home, he pulled a beer and a container of fresh wonton out of his fridge. He heated the wonton on his stove, popped the beer and sat down in front of his computer. He looked up nanotechnologies and started reading. He had studied it in school as a part of his doctoral program, but the field was still in its infancy, and he became more interested in the origins and mutations of microscopic life and focused his research there. The material in the petri dish piqued his curiosity. Why that shape and why did they cluster, and what where they supposed to actually do? He wondered even more basically how could any device that small actually perform a function and what type of function would it be? He read that there were four types of nanorobotic devices: switches, motors, shuttles and cars. A 'switch' is a nanorobotic device that changes its shape in response to environmental stimuli in a process that is called "conformational change." The stimuli causing the change might be a chemical reaction or heat or ultraviolet radiation. A 'motor' uses energy derived from the change process to move around molecules in its orbit. 'Shuttles' carry molecular compounds like anti-cancer agents to targeted locations. 'Cars'—the most advanced of the four forms of nano-robots—have appendages that can be used for locomotion and steering. The appendages may be actual wheels, but they also could be tracks or tails or tiny hairs or extensions like arms.

Brian also studied several options for powering nanorobots. Power might come from traditional micro-capacitors and mini-generators that create and store electrical power to a special wrap called a piezoelectric membrane that transforms magnetic fields or radiofrequency (RF) radiation into electrical power. Nanobots can also be powered by electrochemical stimuli like neurotransmitters in the human body. The earliest proposed uses of the nanotechnology were medical. Tiny drills that would pop cancer cells, isolating and cutting off blood flow to the cells. Nanorobots could "paint" cancer cells and prepare them for targeted chemical and RF therapies. The latter focused heat generated by high intensity RF emissions on painted cells and burned them away from surrounding tissue without harming the non-painted tissue. A newer application destroyed pathogenic mRNA—mutated RNA strands that were giving birth to new cancer cells. Beyond medicine, researchers were looking at environmental applications. Nanomites might be created to facilitate the rapid decomposition of landfills and floating plastic islands in the ocean, eliminating toxic waste and its harmful effects on the environment.

Still, he was beginning to get the same feeling he had in graduate school. The more he read, the more it felt to him like fantasy and science fiction. Perhaps it was possible to build a single nanobot. But the impact of a single or even small number of nanobots would be undetectable in the physical world. For nanotechnology to have any noticeable impact, it would have to scale. Take all the computers and laptops and pads and smart phones that had been manufactured around the world over the past 40 years and reduce them to nanoscale and you could fit them all in the palm of your hand. A strong wind would blow them all into total obscurity.

There could be another option, he thought, allowing his imagination to play, and the fantasy to develop. What if nanotechnology was not the end of the chain, but rather the beginning? What if nanobots merely started a physical process, like the fuse of a bomb. He thought about real world applications. Some cancers, for example, were triggered by the presence of toxic substances, but once the cancer was started, the triggering substance, like smoking cigarettes, could be removed and yet the cancer would still grow, and eventually consume its host. What if, when fighting cancer, you could trigger the growth of an anti-cancer agent, like T cells, with a relatively small number of nanobots. Unfortunately, he thought, as he shut off the computer and headed to bed, even if that were true, you still needed to solve the scaling problem for a therapy like that to make economic sense.

He fell asleep, musing on Isaac Asimov's three laws of robotics:

1. A robot may not injure a human being, or through inaction, allow a human being to come to harm.

2. A robot must obey orders given to it by human beings except where such orders would conflict with the First Law.

3. A robot must protect its own existence as long as such protection does not conflict with the First or Second Law.

Back in the office, Brian returned to the SEM lab. He pulled out the non-biologic RG IV specimen and set up to do further work. He divided the sample into several new samples. The first sample he heated over a Bunsen burner, and then looked to see if there was any change. Nothing he could detect. He tried a variety of acids and still no reaction. At that point, he heard a knock and looked to see Dr. Carrie Comstock standing at the door dressed in a similar hazmat suit. Brian enjoyed working with Carrie. She was a careful and thoughtful scientist, and she had been very helpful to Brian in the past. He held up four fingers, the sign they used to communicate toxicity levels, and she nodded. He motioned for her to enter.

"You must have found something," she said through a microphone in her suit. "You have been incommunicado for two days."

"Stan left something for me but I don't think he is that interested. I am still deciding whether or not to be interested."

"Show me."

He pushed back from the SEM and flipped on a monitor. "Doesn't look like a biologic," she said. "Too symmetrical. Is it a crystal?"

"I wondered myself," he responded. "I ran the spectrometer and it turned out to be a combination of metal and ceramics."

"It's a nanobot?" she responded, picking up quickly on the implication.

"I think it might be. Certainly, it is something manufactured. But I can't seem to get it to do anything."

At that point, almost as if on cue, Carrie and Brian watched as the image started to rotate. As it rotated, the spikes began to move in and out of the sphere, extending and retracting. The effect was mesmerizing.

"Maybe it likes women," Carrie joked.

"Did you bring anything in here with you?"

"Only my phone."

"Can I see it?"

As she pulled it out of her pocket, she noticed it was ringing. "Probably a telemarketer." But when it stopped ringing, the image stopped moving.

Brian said, "Wait here." He ran to get his cell phone and brought it back to the Lab. "Call me," he told Carrie.

"My husband might not be happy," Carrie said, in a light-hearted way—she enjoyed ribbing Brian.

He smiled and said, "Just call me."

She did, and when Brian's phone started to ring, the image started to move again. But as soon as he answered her call, it stopped. He spoke over the phone to Carrie and nothing happened. They tried the experiment several times and the results were the same. As long as the phone was ringing, the image would move. Turn it off or answer the call, and the image stopped.

"Wow," Brian said.

"Well, we know it moves," she noted. "But what does it do?"

Carrie went over to the SEM and pulled out the containment capsule. But before returning it to the glove box, she opened it and started sprinkling it into a new dish. "Be careful," Brian started to say, and then he saw Carrie look at him, her eyes widening. She dropped the capsule into the dish and grabbed her throat. Brian felt his own throat start to restrict. He hit an alarm button and caught Carrie before she could fall to the floor. He laid her gently on the ground. Each lab was outfitted with a medical emergency kit, and the teams there had been drilled over and over again on its use. He stood up and stumbled over to the cabinet but as he reached for it, he felt his legs give way and he crumpled down to the floor. He looked up and for a brief second saw several white suits enter the room in a walking bubble and start to pull him and Carrie to the outer door and then he passed out.

When Brian awoke, he felt his lungs burning and started coughing. He looked around and could see he was in an oxygen tent. Dr. Meisner and several colleagues were standing outside the tent along with Fred Schmidt, who was likewise suited up. Hearing him cough, they put on gas masks and entered the tent.

"How is Dr. Comstock?" he gagged out between coughing fits.

"She's alive," Dr. Meisner responded. "But we have her on a ventilator. What the hell happened?"

"Fred Schmidt happened," he responded between coughing jags. He found it increasingly hard to breath and someone gave him a shot to relax him and he fell back asleep.

It took three days for Brian to recover. While he was recovering, the team ran the same tests on him that he had already run, and likewise determined that the substance was not a biologic, and that Brian was not contagious. Carrie had a rougher time. She went into cardiac arrest twice but pulled through it. By the end of the week, they were able to remove the ventilator. Brian stood by her bedside.

"Do I get a Purple Heart?" she asked feebly, forcing a smile.

"More like a Bronze Star," Brian responded.

Carrie coughed, and Brian said, "Take it easy. It's good to see you on this side still." He grabbed her hand and gave it a light squeeze. She drifted back into sleep.

He joined Dr. Meisner in the Lab's main conference room. Fred Schmidt was present.

"Can someone tell me what just happened?" Brian questioned.

"We still don't know what caused it," Dr. Meisner responded, "but both you and Dr. Comstock went into full blown anaphylaxis in a matter of seconds. We pumped you full of epinephrine and slowed it down but as you can tell, it took days for you both to recover. We are not certain that Dr. Comstock is entirely out of the woods."

Dr. Meisner looked at Fred Schmidt. "I think we are entitled to some answers."

"I don't know what it is," he said. "I brought it here for you to figure that out."

"Where did it come from, Fred?"

"I am sorry, but I am not at liberty to divulge, and even if I could, I am not certain I know. The origin is proprietary information. You know how things work in the Valley. Information is siloed. That is how we protect it."

"That is also how you protect thieves," Brian said. He was angry and justifiably so. Carrie was an important member of the staff, and Brian cared a great deal for his colleagues.

Fred grimaced but didn't take it personally. He needed Brian and this group to work though their issues and take the sample to the next level.

"Can you still work with it?"

Dr. Meisner shrugged as if he hadn't made up his mind. "It is dangerous but that hasn't stopped us in the past. We need to develop new protocols with it. Give us a few days and we will let you know."

Fred stood up and left the room. Looking back at Brian, he said, "I am sorry about you and your colleague, Dr. Johannsen. I will make it up to you."

Brian watched Fred as he left. He didn't need or want anything from Fred. But he knew risk was a basic part of his chosen profession, and if Dr. Meisner wanted to keep working with the substance in the dish, he would continue to support the effort.

He turned back to Dr. Meisner. "Anaphylaxis?"

"Right, a full-blown cytokine storm."

"Do you think it was an allergic response?"

"We don't know yet, but it doesn't look that way. All we know is that your and Dr. Comstock's bodies immediately went into shock in response to the substance as soon as it went airborne. It could be weaponized, which might be why Fred Schmidt is staying mum."

CHAPTER 9.

A Host of Brilliant Ideas

The news of Danny Kang's death hit Van particularly hard. She knew that Danny's dark side, which she had encountered on more than one occasion, should have kept her emotionally distant. She also knew that the good she saw in Danny appealed to her in a way she hadn't felt before. She had her doubts that she could rescue him from the consequences of his bad choices, but she found herself desperate to try. His death ended that fantasy.

Detective Young had been overly complimentary of Van's work following the arrest and conviction of Danny Kang and his associates. Van appreciated it, but it did not feel sincere and did not give Van any confidence in Young's support for her as a detective. The excessive compliments were short-lived. Van found her work being scrutinized in ways it had not been before. Young seemed to enjoy pointing her out at daily meetings and asking for her opinion on matters she knew nothing about. She retreated back to Chess and to Detective Broad. Her analytical work at Chess had been picked up by a new recruit. Detective Robert "Bobby" Davidson was a recent graduate and had studied statistics and computer science at Cal State Fullerton before entering the police academy. Bobby was proud to be a detective, but he had greater ambitions. He had already applied to law school and hoped to join the FBI. For now, at least until he heard back from law school admissions, he was working with Detective Broad in Chess.

"Quite a stint you pulled off, my dear Detective," Detective Broad said in his most affected British accent.

"I suppose you're quite right," Van responded in kind. They laughed.

"Oh dear," she added. "What must I do now?"

"Actually, Van," Broad said, taking a more serious tone. "I do have an idea."

Detective Broad's "idea" was for Van to get herself better acquainted with a new line of medical and pharmaceutical cases that had become the focus of Charlie's work after the Baldwin Hills case. The cases involved complaints raised against doctors and pharmaceutical companies engaging in behavior that exceeded ordinary incompetence and traditional notions of malpractice. Rather, this borderline criminal behavior ranged from a reckless disregard for human safety to the intent to cause harm. Charlie started asking questions after he noticed that many of these cases disappeared under the veil of civil actions that terminated in confidential settlement agreements. The most egregious claims involved death, recklessly accidental or intentional, but the sheen of the medical and pharmaceutical professions often covered up the crimes, which escaped detection for several years, if they were ever discovered at all. Under that same sheen, doctors with ready access to prescription drugs easily hid their addictions and the occasionally disastrous consequences of those addictions. If a botched prescription or surgery resulted in harm and was discovered, the perpetrator usually got off lightly with suspensions and a stint in rehab. Occasionally, a repeat offender lost a license.

Another even darker level involved the criminally insane, who chose the medical profession as a cover or alias. The prime examples of this class were Nazi concentration camp doctors, like Josef Mengele, who collected their dehumanized subjects and brutalized them for no beneficial purpose but to test useless theories of pain tolerance and physical endurance. Even in 21st century America, you could still find doctors, who on their own or in the service of criminal sociopaths, harvested blood or organs without consent while evading the watchful eyes of hospital administrators and medical boards. Van had already run into this one in one of her early cases as a medical examiner on the forensics team. Criminal medical practices like organ harvesting had been commonly treated as urban myths. But the field of clinical psychology actually classified these criminal acts under a mental disorder similar to Munchausen syndrome by proxy—a disorder in which a caregiver, even a parent, intentionally harms someone under their care. The industry's standard manual of mental disorders, DSM-III, called it the Frankenstein effect.

Alvin and Bobby were working with Charlie and had assembled a collection of files they called Medical and Pharmaceutical Crimes. It was only a couple of shelves, and it took Van less than a day to go through. The early cases included, not surprisingly, Nazi doctors on the run who came first to Los Angeles before being chased to South America. These files were thick and identified crimes that mostly occurred in WWII in Germany. There were a handful cases alleging the unlicensed practice of medicine in which a family member complained that someone without a license posed as a doctor or nurse and conducted improper in-home surgeries or treatments, which led to the death or incapacitation of another family member. One file caught her attention. The parents of a UCLA medical student who died in a bizarre accident in a lab on campus had come to the LAPD and asked them to investigate her death. They had already filed a large civil suit against the University and were not satisfied with the University's explanation of what happened. The case was assigned to

Detective Young, and he had accepted the University's explanation that the student died from anaphylaxis after an allergic reaction to a substance in the lab. He suspected that the parents were using the LAPD to strengthen their civil suit in order to get more money out of the University.

The file included press clippings from the time of the accident. The student, Marley Jean Dakota, was a member of a prominent Sioux family living in Cheyenne, Wyoming. Her great uncle, Russell Means, became famous in the early 1970s after he led several protests, the most famous of which occurred in Wounded Knee, South Dakota. The standoff with federal agents lasted 71days and highlighted the massacre of 350 Lakota Sioux, capturing the attention of the press and the nation. Means later became a Hollywood actor, and Marley's essay about his life and personal physical struggles helped her get admitted into the medical program at UCLA. Marley's dream was to become a specialist in Native American medicine, exploring crossover treatments using both Western medicine and traditional tribal cures. She had never complained of allergies, and her immune system had shown no indications of being compromised. She was 19 years old when she died. At the time of the press clippings, the school was refusing to release any details other than that she had had a severe allergic reaction to an unspecified substance in a medical lab. The school reported only that the reaction triggered an anaphylactic response, and Marley had suffocated from a swollen trachea before anyone was able to get her any medical treatment. The parents' civil case had focused on the school's inadequate response to Marley, but they had no details around the substance that triggered her allergic reaction.

Van took the file to Detective Young, set it on his desk, and sat down. "How can I help you, Detective?"

"Charlie and Alvin had me go through our records on medical crimes. I came across something recent."

Young looked down at the file. "The Dakota kid?"

"Yeah. Tell me what happened with this one."

"You like digging, don't you?" he asked, sounding irritated.

"I'm a nerd at heart, Detective Young. You know that. Did you know she was related to Russell Means, the actor who led Wounded Knee?"

"I saw something to that effect, but it doesn't alter my view on the case."

"Which is?"

"There is no case. It is sad but she reacted to something in the lab. Could have been anything."

"She wasn't allergic to anything, according to the records."

"She obviously was. Perhaps something new. Something she had not encountered before."

"Do you think we need to be worried?"

"I don't see why. She was the only one. No one else reacted or complained of any symptoms. Look, you understand what this really was, right?"

"What was it?" Van was careful not to sound disrespectful.

"Her parents want to make their civil case against the University, and they want to use us as leverage. I have seen it before a bunch of times. I have a problem with that."

"Ok, thanks for run down. Sorry to pull it up again."

"There are better cases, Detective. Don't waste your time."

Van picked up the file and went back to her desk. She wasn't convinced Young was right, but she wasn't sure he was wrong. She thought that if she could pursue the case further without raising any alarms, it would be worth the effort. Besides, Detective Broad had exposed her to this line of cases for a reason. Even if that reason weren't clear, she knew she would figure it out in time.

Still, she left the office feeling frustrated and headed to the gym. She had found a women's-only gym near her parents' home in Monterey Park. She liked going thereafter work and sweating out the pressures of the day. The owner of the gym was a small, energetic Cantonese woman named Kimmie Vong. Van enjoyed being around Kimmie for several reasons. Kimmie was very direct and always confident, aspects of a personality that Van respected and tried to emulate. Kimmie was also a great trainer and had studied nutrition and Eastern medicine on her way to getting a Ph.D. in acupuncture. Van had spent many hours with Kimmie learning the nuances of Eastern medicine. It was Kimmie who had convinced Van to up her game with her training regimen and sculpt her body in order to compete in bodybuilding and fitness competitions that were becoming the rage again after steroids nearly killed the sport back in the 1980s. Van was motivated to work hard because her job required that she be in good shape. She knew that she was behind the curve because she had not risen through the ranks as a hardened police officer who became a detective. Van trained with Kimmie for a couple of years before she was able to convince Van to enter a competition. Kimmie had a friend who ran Muscle Beach and had his own entertainment company. She introduced Van to Johnny Bask and his company, JB Entertainment. Van learned from Johnny B that the bodybuilding and beauty contest industry had undergone a sea change in its shift away from human growth hormones and steroids. The competitions now celebrated the variety of body shapes and distinguished what they called a "vintage" body shape from a fitness body shape, and even that from bodybuilding. Kimmie like the vintage competitions in part because the makeup, hairstyle and old-school bathing suits were fashion-centric but also because she could enjoy a normal diet. Both fitness and bodybuilding required extra hours in the gym, and highly a specialized diet that Kimmie had undergone as a younger competitor but that she no longer felt like enduring. Her own feelings didn't affect her read on Van, who she knew was looking for a more rigorous lifestyle, and who she knew could compete at that higher level.

Van had been running her three-mile route almost every morning and going to the gym three nights a week. Kimmie helped her manage her diet and developed a workout routine that varied and prevented Van from focusing on one part of her body to the exclusion of others. Van eliminated breads and meats and began to increase her intake of vegetable proteins and eggs. She learned to make tasty vegetarian dinners and convinced herself that life without wine and red meat could still be enjoyable. She especially enjoyed watching her body tone and firm, filling out with new muscle on her calves, thighs and arms while her core tightened up. Her parents noticed the change and started telling their friends how fit she had become.

Johnny B's competitions almost always fell on holidays like Labor Day and the Fourth of July. It worked well for him because he could get more competitors to participate and more spectators to attend who happened to come down to the beach to enjoy their day off work. Kimmie rented an RV and invited Van to drive down to the competition with her. She parked the RV in the lot behind the pickle ball courts adjacent to the Muscle Beach stage.

Johnny B was good at promoting his events. He had been a fixture at Muscle Beach for decades, and personally knew many of the bodybuild-ing stars of the early Muscle Beach years. He had a troupe of beautiful models who worked his events, directed contestants and handed out trophies to the winners. His competitors ranged in age from mid-teens to 80 years old, and the crowd especially loved watching older competitors whose commitment to fitness showed in their tight bellies and skinny but muscular arms with the extra skin of turkey necks and sagging glutes.

Johnny B's lead judge called the vintage group forward. The competitors emerged from an arched entrance and strode up a walkway, adding their best 1950s pose while wearing full body bathing suits and heels with fishnet stockings and flowers in elaborately styled hairdos. Johnny's models lined them up across the stage and the lead judge walked the contestants through a routine. Van saw Kimmie near the middle of the pack wearing a red polka-dotted bathing suit and a red rose in her hair. Van thought she had never seen such pride and confidence. Kimmie was a pro. After initial poses, the lead judge called out competitor numbers and shuffled the line, moving some contestants from the outer edges to the middle and others from the middle toward the edge. It became apparent to Van that middle was the better place to be. Kimmie managed to stay near the middle to the end and then the judge dismissed the competitors.

Van suddenly felt shy as she heard her group called forward. She stared at the bodies of the women in her class, and they all looked so perfect that she felt out of place. Kimmie came over to her and hugged her, and said, "Kill it babe. You look stunning." Van closed her eyes and, as she walked out on the stage, she could see the judges look at her and start talking to each other. She could not hear them, but she read their lips and knew they were impressed with what they were seeing in her. It gave her a boost of confidence. She walked through a series of poses and moved to the side. Her competitors did the same, gave her a courteous smile, and then showered the judges with little flirty moves as they stood there. Van thought the flirtiness was over the top and not very attractive. They called her number and a model moved her to the middle. Another contestant moved from the other end of the line and then a third. By the time they were finished, Van couldn't tell if she was in the middle or not.

They dismissed the line and as they left the stage, she could see Kimmie carrying a giant smile and clapping for her. They hugged, and Kimmie said, "You did it! Now, let's go get lunch!"

They went back to the RV and Kimmie's parents had prepared a feast. Van tried to eat but the nerves from her performance kept her from having much of an appetite. Kimmie kept telling her how great she did, and, at the end of the day, Kimmie took a second place, and Van, to her shock and delight, left with a first-place trophy. Johnny B made a point of finding Van after the event and congratulating her. He told her the contestants had all been invited to a well-known celebrity's house in the Malibu Hills, and that she and Kimmie definitely should join him there.

The house was well lit up, and Van could see it against the night sky as she drove up the curving and never-ending driveway. The celebrity was an A-lister, who loved any excuse for a party, and the Muscle Beach events had such caché that he could be certain his many celebrity friends would join him. Van pulled up behind a line of cars that were parking along the edge of the driveway. She saw a Bentley and a Rolls Royce hanging off the edge of the asphalt as if they were Fords and Chevys. Van was wearing a tight nightclub skirt and heels but she didn't pull any fashion cards and wanted to be low key. She was looking forward to finding a place to sit and relax—it had already been a long day and she had been on her feet for most of it.

As she walked onto the circular drive at the entrance to the house, she was struck by two thoughts. The house looked like it belonged in England. The arched entrance was a combination of molded concrete and stonework with sharp spires extending above a steep stone-shingled roof. She also noticed that it seemed small. The house was no more than two stories and the entrance hardly larger than a common house. There was stained glass in the portico and a soft orange glow coming through the windows surrounding the entrance. She made her way to the front door hoping to see Kimmie. An older man dressed like a butler asked her name, checked a list he was holding, and allowed her to enter.

The entrance hall was full of people who seemed reluctant to press much further into the house. She slid past them, peeked into the dining room and an attached kitchen that seemed very busy. The dining room table was covered with a variety of dishes. She saw barbecued chicken and racks of lamb covered in garlic and herbs. Different food rings were pressed tightly against each other—artichoke bread and meatballs and sliders all neatly arranged around bowls of various dips. Smartly dressed waiters and waitresses hustled in and out of the dining room snatching up empty platters and replacing them with new exotic dishes. As she purveyed the foods and the activity, an attractive young man in a tight tweed suit with pointy leather shoes brushed up against her and then turned quickly and apologized. He seemed friendly and nice. She stepped down a couple of hard wood stairs into a living room with several soft leather couches and a fireplace large enough for her to stand in without stooping. The room smelled like a mountain cabin. A small fire was burning in the fireplace, or at least it seemed small. She could pick up hints of hickory chips and cedar notes. A long table with a white tablecloth had been pushed against the wall to make room for guests. On the table stood an assortment of wines on one end, reds and whites combined, and a hard liquor assortment on the other end. Bowls of olives, maraschino cherries and sliced lemons and limes stood next to the liquor bottles. Sparkling crystal wine goblets and hi-ball glasses were neatly stacked in the center of the table between the alcoholic alternatives.

"Van!" Kimmie rushed over to her. "Come! Come! Johnny B is here. Let me get you a drink! What do you take?"

Van smiled. Of course, Kimmie would be running around like she owned the place. She made Van feel welcomed and comfortable.

"Can you get me tonic with a lemon?"

They found a corner in a study near a rear sliding glass door with comfortable chairs, and Johnny B walked over with a couple of his friends. He congratulated both Kimmie and Van on their trophies and introduced his friends. Van noticed a couple of Oscars sitting on a fireplace mantle. She also saw the boy with the pointy shoes lurking across the room and trying to make eye contact. She smiled a couple of times and soon he got up his nerve to come over. Johnny B hadn't seen him come over but when he did, he put on a big smile. He turned, and said, "Ladies, please meet the owner of this fine home—the famous actor Martin Richard."

Martin blushed. "Well, my parents are the famous actors, and actually still own the home," he admitted. "But they spend most of their time in New York City and the Seychelles."

Kimmie recognized him. "You were in the movie *Cat's Last Scratch*, correct?" She looked wide-eyed at Van. "I love horror movies, and that was one of the best I've seen." Martin smiled and said thank you. He held his hand out to Van, and said, "And you are?" Van introduced herself. Johnny B boasted on Van's behalf of her victory earlier. Van was careful to appreciate Johnny B and his pride in the competition.

"I am still surprised," she said. "The other girls were amazing."

Martin responded, "I am not surprised." Van blushed. "Would you like to see the back yard?" he asked.

She looked at Kimmie and smiled. "That would be very nice," she said. Kimmie winked at Van and watched as Martin and Van exited the sliding glass doors onto a balcony and down a metal staircase.

The view from the back of the house was stunning. The sun was just setting and the Malibu Hills to the East, loaded with red bark manzanita bushes and coastal sage scrub, were taking on an amber tint. The Pacific Ocean on the West reflected the pinks and oranges in the sky and the dark tips of the Channel Islands fell off the horizon to the North. The balcony was covered in flowers. Pots of blooming azaleas and mums hung from above and the railings were lined with red marigolds. As Van descended the spiral metal staircase, she noticed a small grass area below her with lawn chairs set up to watch the sunset and the lights of a large pool glowed up to the right. She looked behind her into a glassed-in game room with a large pool table, a Golden Tee arcade game and a wet bar. Several olive trees dotted the perimeter of the gardens surrounding the grass area and were lit with small, white light strands. Around the grass and the pool stood clusters of guests. Martin walked up to a group on the grass passing a joint around. Someone offered Van a hit, and she politely turned it down. Martin, who seemed in need of some relaxation, gladly took a hit and passed it back.

"I noticed the Oscars," Van said to Martin.

He laughed. "Not mine. My parents have had some success."

"Would I recognize their work?"

"Are you a movie person?"

"I actually prefer to read," she responded candidly. "But I have seen a few."

"Well, my father is an actor turned director and my mother played the lead in one of his better films. That is how they met."

"Kind of romantic."

"For them it was. They had me, and then got married... But they actually do love each other, unlike so many others out here."

"Are you happy?"

"I suppose. I need to find a way to become my own person. I am known more around these parts as their son and not for my own accomplishments."

"I am sure your time will come," Van offered encouragingly. Martin smiled. A pretty blond with a tattooed arm standing next to him and smoking a cigarette offered them something that looked like ecstasy or molly. Van shook her head and Martin declined, though Van wondered if he were declining on her account. Two forty-ish men saw the blond with the pills and bounced over to the group.

"Don't mind if we do," one of them said, and they took the pills and bounced away.

The tattooed blond looked at Martin, and said, "I am sorry, but I overheard your conversation." She leaned into both Van and Martin, and said quietly, as if to let them in on a secret, "You know that if you want to succeed in Hollywood, there really is only one way." Martin glanced over at Van with a 'here we go again' look but she could tell he didn't want to be impolite so early in the night.

"And what would that be?"

"If your parents haven't told you yet, someone should."

"Go ahead. Please. I'd love to know if there is a formula."

"I wouldn't call it a formula exactly."

"Okay."

"The trick is you need to be a member."

Now, Van thought, this could go several ugly ways. Hollywood had battled a lot of accusations of bias and this drug-toting blond didn't look particularly intelligent. But maybe she had something to say. Maybe she was into Scientology. Maybe she knew something new about the guilds.

"A member of what?" Martin asked, his brow furrowing.

"You've heard of the Illuminati, I am sure."

"I have but educate me."

She smiled. "Of course you already know. It's like this secret society of the world's most powerful people. They control Hollywood, movies and TV, and if you really want fame and fortune, you need to be a part of the movement. Everybody who is anybody is into it. Beyonce and Jay-Z, Madonna, Blake Shelton and Gwen Stefani, Meryl Streep, the entire Sheen family, Bruce Willis and Demi Moore, Ariana Grande, Justin Timberlake and Brittany Speers. All of them."

Martin had met most of them, and he had yet to be invited to an Illuminati party. "Is there a cost to join? A membership fee?"

"Oh well, yeah," she said, laughing. "It's pretty dark if you want to know. You have to really want badly to become an A-lister. They have rituals. There is devil worship and orgies. I don't know," she added almost condescendingly, "but you don't look like you would be a member."

"As a matter of fact, I am," he said with a light sarcastic bite, and Van's eyes narrowed. "My great-great-great grandfather, if you really want to know, was a Bavarian nationalist who opposed the undue influence of the Catholic church and its superstitions in eastern Germany. He helped start the Bavarian Illuminati and persuaded the French hoi polloi to revolt against their monarchy." He leaned close to the tattooed blond, and whispered, "He personally knew Goethe, who was also a member." Then to the group who looked both stoned and mesmerized, he said, "Sad to say that eventually the German government quashed the movement and only a few Illuminati survived. I am the only living descendent."

The tattooed blond stood there for a moment with her mouth gaping, not sure how to respond. She gathered herself, took a draw on the cigarette, and under her smoky breath, she said, "I knew it."

"In fact," Martin added, "we have a secret ritual going on right now. I am sorry to have to leave but, you know, planes to catch, people to meet, babies to kill." He winked at the tattooed blond and pulled Van away toward another group up by the pool.

"That was fun," she said wryly.

"I can't stand it," he replied, "but I suppose that's obvious." His smart phone buzzed and flashed, and he turned away as he took a brief call. "I am sorry, but I need to leave." He pointed to the group by the pool, and said, "Introduce yourself. They are a much more interesting crowd." He turned to leave, and then turned back and smiled, "Very nice to meet you."

The crowd by the pool was more animated, if not more interesting. A heated debate was going on about the new president. "He is a misogynist and a moron," a tall, dark-haired woman was saying.

"First of all, he is not a misogynist," replied a hefty young man wearing glasses and a bow tie. "Unless you think all men are misogynists, but that would be idiotic, and you do not strike me as an idiot. He gives his daughter a prominent role in everything he does, and regularly hires women to lead his projects."

"Those moves are covers for him. He is a playboy and seeks out beautiful women as props to satisfy his ego. You know he had his own beauty pageant, right?" saying this, she turned and walked away in a huff, as if she didn't want to waste her time with someone so uneducated.

Bow Tie looked at Van and smiled. "Most of the misogynists I know hire women as a cover." He shook his head and chuckled. A rather intense-looking young woman, who was standing next to Bow Tie, looked at Van and said, "So what do you think about our new president?"

"I don't think he really knew what he was getting into and I don't think he expected to win," said Van.

"I think you are probably right on the latter part," the young woman responded.

Van shrugged. "My family is grateful to be here and does not take the country and its freedoms for granted. But I don't view that as a political stance. I hope whoever leads us does well."

"That's fair," Bow Tie said, jumping in quickly to keep his friend from pushing Van too hard.

The intense one got the hint but added, "There are a lot of people at this party who would love to see this president fall on his face."

Martin walked back up to Van and the new group. With him was a handsome older gentleman wearing a blazer and jeans with Top Siders and no socks. Van's first thought was East Coast and she soon found out she was right. Martin introduced him as Marshall Turner from Washington, D.C.

"Good evening," Marshall said to the group.

Bow Tie stepped forward quickly, and said, "Pleased to meet you, sir."

The intense one asked rather boldly, "What brings you to the Left Coast?"

Marshall chuckled. "I am heading up to the Bay Area, but I stopped here first to see some friends."

Van was quiet. She had already decided that she would not tell anyone that she was an LAPD detective. She was enjoying the party and entertained by the conversations—not the usual. She didn't want people to feel reserved around her and she was not there to judge. She excused herself and found Kimmie still hanging with Johnny B.

"I am going to get a drink," Van said to Kimmie. "Want to join me?"

"Absolutely," Kimmie responded. As they walked toward the bar, Kimmie asked, "Are you enjoying the party?"

"I am," Van answered. "Some interesting people here."

"Do you find Martin interesting?"

"Sure. I think he is a busy guy. But he is nice and isn't full of himself."

"Maybe," said Kimmie, "he would be a nice person to know."

"Maybe," Van responded and smiled.

They found a couple of seats by the pool. It was dark by now and Martin had set up a couple of heaters so his guests could enjoy the night comfortably. The crowd was getting louder and two fully clothed women had already jumped into the pool. Van could see a couple of rather serious conversations going on nearby. A tall pretty blond was sitting on a small garden wall wiping tears away. Van hoped it was just a bad audition or romantic sadness and not something worse. As she was thinking about it, Marshall Turner walked by and looked down at Van. "We met right?" he said. "But I am not certain I got your name."

"We did. My name is Van and this is my good friend Kimmie."

Kimmie said hi, and Marshall said, "Do you mind if I join you?"

"Not at all," Van replied. He pulled up a deck chair next to Van and sat down.

"It must be late for you," Van said.

She looked at Kimmie, and said, "Marshall is from Washington DC."

"It's a bit late," he said. "I find myself on the West Coast quite a bit."

"What is it you do?" Van asked.

"Whatever people need me to do. I suppose I am a political consultant. I don't like the word lobbyist, but I probably qualify. I connect people. Sometimes they are businesspersons, sometimes politicians, and sometimes both." Marshall was anything but shy. "What about yourselves?"

Kimmie jumped in. "I own a fitness resort for women."

Van added, "That is how we met. Kimmie is my trainer."

"Fitness is a huge industry but complicated to manage," Marshall said.

"Exactly," Kimmie replied, pleased that he seemed interested. "You have everything from corporate megacomplexes to individual trainers working out of their homes."

"Do you think the mega-gyms will drive out the individuals?" Marshall asked.

"They certainly make it harder and not just for individual trainers— any small business. But I don't see how the math works for them. They drive the price down to nothing and have to cover giant leases. Doesn't make sense to me."

"Interesting," Marshall said. "What about you?" he asked Van.

"I am undercover cop," Van said and laughed. Marshall seemed startled just a bit and then laughed as well, getting the joke. "Sorry," Van said. "Actually, I am a chemist," Van said, which was partially true.

"Really?" said Marshall. "Biochemistry?"

"Well," she said, getting a bit nervous that she had opened up a line of discussion that might be better to avoid. "I work with DNA." Kimmie watched Van and stayed quiet.

"That is very interesting," Marshall said. "Have you done anything in the nano space?"

"Why do you ask?"

"I have a couple of nano clients. They are trying to get it going. Nanotechnology is not fully accepted yet. It will be but the public needs to get comfortable with it."

"You are making it more acceptable?"

"I suppose you could say that," he said. "Actually, I am trying to keep it from dying out before it has the chance to prove itself."

"I know very little about it," Van admitted. "I have heard that there are applications in the treatment of cancer, but not much beyond that."

Marshall replied, "A lot of possibilities as I understand it. It turns out there are many important environmental applications. It can decompose oil spills, plastic waste, landfills. That sort of thing."

"Is that what you are working on?"

"Well, let's save that discussion for another time," he said, grinning.

"Yes," said Van. She looked at Kimmie, "And I need to get going. It's been a long day and I have a long trip home. Very nice to meet you, Mr. Turner."

Marshall stood and graciously said, "I hope I didn't offend. Very nice to meet the both of you. I do hope we meet again." Van smiled thinking that she could not imagine why or how that would happen.

CHAPTER 10.

The Star of Bethlehem

F ifty million years ago, a large island north of Australia and east of
Madagascar in the center of what is now called the Indian Ocean
began drifting north through the equator and toward the southwest coast
of pre-historic Tibet. The northeast boundary of this giant tectonic island,
now called India, gradually made its way northeast until it slammed into
the coast of its northern neighbor. What happened next is a matter of
scientific debate, but one theory has the northeastern edge of the island
plunging under the coast of Tibet and forcing that coast tens of thousands
of feet into the sky, forming what we now call the Himalayas. The term
Himalaya comes from the Sanskrit word *hima* meaning 'snow' and *laya*
which carries multiple meanings from 'residence' and 'temple' to 'tempo'
or 'timing' in poetry, speech and music. *Laya* also can mean 'melt' or
'dissolve' and the Himalayas, the most famous, most inspiring and most
impressive mountain range on the planet, the result of a journey across
an ocean and a massive continental collision, in combination, is perfectly
captured as *the temple, or tempo, of melting snows.*

The Himalayan Mountain Range spans 2,400 kilometers or roughly
1,500 miles. The range begins in the southeast in the country of Bhutan
and then runs northwest in a crescent shape through Nepal and around
Tibet to the several states in northern India, then into the disputed regions

of Jammu and Kashmir in northern Pakistan, finally settling at their northernmost point in the Badakhshan National Park in south-central Tajikistan.

Garne "Garny" McDonough, the co-founder of Providia, who broke away after Providia decided its core competency would be video gaming, formed his own electronic medical device company called MetaMed that he set up in Sunnyvale, California, around the corner from Providia. Garny had a long and tortured history with the FDA, and it was only with the help of investment bankers like Derek Whitestone that Garny was able to keep MetaMed operating, drawing its revenue from a small number of myoelectric prosthetics that he was able to integrate into muscle fibers allowing people to control the prosthetic naturally. But Garny's big idea was to push the integration into the Central Nervous System so that motion would be controlled by the brain. Garny's breakthrough came when he discovered MEMS and began using smart dust as a robotic device integrator. He refashioned his prosthetics using robotics and created small chips embedded with nanobots that were receptive to brain waves as a means of controlling the prosthetics. The FDA had not been friendly to the use of electronic brain implants, and most of Garny's ideas ended up in FDA shredders.

The FDA debacles convinced Garny to rethink his business plan, and as he learned more about MEMS and smart dust, he began to envision other money-making applications. One issue that especially caught his attention, and he felt might be susceptible to a MEMS-based solution was climate change. Gary didn't really care whether the apocalyptic scenarios of Senator Al Gore were credible. He didn't care if climate change itself was actually a problem. What he did care about was that a convincingly large sector of the scientific community accepted the evidence that the earth was rapidly heating up, and that at least one cause of the rise in temperature was waste from primarily human activity. Nanobots were already capable of transporting chemicals, and if there were a cost-effective system that might reduce the volume of carbon emissions from cars, factories, landfills, livestock and deforestation by removing it from the air or converting it into water or some other harmless compound, both the government and the industry would pay enormously for that capability. The problem with "direct air capture" was not only its cost but the amount of energy required to make it happen. Even so, the United States government was willing to spend tens of millions of dollars to support technologies advancing direct air capture. Scientists also were exploring carbon mineralization—a normally very slow process that turns CO_2 gases into solids. By exposing CO_2 to certain minerals, the process of mineralization might be sped up, and the gas that is warming the planet could be converted to crystals and made to fall out of the sky like snow.

Garny decided to educate himself and expand his new business network. He attended a series of climate change conferences sponsored by the United Nations and various universities. He studied the Paris Agreement and the Kyoto Protocol, and familiarized himself with the chemical properties of the six greenhouse gases: carbon dioxide, methane, nitrous oxide, hydroflourocarbons, perflourocarbons and sulfur hexafluoride. He met some of the world's top environmental scientists and paid to bring them to his MetaMed offices in Sunnyvale. He introduced them to the engineers in his office working with nanotechnology and encouraged them to collaborate on the use of smart dust for high volume direct air capture and carbon mineralization. He developed a pro forma that he shopped to Derek Whitestone and his favorite venture capitalists, and he got an initial round of $500 million to begin developing an atmospheric carbon scrubbing technology. He would not make the same mistake this time that he made with MetaMed. This time he would prove his technology works and would share its benefits with countries and businesses operating outside the United States. The regulatory Nazis at the FDA would not be allowed to touch his creation until the demand for the product was so great that they would effectively have no choice but to approve it.

Half a billion dollars gave him a lot of options and he had only two criteria. First, he needed to be free of regulation. Second, he wanted to be someplace inspiring. Several of his new environmentalist friends had been to Nepal and a couple had climbed Mount Everest. Garny thought of his new venture as akin to scaling his own Mount Everest and the prospect of living and working in or near the Himalayas thrilled him. The fall of the Soviet Union and its breakup into the many separate nations that had once formed the Union created unique opportunities for a Silicon Valley startup to find an inexpensive, exotic and very hidden base of operations. He searched the Himalayan range for a location and drew some quick conclusions. He decided that Nepal was too touristy and that Bhutan and the states in Northern India and Pakistan were too unstable.

But as his finger tracked north, he found Tajikistan, and Dushanbe— the Tajik capital with 800,000 people. He learned that Tajikistan had resisted the Russian Revolution of 1917 and played a central role in the Basmachi Revolt that along with Uzbekistan, resisted absorption in the Soviet Union. Rather, the two countries formed the Autonomous Soviet Socialist Republics of the Soviet Union, which were maintained until the dissolution of the Soviet Union in 1991. The Tajiks had several disputes with Armenia mostly, because until recently, the largest minority in Tajikistan was its Armenian population. But Armenia was more distracted by its neighbor Azerbaijan, and both of them were a thousand miles away on the other side of the Caspian Sea. Like its southern neighbor, Afghanistan, Tajikistan experienced its own internal conflicts, the results of which were fairly brutal. There were claims of ethnic cleansing, which prompted international involvement, and eventually, the country settled down after it was occupied by an international peacekeeping force comprised of American, Indian and French troops. In fact, Tajikistan had become somewhat of a refuge for the embattled residents of the surrounding countries. War weary and scarred by the religious zealotry of its southern neighbors, refugees fled to Dushanbe, and the population exploded, and Dushanbe became a thriving metropolis. Thus, though not due to its own will or desire, Tajikistan was growing into a pluralistic society with elements of European, Russian, Indian and Middle Eastern cultures all blending together.

Garny took his two lead engineers and flew to Delhi, and then north to Dushanbe. They spent the next week traveling around Dushanbe and then out to the Nurek Reservoir and the surrounding Districts of Republican Subordination, a political division of land managed by the central government not unlike the District of Columbia. They took a small plane to the Jirgatol airport, where they caught a bumpy helicopter ride over the Himalayan foothills through Pamirsky and Badakhshan National Parks to Karakul Lake, a beautiful horseshoe shaped, glacier-fed lake near the border of Kyrgyzstan, 32 miles across and resting at 13,000 feet above sea level. Karakul Lake was known for two reasons. First, it was the location of one of the largest impact craters in the hemisphere, formed by a meteor 20 million years ago. The lake, at its deepest point was 750 feet. Second, it was surrounded by marshes, peat bogs, and pebbly and sandy plains that were home to a remarkable number of unique bird species. BirdLife International identified it as an Important Bird Area (IBA), and the Ramsar Convention listed it as an important waterfowl habitat. The helicopter landed near a small village on the Pamir Highway that had grown up on the lake shoreline. Once a poor and barely surviving village, a small amount of tourism related to the growth of Dushanbe and the annual Roof of the World Regatta revived the village, and it had a small market and a couple of restaurants. Garny and his team suited up and began a trek around the lake, climbing to about 14,000 feet where they found an abandoned Hindu temple built into the cliffs, a thousand feet above the lake. The temple looked across the lake directly to the Himalayas, and Garny knew he had found his dream location for working on smart dust, away from prying eyes and America's robotic regulators.

Over the next year, he flew in construction materials, set up a solar farm for power that he shared with the village, and constructed a road through the mountains to serve the new lab. He also built a helicopter pad so that he could get quickly to Jirgatol, and from there to Dushanbe. A couple of Hindu priests discovered what he was doing and threatened to start a protest, and he gave them funds to build a separate temple on the other side of the lake and they disappeared. After a year, he had a functioning lab operating literally in the middle of nowhere with heated bunks and a full kitchen and dining area. He set up a company and named it TKP Inc., which stood for The Karakul Proposition. His team initially comprised American, Russian and Swedish climatologists, whom he had met at various conferences in Geneva, Warsaw and Doha, and also through Columbia University's collaboration with the United Nations Climate Action group in New York. He added to his own team from Sunnyvale biomolecular engineers from the University of Chicago and MIT. He got them to join him in Tajikistan to develop this world-changing technology, both by convincing them to buy into his vision to develop a technology that might mitigate global warming, and by giving them each a compelling salary and a 0.5% profit share in any products developed out of the Lab. He added the incentive that the profit share would double to 1.0% for any products finalized in the first twelve months. But in order to be a part of the team, there were two conditions. First, they had agree to living at the Lab continuously for a year, and second, they had to sign a nondisclosure agreement, which if they violated, they would forfeit any profit share and unpaid salary.

Garny had a singular vision for TKP. Producing a nanobot that could direct air capture carbon dioxide molecules was a first step, but he suspected that would be easy. What he needed, and the specific capability that would launch him ahead of his Silicon Valley counterparts, was a new means of ultra-high-volume manufacturing. He had left his competitors in the slough of impenetrable regulatory hurdles and political and social opposition to MEMS and wanted to prove it made a difference. Garny had read about the possibility of self-replication in Eric Dressler's 1986 work, *Engines of Creation*, but the actual means to trigger self-replication technology remained elusive and mostly science fiction over the intervening decades. Still, Garny had come up an idea.

The team settled into its remote mountain retreat. Several members made special requests for foods that reminded them of home, and Garny had a supply chain set up to bring special delicacies and supplies regularly to the retreat. He softened on his insistence that his team remain at the retreat the entire time, and he organized special trips around the region for them to enjoy. But the team was well aware that they were there to develop something novel and highly challenging, and that they were incentivized to get it done within 12 months. He had a well-known motivational speaker brought in to lead brainstorming discussions that were held in the Lab's ornate conference room, with a marble table Garny had handmade in Dushanbe, and a reinforced plate glass window that looked out over the lake and onto the Himalayas.

Garny stood at the head of the horseshoe-shaped table, framed by the mountain scene behind him. He listened to some good, even brilliant ideas about the conditions necessary for something non-organic to grow—most of which focused on the nature of crystallization inspired in part no doubt by the harsh wintery conditions of the mountain lab. He allowed all those ideas to play themselves out, and then launched into his own:

"So how do you solve the problem of self-replication? You start by accepting that you are not God. You are not being asked to create something out of nothing—*ex nihilo*. But, in fact, you do not need to be a god. The building blocks of life do not require magic—they only require two things: coincidence and attraction. The right particles have to meet at the right time. And they have to want to meet. So how do you increase the probability of that combination? That part is easy. You find the elements common to the solution, and you increase them until they reach a saturation point—in short, you increase coincidence to the point where there is virtually no instance in which the elements do not meet. You increase co-incidence to the point that coincidence disappears. The problem then becomes attraction. How do you take elements that otherwise exist completely independent of each other and induce them to combine. How would you take a room full of hydrogen and oxygen atoms and turn that into water?"

"That is nothing new," replied Dr. Sadifur Farroush, one of Garny's key MIT colleagues. "You charge it." He paused. "Very carefully, mind you." The room laughed and Dr. Farroush continued. "Electromagnetism. The right temperature and the right charge and electrons begin to fall like pebbles, and snap! Hydrogen rushes in to fill the gap, and you get H_2O—water, enough of which becomes rain. There it is."

"Okay," said Garny. "Thank you. Simple question, simple answer. But we are not trying to make it rain. So let's talk about something more complex. How does a cell replicate?"

"Cytokinesis," answered one of the biomolecular specialists.

"Talk us through that," said Garny.

"Cytokinesis is the process by which a single cell splits into two cells." He went on to describe spindle apparatus and chromatids and all features needed for cell replication. The question everyone was asking themselves as he spoke was how to take a biological process, the miracle of life, and convert it to a mechanical process.

"Okay," Garny concluded. "We know that life self-replicates. We need something that is not life to do the same. Again, let's return to the question of attraction. Dr. Farroush proposes electromagnetism. No doubt an element. Here is what I propose, and then I would ask you to take it and break it apart and see where it takes us. I have been intrigued recently by viruses. We know that they exist in a passive state outside their host cells as virions—miniature protein packets that have no impact on life. The magic of viruses is that they find a way to fake attraction. They lure host cells into consuming them and that is where their devilish impacts begin, because it is only after they are inside a host cell that they begin to replicate at paranormal speeds. I propose that we find the magic trigger of viruses and convert that into a mechanical process."

His comments started loud conversation as the group broke up and the teammates returned to their labs and cubbies to begin to build a virus-based model of nanorobotic self-replication. Within six months, they had constructed a nanorobot capable of capturing CO_2. The new nanorobot was controlled by a central sphere with spike-like projections that moved in and out around the sphere's vertical and horizontal axes. The vertical spike at the southernmost end of the sphere was slightly larger than the horizontal spikes at the equator, and the northernmost spike, employed a gyroscopic effect to keep the nanorobot vertical. Someone noticed that it appeared to sparkle like a star in the night sky. Garny named it the *Star of Bethlehem*, after the star in the Book of Matthew that guided the three wise men to King Herod in Jerusalem. As the story goes, Herod called his scribes, who then cited scriptures about the Messiah, and those discussions eventually led the wise men to a Bethlehem stable in which the newborn child of Mary and Joseph lay swaddled in a manger.

Within nine months, The Karakul Proposition's team used Garny's virus concepts, and identified the conditions required for basic self-replication. The problem was that the process was too slow. They needed an engine—a feature capable of driving replication at higher speeds. Someone suggested superconductivity, and the team quickly realized that the solution was not in the process; it was in the materials they were using to fashion the nanorobots. They converted the nanorobots to a superconductive ceramic design, and self-replication took off like a flash. At this point, the only limiting factor that contained the volume of the production was the size of the chamber in which self-replication occurred. Garny was beside himself. His experiment was working, and he wanted to introduce it to the world as soon as possible.

There was another small problem. As with any new technology, accidents occur, and Garny had lost several of his team members to heart attacks and strokes that seemed to be caused by food or other allergens present in the Lab. He suspected that the elevation was a factor, but he also credited the speedy results of his team to the low atmospheric density at 14,000 feet. It was the closest anyone had come to manufacturing in the pure vacuum of space, and to Garny, it was a necessary and acceptable risk. The accidents were unfortunate, and Garny was overly generous to the families of the deceased scientists.

CHAPTER 11.

A Genius, a Billionaire and a Lobbyist Walk into a Bar

The shock of the smart dust exposure stayed with Brian for several days. The specific lab he had worked in was still closed, following protocol for spills of any toxic or infectious agents, and the advanced protocol for Risk Group IV contaminants. The Lab had placed Dr. Carrie Comstock on paid leave for 90 days. The Tran Labs was well known for taking care of its employees, and Carrie had already been told that if she were concerned about returning to Bainbridge, the Lab would find her another posting. Carrie came from a military family. Her goal was to advance research on infectious diseases, and she knew the best place to do that was at the Tran Labs. Within two weeks, she was back at work with Dr. Johannsen. He marveled at her stamina and strength. Carrie's resilience gave Brian courage to resume his review of the nanoparticles in the petri dish. He dug into MEMS and learned the different functions that MEMS devices were capable of performing and the different features that had been built into these devices. He asked Carrie what purpose she thought the spikes served, and they posited initially that the spikes were intended to latch onto and penetrate something like a cell membrane. The spikes allowed the device to act like a virus.

They convinced T cell lymphocytes to consume the nanobots. But at that point, even though the cell itself was reacting to this foreign object, the device would go dormant and seemed to serve no further purpose. One possibility was that the only purpose served by the device was to activate killer cytokines, as if it were a biological weapon. But it was just as likely that the cell's reaction to the device was unintentional, whether or not anyone else had encountered the same reaction. They assumed something somewhere had happened, which would explain why the petri dish was labeled Risk Group IV. Brian and Carrie both agreed that building a microrobot for the sole purpose of eliciting a cytokinetic response was too simple an answer, notwithstanding Occam's razor and the notion that the simplest explanation is usually the correct one. Anaphylaxis might be used as a weapon, but it made no sense to go to the trouble of manufacturing a microscopic robot just to cause an allergic reaction, however powerful.

Brian knew that MEMS engineers were working on a use in the treatment of cancer, and he thought maybe the device could be programmed to target specific cells, and then some other force, like electromagnetic energy from something benign like radiofrequencies, might cause the device to attack and kill the cancer cells, something like a B cell lymphocyte. Or perhaps the EME would simply heat up the device and burn up the cell from the inside out. Brian experimented with various frequencies, but it was the same in every case, nothing happened. It was Carrie who suggested that the purpose of the spikes might not be for penetration and damage, but rather to grab something. They tried mixing the devices with blood. There was activity but it seemed hardly detectable. Carrie thought she noticed an attraction to CO_2 and that triggered the break-though.

Brian had a nurse at the Lab withdraw blood from one of his veins and contain it in a vacuum so it would not become oxygenated. They combined the nanomaterial with the de-oxygenated blood and the little robots went wild, flying around red blood cells that were emitting carbon dioxide molecules and snatching the molecules out of the plasma. Each robot grabbed hundreds of molecules before it went dormant. They decided to try an experiment with gas. They filled the vacuum chamber with carbon dioxide, and then opened a container with a minute bit of the petri dish substrate. The devices activated immediately and flew around the chamber like a dust storm and the CO_2 levels dropped rapidly as the CO_2 stuffed devices collected on the bottom of the chamber. Brian and Carrie were amazed at the singular purpose these devices seemed to serve. But they still had no idea what the larger purpose might be.

Brian and Carrie wrote up the results of their studies. When they were done, the report was more than 100 pages long and complete with details not only regarding the makeup of the particles but also their structure and apparent function. The report included images from the electron microscope depicting CO_2 capture. They also found evidence of self-replication but included that in an appendix because the process was not apparent and didn't make sense to them. Brian and Carrie presented the report to Dr. Meisner, who was friendly to Carrie but still angry about the accident and the effect of some of the local press on the Lab's reputation.

He flipped through the report and asked them only "What does it do?"

Brian replied, "It captures CO_2."

Dr. Meisner was impressed, not an uncommon response to his staff's scientific analysis. "But what purpose might that serve?"

"I don't know. Fight global warming?"

Dr. Meisner laughed. Brian looked at Carrie, and they both chuckled as well. "We can't come up with a good medical reason for capturing CO_2. When oxygen levels drop, CO_2 levels increase in the blood causing hypoxia, which can become toxic, but the usual solution is not to try and reduce CO_2. The solution is to add oxygen."

Dr. Meisner crossed his arms and touched his chin. It was one of his typical moves when he wanted you to think he had a brilliant idea. "Industrial applications?"

"Yes. Possibly. If you could manufacture enough of these, they might have some impact on carbon emissions. Perhaps they could be used in some kind of advanced catalytic converter and reduce industrial pollutants. It's a thought. But the volume that you would need to have any real impact is so great, even that application is tough to imagine."

"The problem," Brian added, "whether the application is industrial or medical, is the cytokine storm these particles cause in humans. Whether or not they might perform some useful task, the risk that they would get released to the general public is a risk too great to imagine."

Dr. Meisner stood his ground but his tone became dismissive. "All due respect to both of your frightening experiences, but toxicity is rarely a justification for impeding progress. Give it some more thought. Maybe we should get Fred back and see what his reaction might be."

Carrie was beside herself when they left Dr. Meisner's office. "Can you believe that?"

Brian had seen enough of it to not be surprised. He knew that Meisner needed any ideas coming from the Lab to be his own first, before they would be allowed to trickle down to staff, and if he didn't have an idea, he wasn't interested. He thanked Carrie and told her that without her input, they wouldn't be where they were now. Whether or not it would lead to anything ground-breaking, or at least interesting, was yet to be determined. Brian did not have much interest in meeting Fred, but he acknowledged that Fred was a smart guy and might add something. He took off in the Gold Wing for home. The days were getting shorter now and it was already dark, not his favorite time to ride. But the road was fairly open, and as he was passing through Grand Forest West, his phone buzzed. He clicked on the Bluetooth in his helmet. "Hello!" he shouted, slowing the bike to reduce the engine noise.

"Dr. Johannsen!?" someone on the other end also shouted.

"Yes? Can I help you!?" Brian spoke still loudly.

"My name is Marshall Turner! I am here with Fred Schmidt!"

"Just a minute!" Brian pulled the bike off the road onto a side street and shut it down. "I'm sorry. It sounded like you said you were with Fred Schmidt."

"I am. We are here at the Harbour Public House having a pint. Do you have time to join us?"

"I know the place. I am less than15 minutes away. I'd be happy to meet you guys there." Brian jumped back on his bike and took off down Miller Road, which turned into Fletcher Bay Road. He made a left on High School Road and then right on Madison Avenue, which took him most of the rest of the way. Harbour Public House had a small bar that looked out over Harbour Marina. As Brian rode, he thought about what he might say to Fred Schmidt. He expected it to be a pretty candid night. He shut off the bike and walked into the bar with his full leathers on. Fred noticed him right away and came over to the hostess and motioned him in toward the bar where they had a window view of the marina's night lights. Seated at the table were Marshall Turner, whom Brian assumed had called him, and Dr. Stan Meisner. Brian was surprised although he showed no reaction.

"Stan."

"Hello, Brian. Good to see you."

"And Mr. Turner, I presume?"

"That would be me. I have heard a lot about you, Brian. Dr. Meisner had some remarkable things to say. It's a pleasure."

"You good with Guinness?" Fred started.

"Who isn't?" Brian answered back and sat down.

Mincing no words, Fred started the conversation. "It seems that I am the one responsible for almost killing Dr. Johannsen and his colleague Dr. Comstock."

Brian could see that Fred was not afraid to speak his mind. Even though he still was mad, Fred's candor started to win him over.

"Well, in all fairness," Brian said, "there was a warning label. Once we realized what it actually was, we let ourselves get too relaxed."

Dr. Meisner jumped in. "And what was it, Brian? What did you find?"

Brian studied the table, gauging to see if he was explaining something they already knew. But their interest betrayed them. They stared at Brian, hungry to hear what he had to say. "Ok. Well, the first thing we noticed was that it wasn't biological. So the dish was mislabeled. It should not have said Risk Group IV. But in fact, it turned out to be just about as dangerous as a Risk Group IV or Biosafety Level IV substance. It caused an almost immediate anaphylactic reaction in my colleague Dr. Comstock, who, as Mr. Schmidt indicated, almost died from it."

Marshall Turner responded, "Just to keep everything on the right level, because not all of us here are highly regarded members of the scientific community, what did you call the reaction you and your colleague had, and what does that mean?"

Marshall came across as sketchy to Brian. He assumed he needed to be careful around him. "It's nothing more than a severe allergic reaction that causes a lot of problems but the most serious is that your lungs and your throat begin to swell up. You can suffocate if it's not treated correctly, and doctors hate it because it is very hard to control."

Dr. Meisner tried to redirect the conversation back to what actually interested Fred Schmidt. "That's good, Brian. The nanoparticles—what are they for? What purpose?"

"I guess that's the billion-dollar question" Brian answered with a smirk. Fred chuckled at the joke, but he reminded himself of the uncertainties of working with a wunderkind.

"The most we could figure out in the time we have had so far is that they seem especially attracted to carbon dioxide."

Fred responded, "So would you consider them shuttles?"

"If what you mean is a device that transports some type of medicine to damaged cells, no. Not in the true sense of a nanobot shuttle. They do carry CO_2 molecules but not to any destination. As soon as they acquire as many molecules as they can carry, they go dormant and settle at the base of the chamber."

"Like a decontaminant?" Marshall asked.

"I suppose."

Fred said, "Ok. Let's assume we are looking at a CO_2 filtration system. Does it seem efficient? Can a small amount of these particles filter a large quantity of CO_2? Perhaps on something like a spaceship, where CO_2 filtration might be especially important?"

"Not certain about that particular application, but it will take more work to figure out. If what we are looking at is an environmental application and not a medical application, my first guess is no. You would need real volume to have any broad impact."

Marshall thought about Providia's request for the rights to control nanomanufacturing but said nothing. Fred's wheels were spinning.

"Let's assume there is something here. How do we deal with the effect on humans? Can we assume this is something we can get a hold of or not?"

"Right now, there is no way to know. Dr. Comstock's reaction was immediate and almost immediately fatal. It's only because we are a Biosafety Level IV lab that we contained it and saved her life. Honestly, we can't take this lightly."

"But you can study it," Fred said. "Let's give it another round. I want to know the use cases and I want to know if we can make it safe. I don't care how much it costs."

Brian saw Dr. Meisner's eyes light up, but he quickly composed himself. "We'll let you know what we need, Mr. Schmidt."

"One more thing," Fred added, and looked over at Marshal. "I have heard that Providia has AI software that might help with manufacturing."

"One of the few," Marshall responded, keeping his cards close.

"Derek Whitestone sent his team over to gauge how far along they were. His sense was that they were very close. Is that your sense, Marshall?"

"They have spoken with me." Marshall knew this game well. He knew that Fred expected absolute candor, and he knew that they might have told Fred about their interaction with him, but he did not know that for sure. "I would say they are close because they seem to think they need some help in Washington."

"Are they going to get it?"

"I don't know yet. It's not a done deal."

"All right, well, whatever is happening there, if we have something here, we are going to need to be strategic. More to discuss, then. Very good, gentlemen," Fred concluded.

Brian drained the pint in front of him and cordially dismissed himself from the group and headed back to his bike. Dr. Meisner did the same but he was more of a Jaguar guy. Fred and Marshall sat there a bit longer.

"I like the kid," Marshall said.

"Still to be determined," said Fred. "He has real potential. Let's see what he can do with it."

CHAPTER 12.

Trials by Ice and Fire

Garny locked himself in his office adjacent to the Lab's main conference room. He removed a picture hanging behind his deck of which he was especially proud. The picture was taken in Warren Buffet's lodge in Sun Valley, Idaho, and showed him standing next to the top CEOs in the country including Jeff Bezos from Amazon, Elon Musk from Tesla, Tim Cook from Apple, Fred Schmidt from Grindle, Larry Ellison from Oracle, Larry Page from Alphabet, and Lloyd Blankfein from Goldman Sachs. He opened the safe behind the photo and pulled out an Iridium satellite phone he had been using to stay in contact with the world while his team labored in the labs below.

"We did it."

Franklin Everhart, billionaire playboy and founder of the philanthropy WeGive.com listened. Franklin was the son of William Everhart, the real estate mogul who built most of downtown San Francisco, and Garny's best friend. He had helped Garny get Providia off the ground.

"What exactly did you do?"

What Garny did was build a massive self-contained vacuum chamber at the foot of the ridge surrounding Karakul Lake. He hired local labor, who willingly dug a giant hole that Garny had reinforced with steel and concrete and covered with a dome the size of five football stadiums. The labor cost him next to nothing, and he imported most of the materials from Russia. Ministers from the Tajik parliament came by regularly to watch the progress of the giant chamber, and to pick up their consulting fees for helping Garny manage through the various departments in Dushanbe authorizing the build. Garny had promised them that when his work was finished, he would turn the chamber over to the Tajik government to be used as a giant stadium. When the dome was complete, Garny installed blowers around the perimeter of the chamber and attached directly to each blower were six Mitsubishi marine diesel engines with their exhaust manifolds connected to the blowers. He set up cameras around the chamber that were tied back to monitors in the conference room and placed sensors in the floor and also attached them to the beams holding up the dome. The team programmed the sensors to read CO_2 levels.

While the dome was being built, Garny's team worked feverishly to produce as many "stars" as they were now called as possible. They had built several star chambers and over time were able to produce about a 100 billion stars that made up about 1000 pounds of star goo. They discovered that by freezing the goo, the stars remained dormant and stopped replicating. A couple of scientists were suspecting that a connection existed between active goo and the life-threatening allergies their colleagues were developing. Running outside into the subzero temperatures of the Karakul winter had saved many lives, and they noticed that freezing the goo kept it fairly stable and safe to work on.

When the chamber was complete, Garny gathered his top scientists in the conference room. They popped on the monitors and the computer screens reading the sensors. They watched as crews dressed in hazmat suits and oxygen tanks wheeled a dozen large stainless-steel containers into the chamber and placed them on marked locations scattered around the chamber. Each container had a heating coil that was powered by electricity. The containers were plugged in and the crew left the chamber. Garny pressed the start button and red lights flashed in the chamber. A second switch started the diesel engines in the blower rooms. Sensors started to pick up detectable amounts of CO_2 and gauges on the monitors' screens started to flicker. A third switch started each of the blowers in sequence, and flashing yellow lights attached above the blower portals popped on in sequence around the chamber. The process was impressive and remarkably beautiful like a laser show at a rock concert. The gauges jumped and then slowed as a needle measuring CO_2 density moved from green into yellow and then hovered at the edge of red. Once the blowers were turned on, the containers were powered up and the heating coils began to glow. When the container's chamber holding the frozen star goo reached 250 degrees, the lids on the containers slowly parted and a small dark cloud emerged at the opening. The cloud dissipated almost instantly, and the team stared at the CO_2 gauges. Nothing happened. If anything, the needle was moving deeper into red. "Maybe it is not enough," Garny heard someone say. It is enough, he thought, making himself believe. The nanobots will self-replicate until they reach a threshold. There is capacity in this chamber for trillions but Garny knew he didn't need trillions. He needed just enough.

Suddenly there was a pop and the monitors and screens went dark.

"What was that?" Garny screamed at the team. "What just happened?"

"It's okay," said one of the engineers in the corner. "Give it a second. The servers are programmed to reboot once a day. We should have turned it off but don't worry we are okay."

"Holy shit," Garny heard Farroush mutter under his breath.

Then, just as quickly as they popped off, the screens popped back on. Only now the CO_2 needles had dropped to green. The room held its breath.

"Is that a glitch?" one of the other engineers asked.

"We can check," said the first engineer and he clicked on a time bar to the moment just before the screens went dark. As he pulled his mouse over the time bar, the room could see the needles move into the red as they had at the start of the experiment. Then, at the moment the screen went dark, the needles dropped to zero, but the monitoring program began to run before the screens came back to life. The time bar caught the needles jumping back up to red, and then, over several seconds as measured by the monitor, gradually move down into green. Garny let the experiment run for a few more minutes to see if there were any changes, and then shut down the diesel engines and the blowers and the needles fell to just above zero where they hovered.

"Did we just see that?" someone asked, and, after a brief moment of silence, the room erupted and the scientists started laughing and dancing and slapping Garny on his back. Someone had snuck in champagne, and they popped the cork and celebrated. Garny smiled, but he wasn't entirely happy. He knew he would have to repeat the experiment and that it might take weeks to get back to where they were today. But it was not a bad start. The hazmat crews moved back into the chamber and began washing all the dust that had gathered on the floor into collector drains. He let the team celebrate that evening before informing them the next morning that it would need to be repeated. No one complained. All of them knew that it had not gone perfectly and that there were still questions, but they were confident they could repeat it.

And they did. Over the next twelve months, the team ran the same experiment four times, and each time the results were the same. They also experimented with "washing" the CO_2 residue and reusing the particles, but the used nanobots did not act as efficiently as new nanobots and they gave up trying, and the disposed the used nanobots as waste.

On the satellite phone, Garny said to Franklin, "High volume direct air capture works."

"Really?"

"Yes. We built a massive domed chamber measuring over 500 million cubic feet in volume, flooded it with CO_2 to just under 4,000 parts per million, the average level of emissions measured from the opening of a smokestack at a coal burning plant. Atmospheric CO_2 levels in this region are under 350 parts per million. Within 20 minutes, the saturation level drops to 1000 parts per million, and in under 45 minutes, it returns to between 350 and 400 parts per million."

"So what happens if you do nothing?"

Garny expected the question. Franklin was smart and not someone easily fooled.

"Remember that the drop in saturation occurs despite the fact that engines pumping CO_2 into the chamber continue to run. So there is no question that something is happening to reduce the CO_2 levels that are present in the air."

He continued, "But it is the right question and we tested for that. If you shut off the engines and open the vents, it takes five hours for the levels to return to atmospheric levels."

"And how much of the material do you use?"

"We started with about 1,000 pounds of frozen star goo divided into 25 containers, each holding about 40 pounds of the frozen goo."

"And it is dormant as long as it is frozen?"

"Dormant enough. A small amount remains active but not enough to have measurable impact."

"How long does it take to manufacture 1,000 pounds of frozen goo?"

"We have it down to two months. But that is something we need to improve. A thousand pounds may be good for a one-shot treatment in an industrial zone, but nowhere near enough for an on-going application or for anything broad scale."

"We can work on that. Congratulations. It is an amazing accomplishment."

"I think so too. There are some issues with safety, but we think they can be managed. I think it's time to present."

"Ok," Franklin said. "See you in Paris."

The next morning, Garny called his team together. "I want to thank you for the sacrifices you made to make this day happen. I am sorry it needs to come to an end, but I am certain most of you will be happy to return to your families and begin your next journey. No doubt our paths will cross again but for now let me say, well done!" Garny kept a skeleton crew on at the lab. He had not decided whether or not to shut it down completely. But it was time now to stop spending money and to actually sell the product. He also needed to find a place to manufacture the star goo in much higher volumes than he had created for his experiments.

Davik Gregorian joined The Karakul Proposition early on as a construction worker helping to redesign the Hindu temple into what became the Karakul Lab. He had grown up in Dushanbe as an Armenian minority and was fiercely ambitious. He wanted desperately to prove his value not only to his family but also to his Tajik bosses. He watched the parade of international scientists and politicians run through the grounds and dreamed of becoming a central part of its operations. His ambition and his intelligence served him well, and the Tajik bosses quickly promoted him through the ranks to construction manager. Eventually Davik became the lead construction manager and was responsible for managing the construction of the giant dome. He hired all the available crews from Dushanbe and pulled in additional crews from Tashkent, Uzbekistan, and at one point had 1,000 construction workers reporting to him. Davik had studied English in school and often served as an interpreter for Garny during construction meetings. The money Davik made allowed him to build a nicer home for his family in Dushanbe, and when he was able to get away from the job for a few days, he would return home to feasts and joyous celebrations. When Garny closed down the Lab, he made a point of seeking Davik out and complimenting him on a job well done. He told him he would pull strings for Davik to find a job with a large construction firm in Dushanbe. Daviik thanked him and politely declined, indicating that he had made plans to start his own firm, and Garny was pleased and offered to point business in his direction should any arise.

Davik was happy. The few years of hard work for Garny and TKP had paid off very well, and he could only see a bright promising future. He drove down to the Dome entrance to watch the crews clean up the residue of the last experiment. He put on his hazmat suit and wandered around the Dome, ensuring the quality of the clean-up effort. He had built a special storage room for the 25 stainless steel containers holding the star goo. The storage room was outfitted with several freezers to keep the goo frozen until the experiment began. As he was chatting with one of the clean-up crew's managers, he saw one of the Lab scientists enter the storage room. Davik knew the scientist was an Armenian software engineer whom he had befriended. The engineer had actually come from Armenia to join the team, and Davik wanted to say goodbye before it was too late.

As he entered the storage room, he could tell something was odd. The engineer had gone inside one of the freezers and ordinarily would have no business being in the freezer. Davik called his name and got no response. He walked to the freezer door and leaned in, calling his name again. The engineer turned toward Davik, and he saw that the guy had been leaning over an open container and scraping frozen star goo into a small, glass petri dish with a knife. The engineer smiled at Davik and set down the dish on a shelf. Davik looked at his friend, as if the scene made no sense. The man walked toward him, and Davik realized a little too late that he was intent on stealing some of the star goo and getting away with it. The engineer was on him fast and slammed Davik against the wall. Davik saw the knife and tried to knock his arm away but the engineer was quicker and had already planned his attack. He slashed deep into Davik's suit, cutting Davik's belly open and then slammed the blade up through the cut toward Davik's heart. Blood rushed onto the freezer floor and crystallized. Davik stared into his Armenian friend's angry eyes until darkness descended, and he crumpled to the freezer floor. The engineer wiped his bloody knife and gloves on Davik's still body. He closed the blade and shoved the knife into the pocket of his hazmat suit. He then grabbed the dish, sealed it and closed the container lid and exited the freezer, leaving Davik's cooling body inside. Slamming the freezer door closed, he removed the bloody hazmat suit, tucked it under his arm, and quickly left the Dome. At his car, he tossed the suit into a case that he placed in the trunk of his car and headed to Dushanbe International Airport to return to his home in Yerevan, the capital city of Armenia.

CHAPTER 13.

Marley Dakota

Back at the Bureau, Van decided to take a run over to the UCLA Lab where Marley's accident occurred. She studied a map of Westwood Village and the medical campus and found the lab where Marley had been exposed. It was called the Lyndon A. Rutter Center for Cellular Engineering. She parked in Parking Structure 2, and walked over to toward the Biomedical Sciences Research Building but was distracted by a sign that said "Bomb Shelter Bistro." It was almost lunch and Van was hungry, so rather than go right into the Lab, she headed for the Food Court and settled down with a Diet Coke and vegetable soup. A few medical students sat across from her and she heard them talking about a lab, although it wasn't clear which lab they were discussing. She got up to clear her tray and walked by the students.

"I'm sorry to interrupt," she said, "but were you talking about the Rutter Center Lab?"

Somewhat irritated by Van's eavesdropping, one of the female students responded, "Can we help you?"

"I apologize but I did overhear you discussing the Lab. I am an LAPD detective investigating an accident that occurred here about six months ago."

A male student calmly replied, "Don't worry about her. Would you like to join us?"

Van smiled. "If you don't mind." She dropped off the tray and dumped her dishes in a bin and returned.

The male student said, "We are very familiar with the Rutter Lab. What can we do for you?"

"I am here about what sounds like a tragic accident in which one of the medical students working at the Lab died."

"You mean Marley," he said.

"Yes. Marley Dakota. Do you know what happened?"

One of the other students jumped in. "None of us were there, but we knew Marley very well."

"Do you think she was doing anything wrong?"

"As in unethical?"

"Not exactly. Did anyone describe her work as careless? Do you think she died because she made a mistake?"

"Marley was one of our top students and her specialty was lab work. She was given that job and a reward for getting straight As in all her labs."

"You don't think she did something that caused her death?"

"That is a lot of strangeness about Marley's death," another student responded, who had overheard from another table and moved over and stood at the table to listen to the conversation. "I worked in that lab until they shut it down, but they didn't really shut it down. Marley was working on something new that the faculty didn't want disclosed."

"How do you know that?"

Another student, who had joined the growing group, said, "Because she told me."

"She told you?" Van responded incredulously. "Did you ever talk to the police?"

"Nope. No one ever asked."

"What exactly did she tell you?" Van pulled out a note pad and started writing.

"Do I need to be worried about talking to you?"

"As long as you didn't have anything to do with the accident, you have nothing to worry about. If you want an attorney, I can wait."

"No that's okay. I was Marley's roommate. I am still so sad about what happened."

"Can I get your name?"

"Sure. My name is Dawn Bordrider."

"Can we make room for her?" Van asked the group, which immediately slid closer together and allowed Dawn to join them.

"I am sorry for you," Van said to Dawn. "Did you know Marley well?"

"Marley and I were roommates for our entire second year of medical school and the beginning of our third year. Marley was a wiz at the lab and began tutoring a number of first- and second-year medical students who needed help."

"Did she tell you what she was working on?"

"No. She did say that the lab faculty asked her if she wanted to assist, and of course she said yes. They then told her that it was something that required her utmost discretion, and that she could not talk about it with anyone—even her family. She knew that they were going to close down the lab temporarily until their review was completed. She also told me that more than one lab was getting involved."

Van wondered whether what happened to Marley might have been intentional.

"How did Marley die?"

"The official word was that she had a severe allergic reaction and went into anaphylactic shock. We haven't heard anything more. The paramedics and fire trucks came to the lab first, and then some special hazmat van took her body. And they sealed the lab for over three months. It has only opened up again recently."

"You say official word. Is there an unofficial word?"

"We think she came into contact with something lethal. Marley was a fitness freak, and a health nut. She drank a lot of weird teas that she said her Sioux tribe used for medicine and in rituals. Nothing ever phased her. I never even saw her get sick, let alone deal with any allergies."

"Any idea what it might have been?"

"We can only guess. UCLA Medical is a top school and guards it reputation very carefully. Maybe they were doing something for the military, working on an antidote to some weaponized germ warfare. But the truth is, we have no idea. Marley kept it quiet."

"Did Marley ever say what other labs might be involved?"

"No. But I saw her going into this building over here, and I had never seen her do that before."

Van looked at what Dawn was pointing towards. The building wasn't unlike any other around the food court.

"Do you know what is in there?"

"Some nano-something institute."

"Any idea what they do?"

"Not at all. I'm sorry but medical school keeps us pretty busy."

"I understand. Thanks, Dawn, and thanks to everyone. Do you have a number, in case I need to reach you?"

"Sure" Dawn replied, and gave it to her.

The crowd, which had attracted several more students only because they saw something happening, began to disperse. Van reached out to Dawn and the male student and said thank you. They asked her if she thought a crime had occurred, and she honestly told them that she didn't know but that was part of what she was there to find out.

The first thing Van did after lunch was go to the building that Dawn had pointed out. The doors were all closed and the lights were out, so whatever was in the building was not active at the moment. She saw a bulletin board. Tacked to the board was an announcement about a lecture on the ethics of microelectromechanical systems (MEMS) and medicine. The lecture was sponsored by the California NanoSystems Institute.

Van left the Institute and headed back to the Rutter Lab. As she entered, there was a security guard and she had to walk through a screening device. She had to pull her badge out, which along with her keys and phone was placed in a bowl and bypassed the screening device.

The security guard asked, "LAPD?"

"Yes," replied Van, candidly. "I am a detective and I am here to ask some questions."

"Just a minute please," he said, as he handed her badge, keys and phone back to her. "Do you mind waiting over there?" He pointed to a bench against the wall. Van shrugged and went over and sat down. She could see the guard make a call, and within a few minutes, a tall, bespectacled woman approached her.

"Hello Detective. My name is Dr. March Fielding. I am the director of the Rutter Center. How can we help you?"

"Hello, Dr. Fielding. I am Detective Van Eng of the LAPD, but I gather you already know that. I am here with a few questions about the tragic accident that occurred a few months ago in which one of the medical students died."

"It was terrible, Detective. Very unfortunate and tragic. No one here knew anything about the student's condition."

"Do you mind if we go to your office?"

"I don't have much time right now, Detective. Perhaps you could call and make an appointment."

"This is not optional, Dr. Fielding."

"I figured as much. You are aware that there is an on-going litigation, and I have no way of knowing if you are here to assist the students' parents with their case. I was told by Detective Young that the case would be closed and that the LAPD does not facilitate civil litigation. I am sorry but if you have a subpoena, then I am happy to speak with you in the presence of my attorney."

"Did you close the lab after the student's accident?" Van pushed back.

"We did, as would any University office in a similarly sensitive situation. Now I must ask you respectfully to leave. Present me with a subpoena and I would be happy to answer your questions with my attorney. Good day, Detective Eng," Dr. Fielding said, as she turned and walked away.

Van had not known what to expect from the Rutter Center's leadership, but she wasn't surprised. She wanted Dr. Fielding to know that she would not be intimidated. If Dr. Fielding truly had nothing to hide, then she had nothing to worry about. But Van sensed she was worried.

On the way back to the Bureau, she got a call from Detective Young. "Please report to me immediately when you return," was all he said. Van wasn't concerned or surprised. She expected the University to call Detective Young. She reported to his office as instructed.

"I told you this case is a waste of time."

"I don't believe it is."

"How is that?"

"You trusted the University. I understand that. But the science is incomplete."

"The science."

"Yes. Nothing in the record supports Marley being allergic to anything."

"That is not a surprise. We all have hidden allergies, and we have the ability to develop allergies. I never knew I was allergic to grass until I started golfing."

"What we know is that Marley died from anaphylactic shock. What we don't know is what caused it."

"Some chemical in the Lab."

"Did you know that Marley was a lab tutor for the medical school?"

"I had not heard that."

"That means that she was so skilled at lab work that the faculty asked her to tutor other students."

"Okay."

"You don't develop that skill without spending a great deal of time in the lab. After over two years of lab work, Marley never reported any type of reaction, allergic or otherwise."

"How do you know that?"

"Because I interviewed her roommate. In fact, I interviewed her roommate and several other medical students. Marley was at the top of her class. The Lab even asked her to participate in a study that they wanted kept a secret."

"What was it?"

"I still don't know but I believe that the investigation is not done, and with due respect, I would ask that you allow me to continue it."

"I'll consider it. Anything else?"

"Yes. Two things. First, she apparently was spending time at the California NanoSystems Institute. There is a lecture I want to attend tomorrow night."

"Ok."

"Second, I went to the Rutter Lab, where the accident took place and I met Dr. Fielding. She will not talk to me without a subpoena. She is concerned that our investigation might be used by Marley's parents in their litigation."

"Sounds reasonable on her part. I told you I don't like being put in the position of facilitating someone's civil case."

"Well, I can go get a subpoena or you can convince her to talk to me. I don't care about the civil case and I will agree that our conversation will be confidential—as much as it can be."

"I still think you are wasting your time, but I'll give this to you for now. I'll talk to Dr. Fielding."

Van thought to herself, he has to give this to me. It would look very bad for him if he ignored this evidence.

"Thank you, sir."

Young spoke to Fielding and she eventually agreed to be interviewed by Van, but she wanted assurances it would be kept confidential and she wanted her attorney present. She also wanted one more thing—immunity from prosecution. That last request was a hard pill for Van to swallow, but it also convinced Young to let her continue the investigation. If Marley's death was as innocent as Young was led to believe, why was Fielding so concerned?

The next night Van returned to the campus and found the lecture on ethics and MEMS being held in Boyer Hall, across from the California NanoSystems Institute and adjacent to the Rutter Center Lab. She sat near the back of the room, trying to be inconspicuous. A representative of the

Institute opened the lecture and invited a state senator to introduce the speaker. The senator hailed the speaker as a leader in the ethical analysis of new technologies. The lecture was titled somewhat ominously: "The Dark Side of MEMS: Ethics and the Nano Revolution." The lecturer was a short, balding, elderly man from the faculty of the University of Madras in India. He walked through the different types of nanoparticles and some of their positive use cases, like hyper-focused chemotherapies and immunity boosters that might be used in fighting AIDs and other immuno-deficiencies. She was especially intrigued by a line of research in which nanobots were used in the brain to fight Alzheimer's and age-related dementia, but Van quickly picked up on a strong negative bias the speaker had toward nanotechnology. The primary focus of his discussion was the toxicity of various elements used in nanoparticles when they were employed at a nanoscale, and the side-effects of this toxicity on the human body. His list of impacts didn't seem much different than a standard list of contraindications of any medicine or vaccine—stroke, blood clotting, inflammation, arrythmia, high blood pressure, cardiac arrest, cancer, death, etc. Van was particularly interested when he said certain nanoparticles might cause "pseudo-allergy". His explanation of "pseudo-allergy" was complex and involved something called cytokines, which she had learned about in her studies, but she didn't follow the explanation very well. He also discussed the dangers of self-replication, which sounded particularly frightening to Van but also unbelievable. How could a microscopic robot make a copy of itself? In the end, the lecturer advocated for an international oversight body and laws restricting the experimental use of nanoparticles in medicine and other applications like environmental science. When the lecture was completed, the senator approached the lecturn and shook the lecturer's hand rather vigorously and posed with a large smile for pictures. The audience stood and applauded, but Van couldn't tell if the excitement was over the remarks or the senator's political future, which seemed very bright.

Van walked outside into the warm night and smelled a combination of brick and jasmine. She was surprised to see Dr. Fielding, who was doubly surprised to see her. She walked over to Van, and said, "Hello, Detective. Did you find the lecture interesting?" Her tone was not as hostile as their first encounter.

"Hello, Dr. Fielding. Good to see you again. To be honest, I know nothing about the subject, and I'm not certain I know that much more now, but I do find advances in technology like this inspiring."

"Do you agree with his concerns?"

"I don't know. I don't know enough to agree or not agree. What about you?"

"Let's hold off on that one until we speak. Have a good night, Detective."

Fielding's response puzzled Van. It gave Van the impression either that Fielding wanted to speak with her or maybe she was sensing that Van was getting close.

Van called Dawn the next morning. She asked Dawn if she had met Marley's parents, and if so, did she know how to reach them. Dawn said they lived in Cheyenne, Wyoming, and gave her their number. She called them, explained who she was, and expressed her condolences over Marley's death. She said she had a few questions and they seemed eager to talk to her. They said that they thought the LAPD had closed the case. Van was careful not to give them any reason to think the case was being reopened or that there were any suspects. She explained that she found the facts incomplete and was performing a Bureau double-check on the case. Marley's parents never viewed Marley's death as anything more than a tragic accident, but they were mad at the way the University had treated them and refused to share a detailed explanation of what had happened. They told Van that they didn't care about the money. They just wanted the University to take some accountability for what had happened, and they weren't entirely certain that Marley's death needed to happen. Maybe if the University had acted more quickly, their brilliant and beautiful daughter might still be alive.

Van asked if an autopsy had been performed, and they said yes, but that it had been closely controlled by the University medical staff and that Marley's body had been placed in a body bag. They were not allowed even to see their daughter's body in person before they buried her—they had to identify her by looking at photographs.

"But she died of anaphylaxis correct?"

"That is what the University doctors told us. There was no independent verification."

"But I don't understand why they placed her in a bag. Did she have some kind of infectious disease?"

"Nothing they indicated."

"Did they say that whatever she reacted to might cause the same effect in others?"

"I'm sorry, Detective, but we were in shock. We didn't really dig into the details. We thought your police department would take care of that."

"My apologies. One last question. Did Marley tell you anything about what she was working on?"

"No. She told us it was secret and that she had agreed not to discuss it."

"Ok. Thank you for your time. If anything else occurs to you, please reach out."

Before she interviewed Dr. Fielding, Van wanted to know more about the Lyndon A. Rutter Center for Cellular Engineering. She learned that the Lab became famous by being the first to connect cellular engineering, a euphemism for stem cell research, with virology, developing novel defenses against uncontained cell replication. So strange, she thought, that a lab with that level of expertise would allow anaphylaxis to get out of control. She also read about the Lab's T cell research and advances in the fight against cancer. So what might Marley have been involved in that needed to be kept secret? Were they doing work for the military? The research did not lead Van in any particular direction. The only controversial work at the Lab was stem cell research, but the opponents of that effort were fading away as the field shifted from the use of fetal stem cells to manufactured stem cells.

The meeting with Dr. Fielding was set for Friday morning. Van agreed to meet at the University. She thought there was nothing to be gained by interviewing Dr. Fielding at the Bureau except to make her more nervous and probably less candid. She invited Detective Young to join her. When they arrived, Dr. Fielding did not look well. They had an immunity agreement, but Dr. Fielding's attorney insisted that they sign a form he had prepared, which, along with immunity from prosecution included protection from the disclosure of Dr. Fielding's comments.

Van began the questioning.

"Are you feeling ok, Dr. Fielding?"

"I am fine. I will let you know if I get uncomfortable."

"Do we have water?"

"We have a fridge with cold water. Would you like some?"

"If you don't mind."

Detective Young was getting restless. Dr. Fielding looked at him and smiled. "Thank you for all your help, Detective Young. You made a very difficult situation tolerable."

"Thanks. I understand. My colleague here has raised some legitimate concerns that I am certain you can address. I suggest we get through with this."

"Fine with me."

"I don't want to waste your time either," Van said. "Marley Dakota was a student here at UCLA and she worked in your lab, correct?"

"That's true."

"What did she do?"

"Initially, she worked as an assistant to the staff technicians, taking notes, getting supplies, cleaning equipment."

"Was she good at her work?"

"She was excellent and for that reason we found some exciting experiments for her to join."

"Did those experiments have anything to do with the Lab's work on viruses?"

"They did, yes."

"Did she have any difficulty with that work? Any concern about infection or reactions?"

"We taught her Lab protocol, and she followed it perfectly."

"When I spoke to you for the first time, you mentioned that no one knew about the student's condition. Do you recall saying that?"

"I do but it was a misdirection."

"Excuse me?"

"It was a misdirection. Marley did not have any conditions—at least none that I knew of."

Detective Young shifted uncomfortably in his chair. He jumped into the conversation. "But she did have a reaction that led to her death, correct?"

"She did, Detective Young. But not because she was uniquely susceptible."

"Maybe you should tell us what happened," Van suggested.

Dr. Fielding looked at her attorney, and she nodded.

"Marley was a superb student. She had a vision for the work she wanted to do and she was a good scientist. She believed that there was a science behind the tribal cures of her ancestors and she wanted to understand that science. She knew microbiology was the only way to really validate those medicines and cures. She believed that if we understood better how they worked and why, that would advance not just respect for her tribe but also Western medicine. She had the ambition and self-direction of an idealist, and we look for that in our field. So when an opportunity arose to include Marley in something special, we did. An acquaintance of mine, who has been very helpful connecting high level philanthropists to the University, and in particular to our work in medicine, contacted me about nine months ago. He told me he was sending me something that would interest us here at the Lab. He understood that University labs had become highly competitive and that it was new developments that drove not only funding but private sector opportunities. He said that what he had might be a break-though, and that if we were the first to unveil it, it could advance our work here by decades."

"I hope you can understand why I was interested. The pressure here to keep money coming in is intense. We do it well, but it is not easy."

"What was he sending you?" Van asked, trying to keep Fielding on track.

"He sent his assistant who was carrying a Biosafety Level IV case in her backpack. Let's just say, it was not the most responsible method of delivery. We opened it, and inside was a petri dish that was labeled Risk Group IV. Do you know what that means?"

"It is a high-level infectious disease," Van said, recalling her own work in the lab. Fielding was impressed.

"Do you know how high level?"

"I don't recall."

"It is a level of disease on the order of ebola and the bubonic plague, meaning if released it can cause a widespread pandemic that has no cure."

"Holy shit," Young responded.

"We understand how to work with Risk Group IV material. It requires highly specialized training, and we have that capacity here. We also believed we could train Marley on how to handle it."

"But you were wrong," Young said. "And she exposed herself." Van was thinking the same.

"That is not correct, Detective. We studied the contents of the dish, and it turned out not to be Risk Group IV at all. Instead, it was mechanical."

"MEMS?" Van asked.

"Exactly. There was no biological material at all in the dish. We sent Marley over to the NanoSystems group that held the lecture you attended this week to see if we could get some expertise. They told Marley that it should not be hazardous as long as she wore protective gear. We were beginning to explore the contents when Marley got exposed and died almost immediately of acute anaphylaxis."

"How did she get exposed?"

"We have different level hazmat suits here. The high-level suits are bulky and difficult to work in and we don't use them unless there is real danger. Marley and the technicians working with her were wearing the lighter suits. They opened the dish and the devices activated immediately, penetrating her mask and causing a severe allergic reaction. She wasn't the only one who died."

"What?!" Young jumped out of his chair.

Van grabbed his arm and pulled him back down. "How did we not know this?" Van asked.

"We buried it," Dr. Fielding responded. Young put his hand to his head.

"How many people were infected, if that is the right term?"

"The two lab technicians with Marley both died. They did not react as quickly and we were able to get them transported to the hospital and ventilated, but they didn't make it."

"Is that why you closed the Lab for three months?" Van asked, and Young shot a surprised glance at Van, not realizing she already knew this.

"Yes, but there is more."

"Christ," said Young, not believing anything he was hearing.

"I was in that lab with Marley and I ended up in the hospital also."

"But you survived."

"Yes," Fielding sighed. "I was by the door to the lab talking with a colleague. I saw Marley drop the dish and grab her throat. The technicians tried to reach for her but they collapsed as well. I jumped outside and slammed the door closed, but not before inhaling a small amount of whatever it was that escaped that dish. I was allowed to leave the hospital but my lungs are severely burned, and I probably will need a lung transplant to survive." Dr. Fielding was fighting back tears. "I saw so much promise in Marley. I take her loss very personally."

"Her parents are suffering also," Van said.

"I know."

"You kept them away from her to keep them safe, right?"

"Right, but the University has faced a lot of blows recently, and our attorneys are some of the best in the country. They engineered the University's public response, and Marley's parents got caught in the crossfire."

"Is there anyone who can explain why these nanobots cause that kind of reaction?"

"Honestly, we haven't gotten that far."

"Who was your acquaintance who delivered you the dish?"

Dr. Fielding sighed. "Derek Whitestone. He is an investment banker in the Silicon Valley. His assistant was a young woman named Cheryl Brown. Apparently, she had been a student here at UCLA."

"The dish?"

"We have isolated it in a lab freezer that is locked and coded. We closed the lab for three months to ensure that any remnants of the material in the dish are gone and the lab is safe."

"Ok. That is enough for now. Thank you for your time and candor."

Van drove Detective Young back to the Bureau. He was seething the entire way. Van was concerned that some of it was directed at her. But she knew now that her efforts had been worth it, and there was much more to do.

CHAPTER 14.

Anaphylaxis

D r. Aida Barasian dropped into her desk chair exhausted. She didn't remember working this hard since she was in her residency program at Georgetown University Hospital in the United States. She heard a code blue called and waited. Another death, but at least they didn't call her name. Then, just as she was drifting asleep for the first time in 16 hours, she heard "Barasian. Paging Dr. Barasian." Her body fought the fatigue, but she forced herself to stand and head out to the hallway.

Lined against the walls of the hallways in Erebuni Medical Center in south Yerevan, patients laid on cots moaning. IVs dripped trying to keep patients hydrated, and in some cases, anti-inflammatories were being administered through the same IV. Most of the patients had oxygen masks. Dr. Barasian made her way past shouts of "Doctor, please!" to the central desk. The lead nurse practitioner in charge, Nurse Arakelian, reported that the line of cars at the entrance to the emergency room was growing. As each car pulled up, paramedics and physician assistants were interviewing the occupants and deciding whether or not to allow someone complaining of being sick or having difficulty breathing to be admitted. This triage effort had begun two weeks ago when the volume of new patients skyrocketed. Most patients were experiencing light symptoms, but a handful of those cases inexplicably escalated, and in some instances, the patients died. That uncertainty created a panic in the Greater Yerevan population of more than a million people, and at any indication of the illness, they jumped in their cars and headed to the hospital.

Dr. Barasian shook her head. There was no room at the Republic of Armenia's largest medical institution. Beds only opened up as people died and bodies were bagged and removed. She said to Nurse Arakelian, "Tell them to start Level 5 Protocol."

Nurse Arakelian had seen it all and was rarely moved. But when she heard Level 5, she cringed. That meant that Dr. Barasian was rationing care by ordering the front line staff to reject rather than accept patients in the greatest need, in most cases signing their death warrant. The strain on the staff would be very hard as family members screamed at the staff to let their loved ones into the hospital to get medical care. The situation became so dire that staff started filling syringes with a placebo just to placate family members and pretend patients were getting some care.

The chaos that now reigned in Yerevan was due in part to the unknown source of this strange new illness. Officials were calling it a new strain of flu, and some were claiming it was bio-terrorism, and that it originated in Azerbaijan. But, in fact, no one knew the source of the disaster, no one except a software engineer who had spent the last two years in Tajikistan, and he was dead.

Hayk Hovhannisian had battled his way out of poverty in Yerevan. He was beaten regularly by his alcoholic father, whom he hated for the way he treated his mother. When he was 14, he ran away and joined an Armenian gang called the Black Hoods. Hayk knew how to be ruthless and was willing to do any deed called upon by the gang's leadership. He rose quickly within the gang and was made the gang leader after someone challenged him to assassinate his own father. He waited outside his father's favorite bar, and when he stumbled out of the entrance, Hayk walked up to his father's face, stared at him until his father's welcoming smile turned into a frown, and shot him in the face. Hayk spent the next year as gang leader until he was caught and arrested for armed robbery. He had never been named for the murder of his father. No one imagined a deed that heinous was actually possible. He served three years for the robbery and was released, but only after he had picked up a certificate in software engineering through a collaborative program between the local university and the prison.

After prison, Hayk started his own computer business. Within a year, he was making more money than he did as a gang leader, and this time it was legitimate. He gave money to his mother and expanded his business throughout the city. He began to develop construction management software for the largest construction firms in Yerevan and, at their recommendation, for the companies of the firm owners' relatives in Dushanbe. When Davik came to Dushanbe to sweep up all the construction firms for the TKP Dome project, those companies pulled in Hayk to support them. Davik and Hayk met in the central construction compound situated just off of the main road to the Lab. Hayk immediately ingratiated himself to Davik, and they became fast friends.

But as successful as Hayk was becoming, he still wanted more. He watched with jealousy as the Dome was constructed and as Davik grew closer to Garny. Davik tried to pull Hayk into that relationship, but Garny saw something he didn't like in Hayk that he recognized in himself and steered clear. Hayk observed the Lab very closely and realized early on that the focus of the Lab and its wealthy founder was the goo they were testing in the Dome. He learned that it was composed of miniature robots and thought that, if he could get his hands on just a small bit of it, he might be able to reengineer it and become as rich as Garny. When the project was complete and shutting down, Hayk snuck into the Dome's storage room dressed as an engineer. He had secured a petri dish from the main lab and a knife. He knew they stored the goo in a frozen state, and he figured he would need to scrape it into the dish. When Davik stumbled upon him in the storage room, Hayk did not hesitate. He murdered Davik and left him in the freezer, knowing he would not be discovered for a long time, now that the experiment had been concluded and the Lab was shutting down.

When Hayk landed in Yerevan, he pulled his suitcase out of baggage claim and decided to check on the dish, concerned that it might not be intact. The baggage claim was crowded as vacationers heading to the hot spots on the Black Sea and the Mediterranean on the west coast of Turkey stood in long lines with their families waiting for plane tickets. He found room on the ledge of a window and opened the bag. The dish was still intact, but the flight had loosened the seal and when Hayk went to place the dish back in the suitcase, it fell open.

When happened next was a nightmare straight out of a Hollywood horror story. Hayk grabbed his throat as his trachea ballooned and shut off his airway. As he fought to breath, he saw the same thing happening around him. The people right around him were shocked and confused as they also started choking, their eyes popping out of their heads. Parents in the vicinity grabbed their children screaming until they could no longer breath. A few doctors ran to help before they realized they were struggling to breath also. They pulled out pen knives and were performing tracheotomies first on themselves and then on everyone around them, hoping to bypass the swelling and saving their lives. Blood from the tracheotomies spewed everywhere, but the relief was short-lived, and the doctors and their new patients collapsed. The only ones to survive the initial onslaught were able to get to the doorways, and Hayk watched as they ran for their lives away from the terminal. It was the last thing

Hayk would see as darkness descended and he fell off of the ledge directly into his suitcase and the open petri dish. The heat of his body produced a small black cloud of dense active nanobots that rose around his body and out of the suitcase. The cloud began to move toward the rear of the terminal, drawn to the polluted air near the baggage machine and airport staff unloading the planes. The cloud grew in size as it moved through the jetways toward the planes and trembling bodies piled up in its wake.

Once outside, the cloud doubled in size and began to rain bots as they grabbed CO_2 coming from the planes' engines and went dormant. The people outside grabbed their heads in pain and started coughing. Some grabbed their chests and sat on the ground trying to breathe, but the effect was not as strong as it had been indoors, and for the moment, they were still conscious. The cloud continued to grow until it covered a sizeable portion of Yerevan. Residents of Yerevan noticed for the first time in years that the air in the city seemed to freshen and they walked outside to take deep draws of unpolluted air. Then the dust started falling, and for a moment, everyone standing outside thought a nearby volcano had erupted, and the streets were filling with ash. Unprotected, these thousands of people began to experience headaches and difficulty breathing as it turned out even the dormant nanobots caused an allergic reaction similar to active bots, if slightly less in intensity. Emergency lines exploded, and police, fire and paramedics found themselves racing all over the city trying to collect people with the most severe reactions and get them to the city's hospitals. Hospital beds filled up within a matter of hours, and nurses and doctors rushed to find mattresses that could be placed in the hallways. The City government called for the military to step in and soldiers began delivering thousands of cots until there was absolutely no more room at the hospital. That was when Dr. Barasian made her decision to go to Level 5.

It rained dust for a week. The mortality rate from the new "flu" rose precipitously during the first weeks of the "infection," and then dropped to a manageable number, and the vast majority of the hospitalized recovered and returned home. The City hired hazardous material specialists from England, Australia and South Africa to remove the dust, which occupied half of the city within the city limits. The removal took nine months. Periodically, a pocket of dust would surface and blow about, and a few more serious cases would report to the hospital. But the sun did come out and life in the big city returned to normal. The Armenian Apostolic Church experienced a resurgence, and a new cottage industry of mental health professionals grew and became a credible avenue for help and recovery after the national church embraced it. Dr. Aida Barasian was given a national medal of honor for her management of the health crisis. Hayk Hovhannisian was bagged and buried in a mass grave along with the 356 other victims of the airport massacre, which included in roughly equal numbers both Armenians and Azerbaijanis. His family tried to find him and the general word was that his past association with the Black Hoods had caught up with him.

Back in Tajikistan, Davik's family put out an intense search, engaging the construction firms that Davik had managed as well as the state police. Garny returned to Dushanbe from a highly successful presentation to the Global Climate Change Consortium in Paris, France, and facilitated the search for Davik. Within three days, they found his body in the Dome's storage room freezer. Garny attended the funeral, for which he paid, and deposited enough money into Davik's estate to cover the living expenses of his wife and mother and the education of all his children. He placed the Dome in a trust for the People of Tajikistan and it was officially named the Davik Gregorian World Sport Arena and went on to host multiple international competitions. Garny then returned to

France to begin work on a mass production lab. He still was not aware of the cause of the Yerevan Disaster.

CHAPTER 15.

Honesty Would Have Been a Better Policy

"Explain to me, to us, where we stand now," said Detective Young, as he sat behind his desk at the Bureau. Van stood with her arms folded, leaning against the door jam. Robert Johnson sat across from Young's desk and Charlie stood behind Van listening in on the conversation. Van did not want to offend Young any more than she already had just by asking the right people the right questions, which Young had failed to do.

"Let's start with what has not changed," Van offered. "We know Marley died in the Lab as the result of a severe allergic reaction to a substance she was analyzing for the Lab. We know that Marley's parents do not have any details about what actually happened in the Lab, whatever their motivation behind their lawsuit might be—money or not. We also know now that it appears that there was very little the University could have done to save Marley's life. She died almost instantly."

"Okay," Young said petulantly. "I can agree that at some level, our analysis was not completely off the mark."

"Good," said Van. "What is new? First, Marley was not the only one who died. That matters for two reasons. One, it confirms that other than failing to treat the substance they were reviewing as a dangerous infectious disease, which it was not, the Rutter Center Lab did not violate any standards or protocols. Marley's death, if we are to believe what we heard from Dr. March Fielding—and my instinct says she was telling the truth—was truly a tragic accident. Two, somebody placed a dangerous substance in the Lab without adequately warning the Lab."

"Yes," Young agreed. "What was his name?"

"We have two names," Van responded. "Derek Whitestone and Cheryl Brown."

"Have we learned anything more about Mr. Whitestone and Ms. Brown?"

"We have," said Van. "Derek Whitestone is the principal in a Silicon Valley investment bank called Red Hawk Investments. Whitestone started the bank about 15 years ago with a single client, whose personal portfolio still constitutes a substantial majority of the bank's portfolio. The investor is Fred Schmidt, CEO of Grindle, who we know is one of the wealthiest people in the country."

"How did Derek get access to such a dangerous substance? Did he get it from Schmidt?"

"We don't know that, yet. But we do know, based on Dr. Fielding's interview, that he gave it to Cheryl Brown to deliver to the Rutter Center Lab, and that she did deliver it."

"So," Young said to the rest of the team, "what does this all mean?"

Robert Johnson, not to be outdone by Van, piped up. "If this stuff is that dangerous, where is it now?"

"At the Lab," Van said, "apparently under lock and key in a freezer."

"Do we want to confirm?"

"Fair point," Young said, "but it's not helping us."

"My question," Charlie added, leaning in next to Van in the doorway, "is if Derek Whitestone knew this substance, whatever we are calling it, was that dangerous, why did he trust his assistant to deliver it?"

"Maybe he had no idea what it was?" Young said.

"Well," Van added, "except that it was labeled Risk Group IV, which should be an indicator of mortal danger. He must have really trusted Cheryl Brown. Either that, or she was his best option even if not much of an option, because he was hiding something. In any event, we need to get to Derek Whitestone and Cheryl Brown, and possibly Fred Schmidt. My recommendation is that we hit Derek Whitestone first."

"Do we know where they are?"

"Only Whitestone at this point—unless he has already skipped. We don't know if Cheryl Brown is still in Los Angeles, but Whitestone will know."

* * * * * *

The death of Marley Dakota had made life very difficult for Derek Whitestone. Dr. Fielding called Derek from the hospital as soon as she was in recovery, a few days after the incident.

"Derek."

"Hi, March.

"I am in the hospital."

"I'm sorry to hear that. What happened? Are you okay?"

"No. I am not ok. The substrate you sent to us in the petri dish has killed three people and almost killed me!"

"I don't understand."

"Yes, you do. You put my lab at grave risk without any warning."

"What are you talking about, March? I trusted that your lab was one of the most sophisticated infectious disease labs in the country. You knew it was labeled Risk Group IV."

"Yes, but it wasn't Risk Group IV, was it?"

Derek had not known anything about the substrate when he sent it down to Los Angeles with Cheryl Brown. But Fred called him immediately after the meeting with Brian and told him what the Tran Lab on Bainbridge Island had found. He also told him what had happened to Brian and his colleague, and how lucky they were that something worse had not occurred. Derek recognized quickly that it was a mere coincidence that the Stanford Lab that divided the substrate for Derek did so without incident, because they had no reason to determine whether or not it was biological and treated it as a dangerous infectious disease. But Derek had been too caught up in Cheryl's drama to think about warning Dr. Fielding, and the "something worse" that Fred was relieved did not occur on Bainbridge Island, did occur in Los Angeles. When Dr. Fielding asked Derek if he knew that the substrate wasn't Risk Group IV, Derek lied.

But that lie didn't solve anything for Derek. If anything, it ensured that the University would do everything they could to direct blame back to him and Cheryl Brown. Derek said nothing to Cheryl about Marley Dakota. She was being hunted by Belinda's crew, and they had already made one attempt to snatch her. It would do Cheryl no good to know she might be implicated in someone's death. It wasn't doing much for Derek either. His plan to capitalize on the stolen petri dish had sprung a leak and it was only a matter of time before the ship would go down. He needed a lifeboat and the only place he knew to turn to was Fred Schmidt.

But, in fact, Cheryl Brown did know, or at least wondered. As she was standing in line for coffee at Starbucks, the person waiting in front of her picked up the *Times* and one of the lead articles was entitled 'Tragedy at a UCLA Medical Lab.' She reached forward and grabbed another copy of the paper and stood there trembling as she placed her order. She found a seat and started reading.

AP Wire, Los Angeles -- Tragedy struck a well-known medical laboratory on the UCLA Medical School campus on Wednesday morning. University officials report that a medical student died while she was working at the Lyndon A. Rutter Center for Cellular Engineering. The name of the student is being withheld pending notification of the parents. The school says the student was exposed to material that caused a severe allergic reaction and died within minutes as a result of anaphylactic shock. She was pronounced dead at the scene. Officials provided no further details about the accident.

Cheryl's eyes glazed over the remainder of the article that spoke about the origins and accomplishments of the Lab. The article closed with a reference back to the stem cell controversies 15 years prior.

She set the paper down. Her coffee shook as she tried to drink it. She had already narrowly escaped being kidnapped, and now she wondered if, somehow, she might be implicated in the death of this student. She hoped and prayed that it had nothing to do with the petri dish. She got into her car and drove back to her apartment. As she drove, she frantically studied the rearview mirror for signs of the black Explorer. She pulled into the gated garage and ran up the back stairs to her apartment, avoiding the elevator. She got inside, checked to see if anyone had snuck into the apartment, and grabbed her only suitcase. As she pulled clothes from the dresser and the closet and incidentals from the bathroom, she tried to calm herself down. She needed to reach Derek, but she didn't want to call him from the apartment—she wanted to get on the road and back to the Bay Area, where she hoped she could hide and have life return to normal.

But as she gathered her things, Cheryl had a flash of an insight. What was she doing? She had no idea really about what had happened at the Lab. It was possible, in fact, likely, that it had nothing at all to do with her. But how would she know? She needed to get back there and find out what happened. But she also knew that police might be snooping around, and someone at the Lab might see her and alert the police. She was torn, but it mattered more to her to know that the accident had nothing to do with her. She went back down the stairs with a suitcase and a backpack full of her belongings, slowly opened the door to the garage, looked around and walked briskly to the car, threw everything she had in the back seat and jumped in.

As she pulled up to the campus, she decided to drive around to see if there was any unusual police activity. Every step she took was cautious. She made sure the black Explorer was nowhere to be seen, that there were no stakeouts, and that no one was hiding in a car or at a bus stop waiting for her. She pulled on a hoodie and sunglasses, which on campus made her blend in like a student, and she walked over to the same entrance to the Lab that she had used the first time she was there. She expected to see police tape but there was nothing. She tried the door and it was locked. As she walked to the rear of the building, she saw a group of students laying flowers on the steps to the rear entrance and setting up a memorial. She decided to play ignorant and walked up to the students.

"What's going on?"

They looked at her as if she must be stupid if she didn't know, but one of the students took pity, and said, "You didn't hear about the accident?"

"No, I didn't," Cheryl lied. "What happened?"

"Our good friend died here a couple days ago. There was an accident in the Lab, and she got infected and died."

"We don't know if she was infected," another student responded.

"Well, whatever it was," a third student joined in, "she was working on something secret."

"It wasn't that secret," the second student said. "I was there. Somebody brought in a petri dish in a biohazard case to be reviewed by the Lab. I saw the dish. Maybe I am lucky to be alive."

Cheryl felt her knees buckle. She tried to stay calm. "I am sorry about your friend." As she turned and walked away, one of the students said, "Excuse me, what is your name?" Without thinking and still in shock, she looked back, and said, "I'm Cheryl." The student responded, "I'm Dawn. Thanks for asking about this." She pointed at the flowers and smiled at Cheryl, wondering if Cheryl was really as disinterested as she acted.

When Cheryl got back to her car, she was shaking. The chances of it not being her petri dish that caused the student's death were growing slimmer by the minute. If it was her petri dish, she thought, struggling to control her panic, the same thing might have happened to her while she was transporting it to Los Angeles. For some reason, back then, it had just seemed safe.

As she thought about what to do, she noticed movement next to her door. She looked up to her left, and directly into the open barrel of a very large gun. The man holding the gun ripped open the door and a separate pair of hands grabbed Cheryl and jerked her out of the car. No one else was around. No one else saw Cheryl get stuffed into the back seat of the Explorer with a hood pulled over her head and her hands zip-tied behind her back. The Explorer sped away, leaving the driver side door to Cheryl's car open, and her barely touched extra hot Starbucks latte now cold and sitting in the cup holder. Lying on her side in the back seat, Cheryl tried to pull her wits together. She was thinking that she would do whatever these people needed when she felt a jab in her arm that made her feel dizzy before everything went black.

Rather than call and risk Fred not picking up and possibly shunning him, Derek decided to take the two days it took to drive up to Seattle and give himself time to think. If for some reason Fred was gone, Derek had met people at the Lab there, and could stop by and ask how it was going. Fred would appreciate the diligence, which he expected of Derek anyway. The drive to Seattle can be one of the most spectacular drives in the country. Derek took his Tesla Model X fully charged and headed up the peninsula through downtown San Francisco and over the Golden Gate bridge. Not the fastest, but it was the most scenic way north. He passed San Quentin State Penitentiary and thought about it in a new way. It was, for the moment, not just about "them"—the poor evil souls who sat there waiting to die or rotting away the balance of their lives. This time, when he looked over the tall, electrified walls, he wondered how often you can see the sun. He stayed on the 101 North because he knew there were superchargers for his Model X and he drove on through Santa Rosa, passing the giant vineyards that produced the expensive wines his tastebuds had grown fond of. He passed by Humboldt, one of the many clusters of giant redwood trees sprinkled throughout Northern California and thought about how he almost named his company after these beautiful giants. But he knew, for obvious reasons, that it was far too common, and he settled on Red Hawk, which sounded more aggressive anyway. He spent the night in Crescent City, a beautiful coastal fishing village just south of the Oregon border and remembered for the tsunami of 1964, triggered by the strongest earthquake ever recorded in North America, a 9.2 earthquake in southern Alaska that sent out the killer tsunami, which reached 150 feet at its greatest height. The tsunami hit the city at midnight, killing twelve people and destroying much of the town. Derek was excited about the next day's journey, distracting him and keeping his mind off of Fielding's call and the tragedy at UCLA. He had a fleeting thought that maybe it would have been better for him to head south and check in on the Lab and Dr. Fielding, out of courtesy, but he knew that, if he had, he would be walking directly into Belinda's trap. He needed Fred right now more than anything, and the spectacular Oregon coast would put a check on the panic he felt rising in his chest.

Cheryl opened her eyes. She was no longer sitting in the back of the Explorer, and she had no idea how long she had been out or where she was. She was still cuffed by the zip tie, but the bag had been removed. She blinked through the blurriness, and the image of a tall, thin woman came into view. It took her a second before she recognized the woman as Belinda Armendariz from Ragnar Willowbrook. She also noticed the flirty professor Leonard Freund sitting next to Belinda and chuckled at her own now very real misfortune.

"You find this funny?" Belinda fired at Cheryl.

"Sure," Cheryl's gallows humor continued.

"Well, I don't because I do not take it lightly when someone steals from me."

Cheryl feigned ignorance, even though she knew it was futile. "What are you talking about?"

"The nano dish, Ms. Brown. You stole the nano dish from me."

"Well, if you are up on the news, it looks like I may have saved your life."

"Yeah, I know about UCLA, and I don't look at it that way."

"What way do you look at it?"

"Your impertinence doesn't affect me, Ms. Brown. I am not the one handcuffed to a chair."

"You are right about that," she said, nodding her head and pretending for a moment to let her guard down. "No, but you are the one guilty of kidnapping and drugging me against my will."

Belinda sighed. "Do you want to know why what you did was simply a stupid act? Maybe you don't, really, but I am going to tell you.

Yes, you killed someone needlessly. That is about the absolute height of stupidity. *We* have protocol here, and unlike the unfortunates at UCLA, *we* knew what we were dealing with." Her voice rose as she fired Cheryl, not caring whether or not Cheryl was defenseless. "You and your boss Derek could have been part of a trillion-dollar project to develop nanobot defenses against bio-terrorism, nanotechnical solutions to global problems, and giant medical advances in the fight against cancer, cerebral palsy, Parkinson's, Alzheimer's, you name it. Sweetheart, you would have been set for multiple lifetimes. But no. *You* needed to act on your impulse in the moment and now look at you. You are the captive of an elite black ops squad, who could have snapped your neck in an instant. You are coming out of a drug stupor—not the first time in the banal existence you call life. And you are cuffed and tied to a chair facing me."

"What do you want to know?" Cheryl said quietly.

"Where is Derek Whitestone?"

"I don't know. I was in LA, remember?"

One of the guards raised his arm and Belinda signaled him back. "Is UCLA the only place that has my nanobots?"

"I don't know. Derek was with Fred Schmidt when he talked to me. Fred apparently wanted me fired."

"Yes, Fred is a much smarter guy than the rest of us. But I think he made a mistake with Derek that he will regret. So where is Fred?"

"I don't know." Belinda's hand moved and a fist popped Cheryl on the side of her face. Blood trickled out of the corner of her mouth where her cheek slammed into her teeth.

"Where is Fred Schmidt?!" Belinda's voice grew loud.

"I don't know. I don't know. I promise. Derek left with him. That is all I know." This time a fist hit her square in the face. She lost consciousness for a few seconds.

"Are you with us, Cheryl?" Belinda screamed. "Where did Derek and Fred take my bots?!" she yelled in Cheryl's face, spit spraying from her mouth.

"Go fuck yourself," Cheryl replied. She felt something like a pipe hit the side of her head and she went out cold.

* * * * * *

Derek crawled up the Oregon Coast. But rather than the view calming him down, his anxiety grew. He repeatedly had second thoughts about seeing Fred on Bainbridge Island. But he steeled himself and kept driving. It was midnight when he finally arrived—it had been a long day. The slow trip was worth it. It gave Derek the time he needed to formulate a better story. UCLA was not a back-up to Fred for Derek. It was a back-up *for* Fred. Fred knew Derek to be a conservative investment banker, and as much money as the latter had made for Fred, he had also saved the billionaire millions of dollars on losses that he might have had with poor bets. UCLA was a savings strategy, and Derek trusted that Fred would see the wisdom of it, even as he dealt with the tragedy of it.

Gerard let Derek into the mansion on Bainbridge Island and guided him to Fred's study where Fred welcomed Derek from his long trip and told him there is much to discuss and suggested after a light aperitif that they retire and commence in the morning.

CHAPTER 16.

A Journey of Their Own Making

D etective Paul Young had a problem. He had opposed bringing Van Eng into the Bureau without going through regular channels. He knew that had she gone through those channels she would never have qualified as a detective because they would never send a deaf or hearing impaired person out in a squad car with another officer as a partner. He considered himself sympathetic to Van's situation as a human being, but he would not be the one to risk the lives of fellow officers because he felt sorry for Van. She didn't belong there.

The problem was that Van was proving him wrong—at every point. His strategy with the Vietnamese gang The Rush had barely moved with his team sitting there in their cars surveilling the gang from a safe distance. Van had jumped directly into the middle of things, and brought down two of LA's most troubling gangs, the Rush and El Muerte. Detective Young was fighting with Van and Charlie Darling on his decisions to close cases and they challenged him regularly by bringing them back to life. Now, in a direct affront to his authority, Detective Van Eng had reopened the case on UCLA medical student Marley Dakota and stumbled into what may turn out to be a multiple homicide and who knows what else. Bureau leadership was beginning to measure Van's successes against his credibility, and it wasn't looking good for Young. But he didn't know how to stop her. Every time he challenged her, she rose to the challenge and exceeded it. She seemed to be utterly fearless and he could not understand it. But Young didn't put a bullet on Van's desk. That was Robert Johnson, who thought that he was backing up his boss by scaring Van into submission. That was a stupid move, and Johnson was very lucky that Van realized early on there was no real threat. In fact, she turned the tables on Johnson by exposing him as a weak link on the Bureau's team. She knew he was Young's protégé, for what it was worth, so she let him be. But she enjoyed forcing him to drive into The Rush's garage and watch him almost pee his pants every time.

The interview with Dr. Fielding was the *coup de grace.* Van didn't care about Detective Young's ego or his future career, and as she pressed Dr. Fielding for answers, she knew Young was feeling the sheer force of her will to get to the truth. The real test started now. The frozen petri dish in Dr. Fielding's locked freezer was part of a much larger picture, and Van knew it even if she did not yet know what that picture included. Dr. Fielding had been in the dark and yet was willing to take on a grave risk. But for what?

Van talked Detective Young into letting her take Charlie with her up north to Cupertino, Derek Whitestone's Silicon Valley home and the location of Red Hawk Investments. They landed at the Norman Y. Mineta San Jose International Airport and took a shuttle to rental cars, where they picked up a small SUV and a GPS and jumped on the 880 South to the 280 West and exited the freeway at the base of the eastern edge of the Santa Cruz coastal mountain range and into the home of Apple Computers. They arrived at Derek's house, a modest but expensive home on the Deep Cliff Golf Course. Not surprisingly, they found no one home. They wandered to the back of the house and Van shared with Charlie her impressions, which by now Charlie knew to take seriously. What Van saw was a rarely occupied and probably professionally cleaned house with a regularly manicured yard to create the appearance of being lived in. She predicted that Derek was divorced and found the idea of living in a large house by himself depressing. That didn't make Derek a criminal, just a middle-aged male who preferred to be distracted by work, a circumstance that no doubt worked well for his principal and possible only client, a billionaire who demanded his immediate responsiveness 24/7. It also put him in a category of aging single males who have a tendency to make bad decisions, and, whether or not any of Van's speculations were true, Derek was making bad decisions.

They headed back toward the 280 Freeway and parked at a modest business complex across from the Cupertino Hyatt Hotel. Red Hawk Investments was on the fifth floor, Suite 5000. Van noticed that unlike other investment banks, this one appeared to be intentionally low key. Other than the custom sign on the wall above the reception chairs, which combined reclaimed wood and highly polished copper that ornately spelled out the name of the bank, the office was routine and filled with business warehouse furniture and standard cubicles. The lack of a high-end address and décor could mean that the bank was not very successful, but Van doubted that, even if they basically served only one person, Fred Schmidt. She saw the low-key design as intentional—a conscious decision to avoid the ostentatious side of the Valley and appear to be a smart, conservative bank. If Van had not heard about Derek's connection to the UCLA tragedy, the office alone would have left a favorable impression as did the receptionist, who was friendly and cooperative. Van showed her badge and introduced herself and Charlie as Los Angeles-area detectives who needed to speak with Derek Whitestone about events in Los Angeles. The receptionist told them Derek had left the Bay Area and reported to her that he may be gone for several weeks. She did not know where he was going but, in all likelihood, she believed he was heading to see his client Fred Schmidt, who had just purchased a new home on Bainbridge Island. They asked if anyone else worked with Derek on the Schmidt account, and she told them Cheryl Brown had been working closely with Derek on several matters, but she hadn't seen Cheryl for a few weeks, and there was an unverified rumor that she was let go. Van also asked if there was anyone else with whom they could speak who might have some details on what they had been working on, but the receptionist said she doubted it. They asked for Derek and Cheryl's contact information and the receptionist shared it without hesitation. She also asked for Fred Schmidt's contact information and the receptionist said that unfortunately that information was confidential, and that she would be happy to share but only if they had a court order. Van asked if she knew anything about why Fred and Derek had gone up north. She did. Derek had asked her to prepare a file for a Duc A. Tran Laboratory on Bainbridge Island just outside of Seattle. Van asked if they could see the file. The receptionist had left it on Derek's desk, and went to retrieve it. Van looked at Charlie. "Coincidence?"

"Right behind you, Van," Charlie replied. "I would give my right arm that there is a connection back to UCLA."

The receptionist returned with the file. Van took a quick look and saw a business card and flash memorized it—Dr. Brian Johannsen, Lead Scientist, Duc A. Tran Laboratory for Hereditary Biology. She handed the file back to the receptionist.

"I don't want to get you in trouble," Van told her.

"Well," responded the astute receptionist. "I am not entirely sure what is happening here, but if it is not good, I don't want to be a part of it." She handed the file back to Van.

"I can create another. I have copies."

"Thank you. If anything does come of this, we will remember your cooperation."

Van and Charlie went back to the car. They sat there going through the material in the file. In it, among what appeared to be white papers, were a pamphlet and a couple business cards, a handwritten note from Fred Schmidt to Derek. The note was on letterhead with an address on Bainbridge Island. It read:

> D: It is the middle of the night, and I can't get today's meeting out of my head. I think B and RW stumbled into an invention not of their own making and do not fully understand the effects. Dr. J broke it down. This is big. Take care buddy and get yourself back up here asap. F.

Van looked at Charlie. "I don't think we stop here. I'll let Detective Young know we are heading to Seattle. You good with that?"

"Absolutely."

✶ ✶ ✶ ✶ ✶ ✶

Cheryl came to in a basement with her hands tied together to a hot water pipe that emerged from the wall above her head. Her head throbbed and her neck ached from holding her head at an awkward angle. Her lip and cheek burned and felt swollen. She tried to shake off the pain and looked around. The basement appeared to be empty. She saw a washer dryer against the wall next to her. She stood and almost collapsed but leaned back against the concrete wall to stay upright. The paint on the back of the pipe was peeling, and she began to rub the zip tie back and forth over the flaked paint trying to break the plastic.

"It's no use, Ms. Brown."

Cheryl turned around and a light was shining in her face. She could hear Belinda's voice and make out a couple of other shapes, whom she assumed were the black ops guards. The voice had changed, softened but not in friendly way. It sounded resolute.

"I don't really care about you, Cheryl. You aren't the first person to try to steal from me. I can tell you this. No one who steals from me fails to regret it. So whether or not you find your way out of this very difficult situation is totally on you. It is no longer in my hands."

"I can't tell you what I don't know."

"Then tell me what you do know."

She looked down. There was no fighting this. No one was coming to save her. No one ever had.

"Okay. I told you I took it to UCLA. Derek had me over a barrel. Either I did what he needed, or I was out. So I took it. He warned me about you. Said you would not hesitate to kill me. I guess I see that now."

"Can we get it from UCLA?"

"I doubt it. It is the subject of an investigation there. It's evidence."

"Okay. I assumed so. Shit."

"But I think there is more."

"More what."

"More of your bots, or whatever you call it. I think Derek gave some of it to Fred Schmidt."

"When Derek kicked me out of the office, he disappeared for a week. I don't know where he went but I'll bet he went somewhere with Fred and they had some portion of the dish."

"Why do you think that?"

"Because Derek had me go to UCLA for him. He did not once mention Fred although he did tell me while I was in LA that Fred was up near Seattle on some island."

"Jesus Christ." Cheryl heard Leonard's voice. "The Tran Lab. It's on Bainbridge Island."

"I'm thirsty," Cheryl whimpered. "Can you get me some water?"

"Sure," said Belinda. She motioned to one of the guards, who grabbed a glass from a shelf, filled it under a tap, walked over to Cheryl, held the glass for her to drink and then put a bullet in her brain. She died instantly.

"Take care of that," Belinda said to the other guard and left the basement with Leonard, who walked away with Belinda but kept glancing back at the grisly scene.

CHAPTER 17.

Mr. President

S now on the ground blanketed Marshall Turner's Virginia estate. An overnight storm had caused a brief power outage and Marshall's back-up generators kicked in, waking him in the middle of the night next to his wife, who he knew would sleep through anything. The wind from the storm howled and he got out of bed and walked to his office, clicked on his desk lamp and sat down in his favorite leather chair still in his pajamas, staring at his reflection in the large window while the heavy white flakes danced in the air, moving left and right at the whim of the wind. He thought of Congress and chuckled. His phone blinked on and a text came in that he recognized was from the White House. *Meeting with Blondie. 9 am.* It came from the President's chief of staff. Blondie was their personal code, poking fun at the man who cared more about his hair than his politics. A midnight text, thought Marshall. Something is up.

A black limousine pulled into Marshall's driveway at 7:30 am. As he got in, the driver handed him a hot grande mocha latte, lightly sweetened.

"You are too good to me, Manfred."

"And you to me, sir," responded Mario Benitez, whose name was not Manfred but who tolerated Marshall and his sense of humor. Mario's military background made him especially valuable to Marshall, who sought his opinion on international military matters regularly. Their drives into the Beltway often gave Marshall a new perspective on matters he had to address. Besides that, Mario could step in as a personal bodyguard if ever needed. But other than the initial banter, this ride was quiet. The only other words spoken were "White House."

"Good morning, Mr. Turner," Marshall heard from several young staffers as he was escorted through the West Wing to the Oval Office. He reached the main double doors, where he knew to wait until he was ushered into the room. "Marshall!" shouted the President in his booming voice. "So good to see a really talented man in our midst. Refreshing, right?" he said, as he sent a scathing look around the room at the generals and cabinet members who were gathered there. "Absolutely, Sir!" said the president's chief of staff with gusto, and the President nodded approvingly in his direction.

"Marshall, Marshall. Please sit down." He pointed at the two couches in the middle of the room that were already full.

"You," he said pointing to Ben Drummond, the Director of the Department of Homeland Security. "Make room for this fine gentleman." Drummond hopped up and the others on the couch moved more tightly together to give Turner the room demanded by the President.

He added, "Would you like some coffee?" and without waiting for Marshall to respond, the President pressed a button and yelled "Bring Mr. Turner some coffee asap."

Marshall smiled and said nothing. A pretty young blond carried in a tray bearing the presidential seal and a cup of black coffee with packets of creamer and sugar, all of which also bore the seal and set it on the table. The President smiled at the blond, and said, "Thank you, honey."

As she was shutting the door, he started: "Okay good. Everyone is here. Looks like we have a major event in Armenia. I got a call from

Vlad last night, and it is not looking good there. Director, please brief us."
William P. Case, Director of the Central Intelligence Agency, had been
standing at the window next to the American flag behind the President's
desk ignoring what was going on in the room. He already had two agents
in the hospital in Yerevan and was demanding to know what was going
on there.

"Here is what we know now. Someone flying from Dushanbe to
Yerevan carried a highly toxic substance aboard without being detected.
The substance was released in the main airport terminal and killed at
least 300 people and sickened hundreds more. Whatever this substance
was, it increased in size and spread over a large portion of Yerevan and
began dropping toxic dust. The hospitals are being overwhelmed with
patients."

"Great," said the President. "Just about what I got this morning
from reading the morning paper. Have they identified the carrier? Was
he Muslim? Madame Secretary, please." He pointed to Secretary of State
Miriam Debourge.

"We don't believe this was an act of terror. Not yet, Mr. President."

"But it is a horrific act," he said too loudly.

"Yes, it is, sir. The problem is that Tajikistan and Armenia do not
have a history of enmity. As you may know, that tension is reserved to
Azerbaijan."

"It could have been an Azerbaijani, right? Maybe he flew to Tajikistan
as a distraction?"

"Yes, it is true that we don't know who did this yet."

"Great. Brilliant," he said with a bite. The President looked at Case.
"Contact the KGB. We know you have channels. See what they know."

Case glanced around the room as if the President had just given out state secrets. He looked at the President, took a breath, and said, "Yes, sir, Mr. President."

"What, you think the whole world doesn't know you talk to the KGB? Get your head out, Bill. Hollywood took care of that one a long time ago. Make the call!"

"Understood, sir."

"Marshall, what do you think?"

"We have good relationship with Armenia, correct? We have the world's top toxicologists. Let's send a team as an offer of assistance to the country. Maybe add some doctors."

"God damn, I love having somebody smart in the room! How's the coffee?" Marshall ignored the question, just as he had ignored the coffee. The President looked at Secretary DeBourge. "Can we pull a team together?"

As she answered "Yes, sir, Mr. President," he looked over at Case, who knew exactly what the glance meant. "And Marshall," the President added, "talk to some of your Silicon Valley buddies. I want to know if there is anything screwy going on."

"Yes, Mr. President."

Marshall called Fred from the car. He didn't wait for a response. "Something has happened in Armenia. I suggest you find out everything you can at your end. I will see you at your place this evening."

"Will do." Fred rarely took instructions from anyone, but his respect for Marshall was immense. Marshall seemed to have the ability to talk to anyone of any rank without fear and with candor. It was an ability that Fred admired most in the people he knew. He had believed that Derek Whitestone had that same skill set, only recently Derek had given him reason to doubt. He went into the kitchen and poured himself an espresso from a machine that was timed to run at 5:30 am every morning. As he was sipping the expresso, Derek entered the kitchen.

"Good morning."

"Good morning Derek. Sleep okay?"

"Not really."

"Want some espresso?"

"That would be nice, thanks."

"Ok, Derek. You look terrible. You going to tell me what is going on?"

"We have a problem."

"And what is *our* problem?" He emphasized the word "our." As he did so, he handed Derek a small double espresso.

"I took an action that I thought was in your best interest and it hasn't turned out well."

Fred paused and studied the floor as if he were actually studying it. "You know what, Derek? I don't want to discuss this right now. Marshall just called about something extremely serious, and I need time to think and to make some calls and see what I can find out. What I want is for you to relax. Take the day and wander around the island. Give yourself some time to think about what you need to share with me and what you don't need to share with me. Let's meet again this evening when Marshall arrives. There will be much to talk about. I am certain of it."

* * * * * *

Dr. Leonard Freund sat in his office chair. The cold-blooded murder of Cheryl Brown in the Lab basement sent chills up and down his body. Belinda had made him rich beyond his wildest dreams, but her dark side had always frightened him—but not enough for him to leave, apparently.

He reached into a lower drawer and pulled out a single malt Scotch. He threw down a shot and then another and then another. His phone buzzed.

"Leonard, my friend. I have good news." It was General Warner.

"Thanks, General. I could use some good news."

"I just attended another climate change convention in Oslo. Everyone is talking about Garne McDonough's proposed solution to global warming. You might recall that he ran a massive test with bot slime and it worked."

"Remind me," said Leonard, knowing the General had not disclosed what was in the petri dish, leaving that discovery to Ragnar Willowbrook. "What do you mean it worked?"

"According to Garny, the bots self-replicated in massive amounts and eliminated a huge quantity of CO_2 from a giant dome."

"What do you care about CO_2 or climate change?"

"I don't, Leonard. But if what this guy says is even half true and we could learn to program these bots to accomplish other tasks, whatever those are, then we don't need massive quantities. We just need enough."

"The bots are gone, General."

"What are you saying?"

"They were stolen out of the lab."

"How is *that* possible? Jesus Christ. Are you kidding me?"

"We know who stole them."

"Well, get them back!"

"Not that easy, General."

"Make it easy!" he shouted.

"I'll keep you posted," Leonard said and hung up. Her heard the General's fading screams and turned off the phone. Doesn't get much better than this, he laughed to himself and took another shot of Scotch.

He looked at his phone. Belinda had just texted him "Get up here immediately." Here we go again, he thought. He sighed. Maybe it's finally time for Montana. Mountains, a cabin, a fishing rod, a book. But no thrillers. He had enough of that.

CHAPTER 18.

Van Meets Brian

Van and Charlie took a bumpy shuttle ride up to SEA-TAC, the Seattle-Tacoma International Airport. Van tried to piece together everything she knew so far. But as she thought about it, she was distracted by the view out of the eastern-facing window. The flight from San Francisco to SEA-TAC ran past the thirteen volcanic mountains that comprise the American component of the Pacific Ring of Fire, also known as the Cascade Arc. These isolated snow-covered peaks start with Lassen Peak and Mount Shasta in California and run north past Mount Hood, Mount St. Helens, and Mount Rainier up to Mount Baker on the stateside of the Canadian Border. Van was struck by their beauty and their isolation, giant lonely monsters whose fearsome volcanic wrath was might be completely dead or minutes away. Very few tourists had even heard of Mount St. Helens until she blew in 1980, killing 57 people and destroying 250 homes, 47 bridges, 15 miles of railways and 185 miles of highway. She left several inches of volcanic dust over the entire city of Portland, Oregon, 70 miles to the southwest. Van counted the peaks as they flew past and studied the closest peak, Mount Rainier, as they landed. The plane pulled up and stopped short of the jetway. The ground crew pushed a staircase out to the plane, old school. Van and Charlie emerged from the plane on the tarmac and took big draws of the fresh Pacific Northwest air. Van could smell the rain and the wet tarmac from a recent shower. Van had not expected to stay long in the Bay Area, and now that she was in Seattle, she was running out of clothes. They grabbed another SUV from the car rental and popped into a Target directly across from the airport. They took the ferry to Bainbridge Island and found a couple of rooms at the Marshall Suites. They unpacked and agreed to meet at Jake's Pickup, a small deli café next to the hotel. They talked about what they knew and what they thought they still needed to know. Van glanced out of the window and saw a black Ford Explorer with California plates pull into the hotel entrance. She didn't think much about it until she saw four fit men in black boots and black fatigues jump out of the car.

She asked Charlie, "Is there a military base around here?"

"No idea," said Charlie, "but Maps might tell us." They looked at a GPS mapping tool on their phones and there was a naval base fairly close called the US Naval Undersea Warfare Engineering Base. But the base was not on Bainbridge Island; rather, it was across what appeared to be called Port Orchard Sound.

"Does the Navy wear black?"

"Well, I think they call it navy blue for a reason," Charlie chuckled. "It almost looks black."

Van knew navy blue from black and the men were not wearing navy blue. "Okay," she said.

The plan was to go to the Tran Labs first. Van figured that there was no longer an element of surprise with Fred Schmidt or anyone associated with him. Derek Whitestone probably already knew they had been to his office, so there was no additional surprise there. If Derek had decided to run, they would have to start a chase and that would be unfortunate. Hopefully, he was smarter than that. But before she met with Fred Schmidt and Derek Whitestone, Van wanted to know as much as possible about the nano matter and whatever else they were dealing with.

They awoke in the morning and headed back over to Jake's for a quick breakfast. The four men were already sitting in a booth, and Van noticed that they did not seem to talk to each other and that they had no apparent interest in her or Charlie. Not yet anyway.

"Let's rent a different car," she told Charlie.

"Really?" he said.

"I have a hunch."

"Then I am with you."

They stopped and picked up a sedan and drove up 305 to Port Madison and found the Duc A. Tran Laboratory for Hereditary Biology. It was a beautiful building surrounded by pine trees, and the peacefulness of the location struck Van, as if absolutely nothing was happening there, when she knew it was the exact opposite. She noticed a large motorcycle with a gold wing parked next to a Jaguar and wondered if it reflected diversity or division in the Lab. She expected to find out. They entered and told the receptionist who they were. The receptionist rang Dr. Meisner and Van added that they would like to meet Dr. Johannsen as well. The receptionist ushered them into a conference room that was built more for work than show. The white board was full of marks and several sketches were pinned on the bulletin boards, one of which depicted something that looked like a star or an alien spacecraft. Whoever this team was, Van knew to take them seriously. As the two scientists entered the boardroom, it was readily apparent to Van who the biker was. Dr. Stan Meisner still wore a tie to work under his lab coat and Dr. Johannsen was wearing jeans.

"Good morning, Detectives," said Dr. Meisner. "I am Dr. Stan Meisner, and this is Dr. Brian Johannsen. How can we help you?"

"Good morning," Van said, introducing herself and Charlie.

"A bit outside your jurisdiction, wouldn't you say?"

"It's called the long arm of the law for a reason, doctor," replied Van, standing her ground. Charlie chuckled and bit his lip.

"I'm not interested in wasting your time," Van went on. "We are here on a matter related to an incident in which three people lost their lives, one student and two lab technicians."

"Do we need a lawyer?" said Dr. Meisner.

"I'd heard it was just the student," Brian said without concern about Dr. Meisner's question.

Van looked at Brian and turned to Dr. Meisner. "That is up to you, Dr. Meisner. We are here to gather information and no one at the Lab is identified as a suspect in the events in Los Angeles. But if you would like to wait for an attorney, I completely understand."

"I am fine for now," he replied.

Van looked at Brian. "You know about UCLA, Dr. Johannsen?"

"Brian, please. We do, but what we know about it is from the news. Nothing else."

"Do you have any interactions with the Lyndon A. Rutter Lab at UCLA Medical School?"

Dr. Meisner responded, "The microbiology community is a fairly small community. We all know each other, and the goal is to advance the science and we all support each other in that goal. We collaborate on multiple projects."

"Well," said Brian. "Don't be fooled. We are as competitive as a pack of wolves. We know we need each other, but we are constantly fighting to be top dog in the pack."

Dr. Meisner glanced at Brian. Maybe we do need an attorney, he mused.

"Ok. The real question is do you know how they died?"

"No," said Dr. Meisner.

"No but," said Brian, "the report was that the student died of anaphylaxis after being exposed to a substance in a petri dish."

"That is correct," Van said. "All of them from the same exposure and the same reaction."

"Well, it is difficult to know whether there is any connection or not," said Brian. "But we had a similar incident here, only we contained it quickly enough, and although a couple of us got really sick, nobody died."

"Can you elaborate?"

"Do you know Derek Whitestone and Fred Schmidt?"

Van and Charlie looked at each other and nodded.

"They dropped off a petri dish that they wanted us to analyze."

"Christ," Van heard Charlie mutter.

"The dish was labeled Risk Group IV. Are you familiar with that classification?"

"We are," Van said. "Ebola."

"Right, or at least that class of pathogen. We are a Biosafety Level IV lab and qualified to handle Risk Group IV, as is, by the way, the Rutter Lab."

"That is how Dr. Fielding described it," said Van.

"March Fielding," said Dr. Meisner. "Very well respected."

"Only you discovered it was not a pathogen," Van said.

Brian and Dr. Meisner shot quick looks at each other. "Exactly," said Brian.

"And you let your guard down," said Van.

"We did and almost paid a steep price."

"Just a question and I still have the same question for Dr. Fielding. Didn't the label Risk Group IV trigger in you some extra caution?"

"The label could have been a warning, and in some sense, it was the best warning available. But it also could have been a misdirection. It could have been a mechanism for hiding the contents and limiting access to a very small group of professionals. Were we being cautious? Yes. What happened here was at least arguably the result of an error in protocol, only we have no protocol in place for the treatment of either medical or non-medical nanotechnology. I am not sure anyone does. It should not have been exposed to the air in any space where people are present. I wish we knew that then. We know it now."

"That drawing over there," she pointed to the sketch of the star/ spaceship on the bulletin board. "Is that it?"

"Yes, it is. It is a nanoparticle that was manufactured by a human being, but we do not know the source."

"You don't know who produced it."

"We don't," said Brian. "Maybe we should have inquired further but we assumed Fred and Derek wanted to keep it confidential, proprietary information."

"Have you figured out what it does?"

"We think so," said Brian this time. "At least what it does in part, whether or not it is what was intended. My colleague, Dr. Comstock—she was the one who almost died—noticed that the bot seems to be attracted to CO_2. We ran some small experiments and these bots seemed especially effective at reducing the volume of carbon dioxide in the air. Once they had reached their capacity for CO_2 molecules, they went dormant and fell on the floor of the chamber like dust."

"Sounds like a solution to global warming," Charlie said, and the room chuckled.

"Maybe you are right," said Brian. "The world is full of irony, and it wouldn't surprise me that a planet-sized problem would be addressed by a robot the size of a microbe."

"Well, it is certainly true that a microbe can cause a planet sized problem," Dr. Meisner added.

"Do you know why it causes anaphylaxis?" Van asked.

"Hard to say yet," answered Brian. "The nanobot is composed of a titanium alloy and a type of porcelain that bears an electrical charge. It just may be the case that this combination of metals and electricity is something the human body won't tolerate but it doesn't know how to destroy it and it overreacts."

"Any ideas on how to contain it, if it gets released?"

"We are working on that," said Dr. Meisner.

"How so?" asked Van.

Brian and Dr. Meisner looked at each other.

Dr. Meisner said, "I suggest you speak to Mr. Whitestone and Mr. Schmidt. For our part, I think at this point, we might want an attorney present."

"Absolutely understood," said Van. "Thank you for your time." She motioned to Dr. Meisner and then to Brian, who smiled. Van blushed just a little, and Charlie smiled to himself. Van needs someone special like that, he thought, as long as he manages to stay out of prison.

As they left the building, Van looked around for the black Explorer. She didn't see anything that seemed unusual, and she and Charlie got back into the sedan and headed south to Fred Schmidt's mansion.

"Are they part of this?" Van asked Charlie.

"What does your gut tell you?"

"Dr. Meisner is reserved, but that may just be his manner. Dr. Johannsen..."

"Brian."

"Right, Brian. He's is definitely willing to talk and sounds to me like he knows his stuff."

"Anything he say jump out at you?" Charlie said to Van.

"Actually, I am surprised no one seems to know the source. It is a manufactured piece of machinery that came from somewhere. Wouldn't you want to know where? Wouldn't that tell you the answers to a lot of questions, including why it was labeled Risk Group IV even though it wasn't a biological substance? Dr. Fielding didn't know where it came from and people died. Dr. Meisner didn't know where it came from and people almost died. The only thing they did know about the source was that Derek Whitestone delivered it, and Derek Whitestone is neither a biologist nor a chemist but rather a Silicon Valley investment banker, and it is very possible he didn't tell them where it came from because Derek stole it."

"So, you are not buying 'confidential proprietary'?"

"Are you?"

"Nah."

"Well, let's see what Fred says. Are you finding this interesting?"

"You betcha!" Van smiled at Charlie, and Charlie nodded and looked out at the Island greenery. Yes, he thought. This was about as interesting as it gets.

The black Explorer waited in the shadows near the Lab. Its occupants saw Van and Charlie leave and thought they looked familiar, but no one placed them. Their focus was on retrieving the petri dish for Belinda and exacting a small price for the Lab's collusion with Derek Whitestone and Cheryl Brown.

CHAPTER 19.

The Butler Didn't Do It

D erek was the first to arrive, or, rather, he was the first to arrive back at Fred's mansion. He took Fred's advice earlier in the day and spent the day wandering around the Island and let Fred's reaction to his explanation about UCLA sink in. He realized how stupid it was for him to lie to Fred, that Fred would see through it in an instant, and that Derek's only salvation, if there was any at all, was to be totally candid with Fred. He resolved to tell Fred the complete truth, that is, that it was his greed and insecurity that caused him to split the contents of the dish and have Cheryl deliver it to UCLA.

Fred had given Derek a key and told him to let himself back in if he had gone out. He locked the door behind him and headed to Fred's office to pour himself a Scotch and soda. It had started to rain, and Derek looked out the windows through the pine trees over the Sound. Rain has two effects on the ocean. If combined with wind, the sea gets stormy and hostile with crashing white caps. Without wind, rain turns the ocean into smooth glass and the only way to see the movement of waves is to stare at the white edge of the shoreline. He was briefly mesmerized and, for a fleeting moment, actually forgot about his problems, and then he heard a frantic rap on the front door. No one else was home yet so he went over and opened it, and there stood the famous Marshall Turner, soaked like a wet dog.

"Derek Whitestone?"

"If you wait a minute, I will get him for you," Derek smiled.

"Well, I'll be goddamned. What are you doing here? No, wait. You and Fred are pretty much joined at the hip, right? Why should I be surprised? Um, do you mind if I come in?"

"Hello, Marshall. Yes, please come in."

Marshall pulled in a suitcase and Derek offered him his room to change in. Marshall joined Derek in the study.

"How are things, Marshall?" Derek asked him.

"Well, Derek, honestly, I might be inclined to say the more things change and so on. But this President is... different. Problem is I can't tell yet whether that is a good thing. But tell me, how are you, and how is our friend, Fred?"

Derek and Marshall chatted amiably for about an hour. For Derek, the distraction was welcome. Marshall had opinions about everything and never hesitated to share them. Had Derek been in his usual frame of mind, he would have recorded the conversation mentally and plotted some of his next investment strategies. But he was not in that state. Rather he was a man standing on the edge of a cliff or a tall building, and an instant away from stepping off. They sipped their Scotch and heard a commotion in the entrance. They heard a voice they recognized as Fred's and another they did not immediately recognize.

"Here let me take that," Fred said to Dr. Brian Johannsen, who had just closed his umbrella but wasn't certain where to set it down.

"Freddy boy!" Marshall shouted, as he emerged from the study into the foyer. Derek followed growing quiet.

"And Dr. Johannsen? What a nice surprise!" he added, when it became clear who had entered with Fred.

"Dr. Johannsen," said Derek. "Good to see you again."

Brian was courteous. He and Fred had spent that last few hours together discussing the nanoparticles and whether or not there were any safe applications, and if not, whether or not they might be modified to be made safe. Brian had pressed Fred on the origin of the petri dish but Fred redirected the conversation, and Brian figured out quickly that the effort was fruitless. Brian was caught off guard when Fred told him that he had an important conversation coming up, and that he needed Brian to be present and would he mind coming over to Fred's place to meet his guests. Brian agreed, and though Fred offered to drive, Brian was used to riding in the rain and said he would follow. Brian had said nothing about the meeting with Van and Charlie. He figured it was not his place. But they did discuss UCLA and the tragedy there. Brian told Fred that if anything like the dish that he and Derek had delivered to Tran Labs was delivered to another location, the outcome would have been predictable. He told Fred that once he identified the bot as a non-biological substance, he himself lost his fear of the substrate, except for the fact that it had been labeled Risk Group IV, and for that reason alone he continued to be cautious. He had tried to stop his colleague from opening it, but he had been a bit slow to respond, and it had been near disastrous for them. Fred said nothing about Derek to Brian. He was still considering a response and had pretty much made up his mind but had not come to any final decisions. Brian was already drawing his own conclusions about Fred and Derek's actions. He was not afraid of talking with Fred despite the meeting with the LA detectives.

The four men met in Fred's study. Brian had pulled off his riding gear and was still drying out but the fire in the fireplace and the Scotch made him comfortable. Fred started the conversation.

"Gentlemen. I want to thank all of you for being here, especially Dr. Johannsen. His continued work on the nanoparticles has been very productive, and we are forming the beginnings of a plan. His perspective on how we might proceed is critical and I have invited him to consider joining any program we begin to develop." Brain smiled but said nothing.

"Marshall, your timing is impeccable, as usual, and I am especially glad you are here with us now. At our last meeting, you mentioned Providia, and as I said then, Derek has done some initial investigation there. Is there anything you can tell us about the AI at Providia and how that might contribute?"

"Yes, Fred, and I am glad to be here thank you but before we develop any plans I am here on a mission from the President and it is directly relevant to what you are discussing. Do you mind if I impose for a few minutes and take us in a slightly different direction?"

"Not at all."

Derek was listening to everything quietly. At this point, he was disoriented. Fred was introducing Brian and talking about a joint effort as if Derek would be included. He wondered if his idea of confessing everything to Fred was the right idea, and he found himself backing away from that ledge. However, at the mention of Providia, he began to think of Cheryl Brown and wondered if she was doing okay in LA. He realized that he had ignored her completely as his own issues escalated, and he only now recognized that it had been well over a week since they had spoken. He had expected Marshall's mission to be political and was tuning it out as he thought of Cheryl, and then he heard Marshall say, "...there is a developing toxicological disaster in Yerevan, the capital city of Armenia.

Hundreds have died from an anaphylactic pandemic that started at the airport in Yerevan, and the hospitals are overwhelmed. Apparently, a cloud that started building at the airport, has grown immense and is raining some kind of toxic dust on the city. We are assembling a team of experts, and Dr. Johannsen, with all due respect to the ideas that you and Mr. Schmidt might have right now, you might consider joining that team."

"Tell me about the dust," said Brian. "What do we know?"

"Very little," said Marshall. "The Yerevan hospital has not been able to identify any particular pathogen that is triggering the anaphylaxis. All we know so far is that the toxin is causing a cytokine storm, and some people seem to be able to manage it and others are dying."

Derek said almost without thinking, "The victims at UCLA died from anaphylaxis."

Fred said, "UCLA? Derek? I heard about something at UCLA—a student dying in a lab. You said victims, as in plural?"

Brian said, "That is the same reaction we had at Tran."

Marshall said, "UCLA? Why are we talking about UCLA?"

Derek started to speak, uncertain what words to use, when there was another knock at the front door. "Excuse me a minute," said Fred.

As Fred was answering the door, Brian looked at Derek and Marshall. "Do you know where the nanoparticles came from? Where they were manufactured?"

"I might," said Derek. Brian and Marshall both looked at him and as they waited for him to elaborate, Fred walked into the room with Van and Charlie.

Marshall started to joke about it being quite the assembly when he recognized Van from the Hollywood party. Her presence seemed to him to be utterly out of place until Fred introduced them, "Gentlemen, allow me to introduce Los Angeles Detectives Van Eng and Charles Darling."

Marshall stifled a laugh. "I believe Miss, my apologies, Detective Eng and I have met."

"Yes, Mr. Turner," Van said. "We met and spoke briefly at Martin Richard's after party. Good to see you again."

Fred then said, "The detectives are here on business. I appreciate that the situation in Armenia may be pressing but I suggest we allow them to conduct their business first."

"Ok by me," said Marshall, still staring at Van incredulously.

"Thank you," said Van. "Hello, Dr. Johannsen."

"Detective Eng." Fred looked Brian, and Brian returned the look and nodded. The entire room heard Fred under his breath say, "Okay."

"Do you mind if we talk to Derek Whitestone alone?" Van inquired.

Derek responded, "I will speak with you Detectives, but it would be wise for me to have an attorney present?"

"Then I am afraid we need to advise you of your rights, Mr. Whitestone."

"Wait a minute," said Fred. "I want to know what this is about."

"We think you may know already, Mr. Schmidt. Might be advisable for you to lawyer-up, if that is what they call it. For now, our primary concern is Mr. Whitestone."

"Does this have anything to do with UCLA?" Fred asked, sensing the situation that he had orchestrated was getting out of control.

"It has everything to do with UCLA," Van said as she pulled out cuffs that Charlie handed her and approached Derek

"Wait a minute," Fred said. "Derek, you need to tell me now, what happened at UCLA?"

Derek looked at Fred, feeling helpless. Van filled in the void. "Three people died at a UCLA Lab handling the petri dish that Derek Whitestone allegedly," she paused, "had delivered to the Lab."

Fred looked shocked. Marshall and Brian were quiet. "That's right," said Derek. "It was a backup plan."

"Derek," Fred looked at him pleading and almost hurt. "I don't understand," he said and then added, "And what is the crime?"

"As it stands," said Van, "criminal negligence and involuntary manslaughter." She fitted the cuffs on Derek and read him his rights. "We are booking him here tonight at Bainbridge PD. He will be extradited to Los Angeles."

"Don't worry, Derek. I will get you out. We'll deal with the rest later."

"Thank you for your time, gentlemen," said Van, as they moved to leave.

"Derek," said Marshall. "Where did it come from?"

Derek turned back. "Ragnar Willowbrook."

After Van and Charlie left with Derek, Fred returned to the study.

"That was entertaining," said Marshall. "Did you have any idea?"

Fred was angry. "I did. But only an idea. I had a plan and now, fuck me, it looks like it needs to change."

Brain said, "Ragnar Willowbrook. Isn't that the lab near Santa Cruz? They manufactured the nanoparticles?"

"Yes, it is," said Fred. "They didn't manufacture anything. They don't have the technology. But I'll bet they know where it came from."

"Derek got the dish from Ragnar Willowbrook, and you brought it to us," said Brian, now confused and deeply troubled at the events going on around him. He looked up at Fred and Marshall as if the entire world had gone crazy, and he didn't know whom to trust or what to believe any more. Then his phone buzzed.

"We need to get back to the Lab now. There's been an explosion and the Lab is on fire."

"I'll take you," said Fred. "No need to go back out in the rain."

"I'll wait here," Marshall said, imagining the worst.

"We'll get you a mask," said Fred. "You're coming with us."

CHAPTER 20.

It's Gone

The black Explorer waited on a side road behind a grove of trees. Clouds were building and the breeze that usually preceded a storm was picking up. A dark gray wall of rain was making its way from the north across Port Madison Bay. Boats raced across the bay to the marina, trying to outrun the storm. The ops team could see Detectives Eng and Darling head out of the entrance and get in a beige sedan. "Find my dish first," the team heard Belinda command. As soon as the sedan was gone, they slipped out of the Explorer with their gear. They set up posts around the perimeter of the building gauging the activity inside. They could see a group of scientists gathered at the window, watching the rain come. "Hold," came the command over the radios. Several staff members left the building to beat the rain home. They then watched as Fred Schmidt drove up, parked and entered the building. The team was disciplined from years in the field. They had waited under much more severe conditions. From the wet heat of southeast Asia to the scorching dryness of Somalia to the icy cold of northern Afghanistan, they had waited for hours upon hours for the right moment to do their duty and follow some command. They were a tight, disciplined unit, always ready to do whatever they were called upon to do. Now they waited and hid outside a modern American laboratory in the thick, green brush of Bainbridge Island in Puget Sound as the rain began to fall. Inside, Fred Schmidt had asked to meet with Dr. Johannsen. He was escorted to Brian's office and stood there gazing out the window at a wall of rain quickly approaching the Island.

"Mr. Schmidt," he heard behind and turn to see Brian removing his hazmat gear.

"Good afternoon, Brian. I hope you don't mind my intrusion."

"What's up?"

"What do we know?"

"Well, we have confirmed self-replication. It's a stunning process, actually, like watching a crystal form."

"It can happen anywhere?"

"We are testing that out but we are keeping the environment very secure. Even still, it is remarkably fast and it speeds up with the introduction of electrical energy and heat."

"What about other uses?"

"That is more speculative. These nanobots are programmed to harvest CO_2, as we have discussed. It does not seem that far-fetched to imagine harvesting other type of molecules, possibly even more complex molecules like hydroflourocarbons or methane. If we could find a way to make it safe, I can imagine uses in a variety of situations, from controlling emissions at refineries and coal-burning plants to improving safety in mining operations. There may be electrical storage applications as well. It is just the beginning."

Fred's smiled and started to glow. "That is what I wondered. We have a lot of work to do. Do you mind joining me with a couple people at my place? I am happy to drive."

"Of course, but I might as well head home from there. I'll take the bike."

Brian packed up and put on his rain riding gear. As they left, the rain began to get heavy. Fred ran and jumped in his car and Brian hopped on his bike and took off.

The ops team waited in the rain, quietly. When Fred and Brian were a ways down the road, the ops team heard the command, "Gear on," and they all put on gas masks with special low vision goggles snapped in place. The next command was "Go." Quickly and quietly, they moved toward the rear entrance. It was locked but they easily pried it open with a small black crowbar and moved swiftly up the stairs. At the third floor, they fanned out. Most of the staff had left but a handful remained. The team deployed knock out gas canisters around the floor, and everyone on the floor crumpled to the ground. The team checked to be sure they were out and searched the labs' freezers and refrigerators. Belinda had described the dish in detail including the Risk Group IV warning and a special code that identified it as the dish containing the nano gel. One of the ops members waited in the elevator lobby. Dr. Meisner and a couple of colleagues were taking the elevator up to the third floor and were casually conversing with each other about golf. When the door opened, the ops member quickly tossed in another canister and as the scientists tried to leave the elevator, he pointed his assault rifle and they backed into the gas, falling to the floor. The door closed and he pushed the button to open it and then dragged out the unconscious bodies, placing them next to each other on the floor of the lobby. He heard someone say, "Got bots," and then the command, "Place charges." The unconscious white coated bodies were all dragged to the lobby area and neatly lined up on the floor. The ops team then quietly exited the building down the back stairs and back into the foliage that surrounded the grounds on the rear of the building facing Port Madison Sound. They made their way back to the black Explorer, jumped in and peeled away with a biohazard case holding the remains of the petri dish. They drove for 10 minutes and then parked. The captain of the unit pulled out his cell phone and dialed a 10-digit number. When he hit send, the charges at the Lab blew and a black cloud appeared on the horizon, but the rain quickly washed it away.

Back at the Lab, staff that had been on the lower level smelled the knock out gas from the third floor, and following Lab protocol, quickly grabbed masks and exited the building. Instead of standing in the rain, they ran to their cars in the parking lot and started calling each other waiting for instructions from Dr. Meisner, but they heard nothing. Finally, someone texted the group and reported that Dr. Meisner and several staff members were missing, and a small handful, including Carrie, who happened to be on the first floor in a meeting in a conference room, put on their masks and ran back into the building. As they were entering, the charges on the third floor exploded, sending a large plume of smoke into the sky and glass and metal and wood chips sprayed into the parking lot. The east side of the building, opposite the rear entrance, collapsed. Several staff members jumped out of their cars as fire engulfed the building and ran to the rear entrance to help those who had just entered. A couple staff in the rescue group stumbled out of the door and fell on the ground coughing. Carrie had made her way to the third floor to discover the unconscious bodies lined up when the explosion occurred that sent her sprawling back into the staircase and she tumbled down a flight of concrete stairs. There was a loud bang as the east side of the building collapsed and all but a couple of the bodies fell into the burning debris two stories below. One of those bodies was that of Dr. Meisner. More staff rescuers came up the stairwell and pulled Carrie, who was bruised and bleeding, out of the building. The lobby floor was slanted toward the collapse and two staff members were hanging on the edge and the rescue team appeared and pulled them to safety.

But the safety was short-lived. When the ops team recovered the petri dish, they had no reason to be concerned that there might be smart dust remaining in the Lab either from the original sample or from the process of self-replication that Brian and the team there had uncovered. In fact, several containers of the smart dust had been stored in a special sealed locker that burst open when the explosion occurred. The explosion shattered the containers holding the additional smart dust and the heat of the fire caused the nano particles to rise, forming a cloud that dispersed throughout the building and into the parking lot.

All of the unconscious bodies that happened to survive the partial building collapse died immediately. But the team members in the parking lot who were following protocol and had their masks on weren't affected. A couple of team members had removed their masks but when they felt the tingle in the back of their throats, they immediately put them back on, and even though they started coughing, they didn't have full blown anaphylactic reactions. Port Madison and surrounding communities were extremely lucky that a heavy and windless rain came through when it did and kept the cloud from dispersing any further.

Van and Charlie were transporting Derek to the Bainbridge Island police station, when Derek's phone lit up with text messages from Fred telling Derek to inform the detectives what had happened and not to return to the Lab. Van told Derek to text Fred and give him her mobile and Fred called Van directly.

"What's going on?"

"Dr. Johannsen is getting reports from his team there. It's still unclear why the explosion occurred but the situation is bad and contin- ues to be extremely dangerous. Several scientists were on the third floor when it exploded, and there have been injuries and some deaths, including Dr. Stan Meisner, the top faculty member there. But there is more that you need to know about. According to Dr. Johannsen, the Lab had been able to replicate the nano particles and was storing a sizable amount in a freezer. Some members of the faculty are reporting reactions but they have masks. We are picking up gas masks at the hospital before we go up there. I am sure police and fire are on their way. We hope to God they know to mask up before they get there."

"Ask them if there is any concern about other infectious diseases?" asked Charlie. The report from Brian came back that possible SARS containment would be required. Marshall, who was riding with Fred and Brian, mentioned what had happened in Yerevan, Armenia. According to Marshall, a large portion of the city had been infected by whatever had been released. The location would need to be treated as extremely hazardous and contained quickly.

"We can pick up masks at the station," Van said to Charlie.

When they got to the police station, there was a skeleton crew. Several officers had gone up to the site of the explosion. Van confirmed that they knew to treat the incident as hazardous and had appropriate gear, and had informed Seattle's HazMat team, who were on their way. Van called Detective Young in Los Angeles and reported everything that had developed. Young told her good work and said to be very careful. They booked Derek at the station. He was led to a cell to be transported to Los Angeles at the earliest convenience, but with the events unfolding at the Lab, it was uncertain when that would be.

Van and Charlie grabbed masks and headed back up to the Lab. The police had set up a wide perimeter, with an outer boundary two miles wide. They evacuated Port Madison and closed all roads going up to the Lab. They taped up an inner perimeter 500 feet around the Lab, and the Lab staff was asked to wait outside the perimeter. Ambulances were on site and transported anyone complaining of allergic reactions to the hospital immediately. The police allowed Fred's car to enter because of Brian, and Van and Charlie's car was allowed to pass. When they got to the scene, they introduced themselves to the local detective in charge. The fire had been put out with foam, and the HazMat team was enclosing the entire building in a tent. All active responders were wearing full Hazmat gear. Charlie told Van that the scene looked like something out of the movie, *Mission to Mars*. Van and Charlie had already informed the police department of their presence on the Island and weren't questioned. The lead detective confirmed to Van and Charlie that there were 10 bodies and a half dozen more, who were injured in the blast when they tried to rescue the missing doctors. He also confirmed that they found evidence of explosive material in the debris. Van told the detective about the black Explorer she had seen earlier in the day with California plates. She suggested issuing an all-points bulletin or APB though by now they were probably pretty far south. She also suggested they look for SUV tire tracks, maybe All Terrains, where they might have parked. With no other leads, the detective called in the APB to include Seattle and all highways south into Oregon.

Van found Brian speaking to the fire fighters and putting on a HazMat suit.

"I am really sorry about your colleagues," she said.

"I need to get in there," he told Van. "I need to find the dish."

"Let me join you," she answered him. "Maybe I can help." But Van had her doubts that the dish would still be there.

She asked Charlie to start talking to the staff that remained in site. She wanted to know if anyone had seen anything strange including a black Ford Explorer with California license plates.

They suited up and walked up to the building and walked in through a temporary containment entrance, a long white tunnel strung with lights.

The rain had stopped, and the air was misting. The day was growing dark and the lights helped them find their way through the debris. The outer East wall had collapsed completely, and Van could see the partial collapse of the second and third stories. The bagged bodies had been laid out on the ground next to the coroner's van. Brian wandered over to the suited-up coroner and let them know to be careful with the bodies given their exposure to the nano particles. They began picking their way through the debris. There was broken glass and shattered lab equipment everywhere. Brian found his monitor and server, but it was partially melted from the fire. He showed Van and said, "That's three years of my life down the tubes." Eventually, they found the small locking freezer in which Brian kept the original petri dish, and they could see marks from the crowbar that showed it had been pried open and broken into and emptied. Van told Brian it was evidence and pointed it out to the local forensics team that had already arrived. They looked around but there was no sign of the petri dish.

"It's gone," said Brian.

CHAPTER 21.

Van's War

Brian didn't go to Armenia, as much as his expertise might have helped. The catastrophe at the Lab kept him on Bainbridge Island, and he worked closely with Seattle PD's forensics team trying to piece together what had happened. Van and Charlie went back to the hotel and booked a flight to Los Angeles, where they planned to have Derek arraigned. But before she left with Charlie, and as they were removing their hazmat suits, Brian told Van he would like very much to stay in touch. Van said of course they would be in touch as the case moved forward and as whatever they learned from the explosion might advance her investigations in Los Angeles. Brian pulled his hazmat boots off and walked over to Van in his loose T-shirt and jeans and socks on the wet grass, and said no, that he would *really* like to stay in touch. Van felt her knees give a little and she smiled.

"I would like that very much," she told Brian.

He blushed and said with some relief, "Okay then."

Charlie didn't waste any time. In the car ride back to the hotel, he said, "That Brian, something about him."

Van blushed and just said, "Charlie," and nothing else. Charlie smiled.

The next morning, they retrieved Derek from the police station, cuffed him, and took him to a special waiting room at SEA-TAC designed for police uses. As they sat waiting for their flight to be called, Derek said to them, "There are some things you should know."

"Okay. Are you certain you want to proceed without an attorney present?"

"Yes. You need to know this now. As for me, it is what it is." Charlie looked at Van as if to say, we need to be careful with this one.

Van turned on the recording feature on her phone. "Okay, tell us what you need to tell us."

"The petri dish was stolen from Ragnar Willowbrook by Cheryl Brown. She hid it from me and then accidentally disclosed it to me."

"Who is Ragnar Willowbrook?"

"Ragnar Willowbrook is the preeminent independent engineering laboratory in the Silicon Valley. Everybody who is anybody developing any biomedical applications tries to get an RW Labs endorsement, except that it is really a false front. The lab has gotten rich off of their reputation, but they have not developed anything new on their own. They are known for stealing ideas and then winning the race to patent the ideas as their own ideas, and they buy top legal talent to ensure that they win those patent cases."

"Do you think they stole the dish?"

"I don't know. They have a lot of inside channels. They could have paid for it."

"But you ended up with it and you elected not to return it."

"Right. I was torn but it occurred to me that Fred might be able to do much more with it through his channels than Belinda could through hers. Honestly, I thought Fred would be impressed, and truth be told, he was."

"So Fred knew the dish was stolen?" Charlie asked.

Derek stared at the ground. "He knew Cheryl took it from RW. He told me to fire Cheryl. Instead, I used her as my back-up option to Fred."

Van asked, "Who is Belinda?"

"Dr. Belinda Armendariz. Her ruthless tactics got her promoted to Chief Scientist at RW and ultimately CEO. I believe that Belinda figured out that Cheryl stole the petri dish, and I am not only concerned about Cheryl but what else Belinda would do or might have already done to retaliate for its theft. I asked Cheryl to deliver the dish to UCLA—that was my back-up plan to Fred. Cheryl drove it down there and had a scary interaction with men in a black SUV. I assume they were Belinda's men."

"Explorer?"

"Yes." Van looked at Charlie. Derek continued, "She said it had been following her down the 5 Freeway to Los Angeles. We suspected Belinda might be on her tail, so we set up a decoy bag that they grabbed off of Cheryl's back. They would have taken her, but a campus security guard was there and intervened."

"Where is Cheryl now?"

"I don't know. I can't reach her."

"You need to give us her contact information. Does Belinda employ black ops?"

Derek got quiet. "Yes." He said looking down again.

"Do you think Belinda could do Cheryl harm?"

"I don't put anything past Belinda."

"Do you think Belinda will come after you?"

"She might. Especially if she doesn't get from Cheryl what she needs."

"You willing to sign a statement?"

"Sure. Whatever you need. I don't care what happens to me anymore."

The three of them flew to Los Angeles and landed at Hollywood Burbank Airport. Van had police vehicles waiting for them. She booked him into the Metropolitan Correctional Facility, a slightly less hostile environment than the infamous Twin Towers correctional facility. Van reported everything that had happened to Detective Young. He knew at this point he need to support her and provide anything she needed to bring this to a conclusion. Van wanted to hit RW Labs as quickly as possible. If Belinda was as hardcore as Derek led her to believe, Van didn't have much time. Belinda could hit anybody associated with Derek, like Fred or Marshall or even Brian, who had been minutes away from disaster at his own lab.

She and Charlie went to Cheryl's apartment. It had been ransacked. Pictures pulled off the walls, furniture torn apart, dishes smashed and knick-knacks scattered about. She called forensics to see if they could find fingerprints, but she doubted they would have been that careless. DNA was more likely, and whether or not it helped, she wanted it. She studied the room. The destruction and debris was random—not orderly or planned. It seemed more angry than intentional, as if someone was sending a message. Like the explosion at the Lab. What purpose did it serve if they had found the petri dish? Retaliation? A message?

She returned to the Bureau and went back into Detective Young's office. "I want a coordinated assault on RW Labs," she said. I want to fight her black ops with our best tactical assault teams. We need to be prepared, and it could get ugly. If what I am hearing is true, Belinda Armendariz is no better than a domestic terrorist, and the material she probably has back in her possession could be weaponized. We need to prevent that."

"We can get SWAT on it, but you'll want the FBI to lead that effort."

"That's fine. Let's get it together."

The FBI maintained an office on the fifth floor of the LAPD's central headquarters to allow for close coordination where needed. Detective Young took Van to the Office and asked for Agent Henry Sams. The LAPD post was not the worst office an FBI agent might fill, but it was not considered high grade. Henry Sams had been with the Bureau for 20 years and was nearing retirement. He had never been viewed as a climber but had managed to hold his job in part due to his good work on several cross-border gang cases. Detective Young and Agent Sams knew each other well. They had a recurring lunch meeting once a month, where they updated each other on new developments. LAPD leadership had a tense relationship with the Bureau but viewed the lunch meetings as beneficial and allowed Young to keep them. For Sams, it was viewed as part of his duty to maintain a connection to the LAPD.

"Agent Sams."

"Hello, Detective Young. Please follow me."

Van was struck by how plain the agent's office looked. There was a small foyer with a couple of ratty chairs and a cheap coffee table. A coffee machine stood in the corner next to a water dispenser and a trash can that needed emptying. Nothing was on the wall except a small, framed sign that said Federal Bureau of Investigation, Los Angeles Bureau. It was a sign that you might miss if you weren't looking for it. She wouldn't have thought twice about it as an LAPD office, but as the central office for the FBI in downtown Los Angeles it seemed very sparse. They went into a small interrogation room with a white table and metal chairs.

"Let me introduce you to Detective Van Eng."

"Pleasure. What is this about?"

"You might have heard about the explosion in Seattle."

"Yes. It is on the wire."

"Detective Eng was there."

Henry's eyes grew wider. "What do you know about it?"

Van responded deferentially. "It's a rather long story, Agent Sams, but it starts with an investigation into an accident at a UCLA laboratory that resulted in three deaths." She walked through her investigation and ultimate capture of Derek Whitestone, who during his extradition to Los Angeles had confessed to a theft that Van believed was connected to the bombing. More importantly, she said, the material that was stolen was extremely dangerous and Whitestone provided information that she believed placed the material in the hands of the person responsible for the bombing who had yet to be detained.

Sams contacted headquarters and assembled a larger briefing that led to a coordinated effort between the FBI, the Bureau of Alcohol, Tobacco and Firearms, the LAPD Detective Bureau and SWAT Team and the Santa Cruz Police Department. The teams set up a war room in one of the classrooms at UC Santa Cruz, about 45 minutes southwest of RW Labs. Agent Sams took the lead for his team and organized command and control for effective cross department coordination. Everyone agreed the operation needed to be tight and that there was no room for jurisdictional in-fighting. They hatched a plan to send a small team to the Lab. If the Lab cooperated, that team would take appropriate action but at any sign of resistance, one team member would text a code and the force would mobilize at the main entrance. Given that they were dealing with black ops, the team knew extreme caution must be taken, and initial cover would be provided by the SWAT unit. In order to prevent the advance team from being taken as hostages, they would be backed up by a small armed SWAT unit and were to advance no further than the main entrance to RW Labs.

The advance team included Agent Sams and Detective Young, Charlie and Van as well as four back-up agents. They left first in two unmarked sedans. Ten minutes behind them was the LAPD SWAT Special Reaction Team in three Lenco BearCat armored rescue vehicles carrying 15 team members. Behind the BearCats, the FBI and ATF drove another four specially outfitted SUVs carrying another 20 agents. Two LAPD SWAT helicopters outfitted to carry another four officers externally armed with fast action AR-15s waited at the University for instructions.

The advance team rolled up to the guarded entrance of RW Labs in two cars. Agent Sams rolled down his window and displayed his badge to the guard, "My name is Agent Henry Sams. We are from the FBI and would like to speak to Dr. Belinda Armendariz."

"Please hold." The guard returned to the guardhouse. He spoke on the phone and then came back to the car. "Dr. Armendariz is not available."

This was expected. "Please let Dr. Armendariz know that we have a warrant to search the premises." He handed the guard a copy of the search warrant.

The guard left with the warrant. He got on the phone again. In a few minutes, the gate opened. "We're in," Detective Young radioed to the support team, which instructed them to move forward, keep out of sight of the guards and wait for further instructions.

The two cars rolled up the long and windy driveway to the entrance. No one was outside to meet them. They exited the car and pulled their guns. The front desk and the lobby were empty. Then they heard Dr. Armendariz speaking over a loudspeaker into the lobby.

"Good morning, gentlemen. How can I help you?"

"Dr. Armendariz, I am Agent Henry Sams of the FBI. With me are Detectives Paul Young and Van Eng of the LAPD. We have a warrant to search the building."

"On what grounds, Agent Sams?"

"There is a judge in Los Angeles who believes there is probable cause to connect this lab to the bombing of another lab in Washington State."

"That is absurd, Agent Sams. We are a reputable scientific institution, not a terrorist organization."

"You are required by law to allow us access."

"Then you must allow my men to disarm you." At that point, several of Belinda's black ops stepped from behind the elevator bay and pointed their guns at the advance team, which immediately raised their weapons at the guards.

"Stand down, Dr. Armendariz!" Agent Sams shouted. "Instruct your men to lower their weapons. We will not be disarmed." The guards did not lower their weapons. Rather, they began to slowly move forward toward the advance team. Van felt her heart sink, but she held her ground as did everyone else. Detective Young was holding his push-to-talk phone in one hand and his Glock-9 standard issue pistol in the other. He keyed the phone, sending a signal to the support team. As he did that, a doctor in a white lab coat appeared from behind Belinda's guards.

"Stop this!" he shouted at the guards. "Ignore him!" Belinda shouted over the speaker.

Dr. Leonard Freund stepped forward toward the advance FBI team with his hands up. He told the guards again, "Lower your weapons," and to the FBI team, he said, "Take me into custody. This needs to stop."

He walked forward toward the agents. Belinda's voice became very calm and grave. "He must be stopped," she said, and one of her black ops fired a shot that knocked Leonard to the ground. The agents immediately returned fire forcing the guards to retreat a step backward as the agents likewise backed away from the guards toward the front entrance. Van dove forward and grabbed Leonard by the collar as bullets whizzed past her head. Two FBI agents jumped in front of her firing nonstop at the guards, and another agent jumped in and helped her pull Leonard out the front door and behind the parked sedans. Van looked down and saw blood staining Leonard's coat. He looked at it and then up at her and smiled. "Do you mind putting a little pressure on it," he said and then passed out.

The support team raced up the long driveway. "We're clear," Detective Young yelled into his phone once all the agents had backed out the front door continuing to fire toward the guards. A couple of agents were hit and bleeding, but they had moved outside as well. The SWAT team positioned two of the BearCats in front of the entrance as the third BearCat smashed the front doors down and slid into the lobby. Officers in the armored BearCat began fired toward the guards from gaps in the windows. The BearCat's surprise entrance into the lobby had shocked the guards, as had Leonard's actions. A handful ran up a rear staircase while the remainder laid down their weapons and surrendered. The remainder of the team went into the stairwell, guns drawn, and began a search, floor by floor for the remaining guards and for Belinda. There were a few brief gun battles, but eventually, the guards all surrendered. As the team brought them out, Van shouted to Detective Young that the doctor needed medical. A SWAT team member pulled out a kit and put a pressure bandage on the wound. Detective Young had radioed for the helicopters and they arrived quickly. They strapped Leonard into a SKED stretcher and flew him over to Dominican Hospital in Santa Cruz.

"Where is Belinda?" Van asked. No one knew. She grabbed Agent Sams and Detectives Young and Charlie, and they began a search of the building. "She could be hiding in one of the sterile labs," she suggested. They ignored the decontamination units and searched room by room, but Belinda was gone. Agent Sams organized a search of the executive offices, including Belinda's office, for evidence of a connection to the Bainbridge explosion. They pulled out dozens of boxes of materials to review.

Van and her counterparts got in the sedan and drove to Dominican Hospital to check on Leonard. He was still in intensive care and being prepped for surgery, but he was alive. The doctors told them it might be a couple of days before he would speak with them comfortably.

Van went back to her hotel. She was still worked up over the day's events and couldn't sleep. She reflected on Leonard's courage and on the courage of the agents who had protected her. She thought about how skillfully Agent Sams had managed the assault. Her phone flashed. She leaned over and it was Brian. Part of her wanted to resist his advances. The other part wanted to melt into his arms. She realized though that she needed to update him on the day and answered.

"Hi."

"Hi."

"How was your day?"

"Pretty intense. I am still shaking."

"Did you get Dr. Armendariz?"

"No, we didn't. She spoke to us and was able to see us, but we think she was connecting remotely. She must have got word and skipped. Or maybe she was just lucky. Anything new up there?"

"Yes. They are dismantling the tent. There are no active nanobots left. All that was left was the used dust. They cleaned and detoxified the site, but it is still a mess. We have had a couple of meetings with the University about reopening the lab elsewhere. They are talking to me about taking over Stan's position."

"Wow. Congratulations, I guess."

"Yeah. I have mixed feelings about it. Could be a dream come true but it's terrible how it has come about."

"Yeah.

There was a brief silence on the phone.

"Van?" Brian said.

"Yes?"

"I miss you."

Van giggled. "Uh, we've known each other how long? Maybe 5 hours tops?"

Brian sighed. "Too much?"

"No," Van smiled and squeezed the phone. "It's not." They hung up. The call relaxed Van and she drifted to sleep.

✳ ✳ ✳ ✳ ✳ ✳

Belinda kicked back in her hotel suite in downtown Seattle, smoking a cigarette, sipping Cognac, and looking out over the night skyline at the space needle. The petri dish sat on the coffee table in front of her along with the laptop that connected her to the Santa Cruz lab. She didn't feel bad about Stan Meisner. His arrogant ass got what it deserved, and the Tran Lab would be in disarray for months allowing her to get a jump on developing uses for the nano gel in front of her. It made her feel powerful to have manipulated the FBI remotely though a secure application on her laptop. She watched as everything played out. Leonard had become a problem now for some time and if he hadn't been taken care of today, he would need to be addressed at some point. The phone buzzed.

"General."

"Doctor."

"Bit of a mess today."

"Don't worry about that. We'll take care of it. National security and all. Of course, someone will need to suffer the consequences.

"That shouldn't be a problem. My team acted on their own."

"I am sure of it. Did you get the dish?"

"Yes, I have it."

"Good. You can fly out here tomorrow?"

"No. I am taking some time off. I'll secure the dish."

"Understood. Stay in touch."

Belinda missed Spain and the Pyrenees. Basque Country. Her family had an estate in the mountains above Errenteria, not far from Pamplona and the Running of the Bulls, her favorite event. She mused that she had "run the bulls" today and won, which like the contestants in that insane Basque contest, meant only to her that she was still living.

CHAPTER 22.

The Beginning and The End

Leonard woke from his surgery. His hand was cuffed to the bed. He laughed to himself, "I guess I made it." He was still surprised that he had had the balls to walk out in front of Belinda's death squad, but he had grown tired of her hardcore tactics, and blowing up the lab and his colleagues on Bainbridge Island had been the last straw for him. He knew it would be tough, but he wanted to get back at Belinda. He pressed the buzzer on his bed.

Detective Young called Van. "The doctor is ready to speak." She grabbed her badge and gun and said, "Meet you downstairs."

They stood in Leonard's room around his bed. The attending physician told them they could have no more than 15 minutes. Leonard smiled and said to Van and her team, "Take as much time as you want. You are the reason I am here breathing at all."

Agent Sams looked at Van. She began, "Dr. Freund, I am Detective Van Eng of the LAPD."

He smiled. "I remember you. You are the gorgeous young agent who came to my rescue. Thank you for that."

Van smiled courteously. "We have a lot of questions for you, sir. But to start, were you aware of the plan to attack the Bainbridge Island lab?"

"Look," Leonard answered, "I am prepared to talk, but contrary to my present appearance, I am not quite as dumb as I may seem. We need an understanding here. I am not discussing anything without a deal."

Agent Sams replied, "We don't have a problem with that Dr. Freund. I just can't guarantee that you won't serve some time."

"Ok, put it in writing and that will be good enough," Leonard said. "Here it is. I don't know that Dr. Armendariz intended the death and level of destruction that occurred at the Tran Lab, but she did instruct her team to find the dish and she told them to make a statement, and they knew that by that she meant for the team to set off an explosive charge. You are aware that the petri dish was stolen from us?"

"We are," said Van. "Derek Whitestone is in Los Angeles in jail awaiting arraignment."

"He'll probably get released," Leonard mused as much to himself as to the group in the room. "Friends in high places, right?"

Agent Sams said, "That's not how we work, Doctor."

"Right," said Leonard. "So, you know Whitestone had an accomplice?"

"Cheryl Brown," Van replied.

"She's gone," Leonard said, remorsefully.

"What do you mean?" Van asked.

"Belinda had her executed in cold blood, after she tortured her into confessing to stealing the dish and to Derek Whitestone's plans in Seattle."

Van looked at Detectives Young and Charlie and shook her head imperceptibly as if to say I am telling you now, I want her in my crosshairs.

"Do you know where the body is?"

"No, but if you search the grounds and the woods around it, you will find a fresh grave. Of that I am certain."

✶✶✶✶✶✶

"Hello, Mr. McDonough," said General Bill Warner standing outside the conference hall at the University of Paris where the annual Global Climate Change Consortium had just concluded. "That was quite a speech you gave."

"General," Garny responded.

"Can we talk?" asked the General.

"We're talking," replied Garny.

"Let's bring this home."

"To the States? I'm open but I left precisely because I would never have been able to accomplish there what I did here. You think I can do that now? You know what my goals are with the technology."

"I do and I support you. Bring it home and we'll make sure you get what you need."

"How about this instead?" Garny proposed. "I'll provide you with a sample. You have your team analyze it and get back to me. Remember, the sample is still dangerous even in small amounts. You need a team that knows how to handle it."

"It won't be the first time," said the General.

The next morning, a biohazard safety case was delivered to the General's hotel room in Paris. Inside the double reinforced case was a tightly sealed petri dish labeled Risk Group IV to ensure proper handling.

✶✶✶✶✶✶

Brian pulled his bike into a gravel turnout to watch the sunset. He parked the Gold Wing and walked over to a rusty metal railing that kept him from plummeting 150 feet to the crashing waves below. Up and down the coastline it was the same. Giant rock pillars and steep stone-faced cliffs all framed the movement of large dark blue waves slamming into the rocks and spraying foam thirty, fifty and sometimes eighty feet into the air. He heard the bleating of sea lions crying for mates and watched seagulls dancing in the wind as it swirled around the steep cliffs.

The sun dropped below dark clouds on the horizon, the drifting remainder of a recent storm, and suddenly sprayed the coastline and the ocean foam with yellow light that gradually turned orange and then crimson. He loved the colors and the feel of twilight. He wondered if he would feel the same about Van. He knew right away that she was special. It didn't hurt that she was sexy as hell and he longed to be with her in that way. But she would be more to him. The University had asked him to take the lead in rebuilding the Tran Labs. He didn't say no. But he needed time to think and to recover, and for now, the only thing on his mind was traveling south. He climbed onto his bike and continued the long and beautiful journey down Highway 1 to Los Angeles.

Excerpt from *Resonance: Book 2 of the Nanobot Trilogy*

B elinda Armendariz awoke in her hilltop villa just outside Errenteria, Spain. Errenteria, was a medium sized town on the coast of Spain, but more importantly to Belinda, it was her home country, the Basque Country. Belinda believed in her people, fashioned herself their queen, as she dreamed about resurrecting the original Basque kingdom, the Kingdom of Pamplona. She had traced her lineage to the House of Jimenez, the monarchic dynasty that ruled over Pamplona for three centuries. It was, in her mind, the Golden Age of the Basque People, and Belinda believed it was her destiny to resurrect the dynasty and bring back the Basque Golden Age. Her rise to CEO of Ragnar Willowbrook Labs in the Silicon Valley and her growing wealth confirmed her grand destiny and, without telling anyone at the Labs, she had redesigned the grounds around RW Labs so that the gardens and sculptures formed the shape of her Basque Country. From her fifth-story office atop the Labs, she could swivel her desk chair and look out her window at the Labs massive gardens and dream of being home.

Now she was home, waiting out the repercussions of the explosion at the Tran Labs on Bainbridge Island, the Lab that was attempting to steal her most recent invention. It was her ops team that retrieved the petri dish and planted the charges and even though it had not been her intention to destroy the Lab, her team got a bit too enthusiastic and the explosion resulted in 10 deaths. Belinda knew she might be hunted if she were tied to the explosion, but she had an ace up her sleeve. General Tom Warner, a five-star general at the Pentagon, knew about the accident and about the petri dish that had been returned to her possession and he would protect her.

She looked at the petri dish and thought about where it had been. General Warner had called her colleague, Dr. Leonard Freund, and arranged for the delivery of the petri dish to Ragnar Willowbrook. The general would not divulge its source or contents, although he did say be careful with it and when they received it, the petri dish had been labeled Risk Group IV, meaning it was not only toxic but potentially lethal. He wanted Belinda's company to figure it out and get back to him with their sense of its possible uses, military or otherwise. Belinda knew that the Pentagon was not always interested in military uses of technology. Several prominent examples of modern advances in technology started with the military and the Pentagon's interest in those advances extended well beyond a simple kill factor. ARPAnet, for example, was a machine-to-machine computer-based communications network developed by an arm of the Department of Defense, the Defense Advanced Research Projects Agency. The military wanted a decentralized communications network that would withstand a nuclear attack. In the 1990s, DARPA shared the ARPAnet technology with several universities that converted it into a nationwide computer communications network and renamed it the Internet. So as Belinda studied the dish, she was not focused on whether or not she had possession of a potential weapon. What mattered more to her was that she was staring at a watershed advance in technology that she could control.

But what to do with it now? Back at the Lab, they were in the process of formulating protocol for its handling, but Dr. Freund let curiosity get the best of him and had made the mistake of giving the dish to a junior technician, as qualified as Sam Waterford might be, for preliminary review. That might have been the first step in the process anyway, but Belinda, who struggled with Dr. Freund's lack of control in several areas, had developed a successful method for handling new discoveries and it upset her when her method was treated lightly. Water under the bridge now, though. Freund's mistake had led to the Labs' likely demise and forced Belinda into hiding. Still, she had it back in her possession and had an opportunity for a fresh start. She would not go back to the States. Too risky. She had more than enough money in several Cayman Island accounts and could start up a new Lab, here in her home country, Basque Country, or perhaps better, just outside what was defined by the Spanish Constitution as the Basque Autonomous Region and near the pinnacle of Basque identity, the City of Pamplona.

* * * * * *

HELPFUL REFERENCES

Fairy Tales by Hans Christian Anderson

The Alienist by Caleb Carr

The Angel of Darkness by Caleb Carr

Engines of Creation: The Coming Era of Nanotechnology by K. Eric Drexler

Radical Abundance: How a Revolution in Nanotechnology Will Change Civilization by K. Eric Drexler

There's Plenty of Room at the Bottom by Richard Feynman